THE BOMB MAKER'S APPRENTICE

ROBERT SANDILANDS

Ordering Information:

Prime Seven Media
518 Landmann St.
Tomah City, WI 54660

Printed in the United States of America

CHAPTER 1

*C*orrie shivered even with his new padded jacket zipped up to his chin the cold dampness of the derelict house creeped into his bones. The bloody thing wasn't worth the effort nicking it from M&S. Had left his old one on the hanger in the changing room, would have been better than this. He glanced over at his friend standing at the opposite side of the bare open window, Danny was barely visible in the dark moonless December night and imagined him shivering, his shoulders hunched over, hands dug deep into his pockets, cursing under his breath. Danny wasn't Corrie's main concern, the bag that lay between them on the floor, contained a bomb, he had no idea who made it or how powerful it was. His instructions were brief, Hussey had given him the address where to plant it, told him it would explode when the zip was opened.

"Not the best way to spend Christmas eve." Danny had complained on their way here.

"The payment for doing the job will make a nice present though, just think of the cash," he had drummed into his friend on the long walk. A sudden cold frosty breeze blasted in through the gaping window. Corrie pulled his hood down almost over his eyes, "step back from the window Danny, away from the cold and in case somebody sees us."

"Who's going to see us? It's too fucking dark, I can hardly see you."

"Best not to take that chance, places like this attract homeless tramp and squatters, they could be sleeping rough here."

"I can tell that by the stink," Danny grumbled, "I'd rather suffer the cold at the window than breath in this shit." He took a reluctant step back, "knowing what's in that bag we've been carrying all the way here, I'm not sure it's worth it."

"Don't worry about the bag, it's safe enough, the zip has to be opened to trigger the timing device. When we do, we have four minutes to get ourselves safe."

Danny shuffled his feet and blew hot breath onto his fingers," why does Hussey want this old warehouse blown up?"

Corrie thought back to the conversation he had with the little black man, "He said something about the owner wanted it done for the insurance."

"I can't see much in the dark, but I'm guessing those old doors will be solid, the locks will be well rusted, it could take a bit of time to get in," Danny complained, half expecting Corrie to snap back at him with an alternative.

Corrie followed his friends gaze and could only see a rough silhouette of the warehouse, against streetlights in the distance. They had come here just as the daylight was fading, had decided that this building offered the best vantage point. What they had discovered was that the whole street had been abandoned by the council and had cut off the power. They stood on the second floor of a derelict tenement house, looking down across from their quarry and could hardly see it. That soon changed when an abrupt flash of light from a car head lights illuminated the warehouse front. Instinct made them take a quick step back. A huge limousine followed by another car pulled up at the warehouse doors.

The interior light came on in the limousine, the driver stepped out with a lighted torch. He went to the rear, opened the boot and lifted out a folded wheelchair.

Danny stepped over beside Corrie, together they crouched close to the gaping window, watched as the driver manoeuvred an obese man out of the rear door into the chair. At the same time four dark figures got out of the car parked behind. Contrary to Danny's assumption, the tall driver opened the door with no problems. He entered the building and a moment later, the place lit up exposing the identity of the four figures standing beside the wheelchair. They were kitted out in combat gear each carrying a holdall and wearing shades, they followed the tall African featured driver into the building pushing the man in the wheelchair. The door slammed shut and from where they were, across the street Corrie and Danny could hear the locking mechanism clang into place.

"That's a bit of a bummer," Danny said in a hoarse whisper, "how are we going to get in there without alerting that lot?"

Corrie tried to think of a way around this problem, when he felt his mobile vibrate in his hip pocket. He snatched it out, looked at the name on the screen, "what?" He cried into it. For a while he was silent, listening to the caller. "we've just watched people go into that building..., what do we do about them?" The phone went dead, all he could do was stare at it, in disbelief.

"Was that Hussey?" Danny asked.

Putting his phone back into his pocket, Corrie nodded, even though it was too dark for his pal to see," that thing in the bag has a backup device, in case it doesn't get opened, half past seven is the time set

"Right, "Danny said, grabbing Corries arm," let's get out, leave the fucking bag here."

Corrie pulled his arm free, "no Danny, we've time to get around back of the building, there's got to be a window or a back way in, we find it and lob the bag inside and do a runner."

"We better start moving now, give ourselves time to find a way in."

"Okay. Grab the bag."

Danny fumbled for a while trying to get hold of the handles, he never got a hand to them, the high velocity round burst his skull open.

Corrie reacted quickly and jumped for the open window, but his reactions were not quick enough. The second round smashed into his spine between his shoulder blades, sending him careering out into the darkness. His body hit the cobbled street below, he never felt a thing, Corrie was dead before his body left the bare window frame.

John Deroche was one of the obese cripple's bodyguard, his orders were to guard the vehicles, against vandals and recent threats of a bomb being rigged to the car and to give warning should the police approach. He was seated in the rear of the second car on the far side from the derelict houses. John was in desperate need to urinate it was this miss-comfort that kept him alert or he would have missed noticing the faint light that came from the upstairs window of the derelict building across the street. He had no doubts as to what the light came from, had to be a mobile phone. Someone must be up there, must be watching the warehouse. He snatched his own phone from his pocket, being careful not to let its light be seen.

Sitting, uncomfortable in his lightweight wheelchair, bought for the purpose of easy transporting in and out of the limousine, the obese Randell studied papers handed to him by one of the four men sat around the work bench they used as a table. As he concentrated, he mumbled and cursed to himself. A sudden barrage of noisy curses came from him when his phone sounded. His tall black driver picked it up off the bench, where it had been placed, held it to his ear for a moment, nodded and handed it over. Randell unceremoniously snatched it and shouted into it, "what is it Darroch?" A long period of silence followed as he listened to his bodyguard's information, "Okay," he replied into the phone, "you stay there, I'll get one of these boys to deal with it." He leaned his enormous body back on the wheelchair and took a long look at the men sat around him, "it seems we are being watched form the building across the street upstairs front room."

The four men looked at each other, started fidgeting and reaching for their bags, Randell's cold sunken blue eyes turned on the man nearest to him, "deal with it, Pat."

"Okay Mr. Randell," Pat instantly jumped to his feet.

Randell held up a cautioning hand, "I trust you'll know what to do if we are being watched. You never know how many we are dealing with, if you think there's too many for you to handle, come back and get help."

Pat decided, the only way he could leave and not be seen was by the toilet window at the back of the building. He lost quite a bit of time squeezing his bulk through it and lost more time stumbling over obstacles in the dark. When he reached the end of the building, he heard the first shot, half a second later came another one. He pressed his back tight against the wall decided, the shots hadn't been aimed in his direction and took a cautious peek around the corner and chanced edging out to have a look at the bare window in question. When he heard the body hit the wet cobbles, he ducked back in behind the wall and scrambled his way back panicking in case the shooter started firing at the warehouse. When Pat returned, he found the others on the floor taking cover beneath the bench.

"Didn't hear any of the shots hit this building," Randell breathlessly said as two of the men and his driver lifted him back onto his wheelchair.

"Well the weapon was definitely fired from that room," Pat assured him.

Settled back in his chair, the big man trembled, his crotch drenched with urine, red in the face with embarrassment, he shot up both arms and shouted, "let's get to fuck out of here."

Pat shook his head and was about to reply when the explosion shook the floor beneath them. The force of the blast blew the old warehouse door in on top of the three men who were sat at the nearest end of the bench.

CHAPTER 2

"You should all be proud of yourselves," said the tall thin man at the lectern and for the umpteenth time pushed his glasses up his long thin nose," you are ten remaining people out of the mob that joined us. We still have to whittle you down even further." He fell silent for a while, to let what he had just said sink in, grinned as he watched the reaction of seven men and three women shuffled in their seats, a few of them glanced at each other. When satisfied they had got the message he continued, "You will each be given a task, that you must be successful at, otherwise you will go, that's if you survive," again he let that sink in," I have no idea what your task will be, and I don't really want to know, all I can say is, do your best and you might survive."

All eyes were on him as he picked up his notes and left through a side door. A long silence fell as they absorbed what they had just learned from the lecture. Only the odd creaking of a seat disturbed them in their thoughts. After what seemed like an age, the oldest member stood up and walked out the lecture room. Soon after, the rest of his fellow students fallowed and joined him standing in the corridor.

Richard Barton, at thirty-six years old was the oldest member in the class to survive weeks of gruelling training. He had often caught himself wondering, what had become of the people who had failed along the way? They all just seemed to have vanished into thin air. One of the girls started to snigger at a joke her mate had cracked, jolting Barton out of his thoughts. A well-endowed blond in her forties Barton assumed, stepped out of a door farther down the corridor and strutted towards them. She stopped with her hands on her hips glared at them, "what's going on here," she demanded and looked straight at Barton.

"We're just about to sing you a Christmas carol," he replied with a smile and heard the rest of the group chuckle quietly behind him.

"That's all we need in this place, a comedian," she hastily commented, "now get back into that lecture room and stay there," she turned on her heels and retreated back into the door where she had come from.

Barton was the last to be seated, he chose the back of the lecture room and had just got settled when she entered by the side door," bloody hell," he whispered to the two men sitting in front," It's Mrs. Nasty big boobs."

She took up her place at the lectern, glanced at all the faces in turn. When she came to Barton sitting at the back, she delayed a moment longer, gave him the nasty eye treatment.

Once she got all her papers sorted on the lectern, she looked around at all the faces, "you will all rendezvous here at twenty-one hundred hours. You will be in the supplied combat gear and carrying a ski mask, that you will put on later. You will each be given a handgun, nine of which will be loaded with a single blank round, one will be loaded with a one live. These weapons will be laid out across a table, so you can choose one at random. They have been specially sealed, making it imposable for you to know which is which." A look of pleasure dawned across her face as she took in the expression on all the faces, she grimaced and continued." You will be picked up with a truck that has been blanked out and taken to a forest. You will then be dropped off at different position, where you will head into the wood to seek out and aim to kill the first person you see." She gazed at them, her eyes darted from one to another as if challenging one of them to question her. "When you have fired off your shot, you will head back to where you were dropped off." She gathered up her papers and without a backward glance strutted out the door she had entered by.

Barton arrived at the same time as three others with two minutes to spare. He grinned and nodded to the members that had already arrived, as he walked to his seat at the back. He noticed a great deal of attention was being paid to the table that had been placed in front of the lectern, where he discovered all the pistols had been laid out.

At dead on seven o clock wearing her combat out-fit, she entered through the side door. All eyes turned to her as did Barton's, surprised that she didn't come in via the main door. The jacket and trousers were rather a neat fit he couldn't help but admire her curves as she passed him. He instantly thought of that old song, SPING IS BURSTING OUT ALL OVER.

She stood beside the lectern and looked directly at him, this time it was more grimace, rather than a disgusting sneer. He returned the compliment, with his broadest smile. She quickly turned away.

She held up her hand and shouted, "okay, I'll call your number and you can come and pick a weapon."

Barton's number was the last, he wondered if this was deliberate. He got up and strolled towards the table, all the while holding her gaze and smiling. Her eyes didn't falter, her expression never changed. When he got to the table, he winked at her, picked up the last gun, turned around in a mock military style and marched back to his seat.

A burly bald-headed man with a walrus moustache, opened the door and stuck his head in and said, "time to roll, Miss. Damston,"

She gave the members an overhand wave towards the open door. With a noisy shuffle and a scrapping of chairs, they all rose and filled out the lecture room, trooped down the corridor, out the back door and clambered into the back of the waiting truck.

Barton was surprised when she jumped in the back, and even more so when she planked herself down on the bench seat next to him and snuggled up a bit too close, he had to admit he welcomed the physical contact.

CHAPTER 3

*A*fter almost an hour's drive the truck stopped. The latter ten minutes or so must have been on a dirt road. They had all been bumped about and Damston was almost on Barton's knee a few times. She pointed out a member sat across from her and said, "okay you first," The man jumped out and the vehicle moved on about a hundred metres, she delegated another member. This went on until only she and Barton remained, "your turn," she said with her hand on his shoulder and said softly "the only person guaranteed to survive, is the one with the live round."

"One chance in ten that it could be me, very comforting," Barton cried as he jumped over the tail board.

"It's not too late to pull out," she shouted after him.

Barton pulled the pistol from his waist band, it felt comfortable in his hand, well balanced. The seal had been welded onto the cocking mechanism but wasn't obtrusive. He released the safety catch and headed into the forest.

He had only gone fifty metres, when he heard the first shot, He slid his ski mask over his head and dropped to his knees behind a young conifer tree, scanned the area around him, listening for tell-tale footsteps when the second shot rang out.

Barton let a good ten minutes drag by, before he got back onto his feet and with stealth proceeded. The only sound he could hear was his own breathing and a distant owl call, from somewhere close by, a fox yelled. A dark figure sprung up from behind long shrubs and fired off his shot. Barton returned fire and was relieved to be able to do so, which meant his opponent had picked a blank as obviously he had done. The figure held up a hand and retreated to his pick-up point. Barton was consoled that he had fired a blank as well. He returned the gesture even although the figure was well on his way and couldn't have acknowledged it. Still treading with care Barton headed back the way he had come.

He thought he was heading back to his drop off point. Every tree looked the same, every shrub and bush identical, he realised he had lost his sense of direction. Prohibited to wear a watch, he had no idea how long he had been wandering around. The light was fading fast as dark clouds drifted past blocking out the moonlight, he tripped and stumbled blindly on.

Two shots blasted out in quick succession, quite close by, echoing through the forest. He dropped to his knees again, counting his own, that's six, another four to come and the exercise is over. The sad thing about it, one of his class-mates might get killed or injured. While still on his knees, more shot rang out, one, two, a long break, then came a third, A few more minutes dragged in, before he decided to take the chance that the last shot would be another blank. Using all his army training in the art of stealth, he continued in his search for his drop off point.

A sudden break in the overcast sky let the moon illuminate the surrounding area. There it was, the dirt track, only a few paces away. Barton decided to make a quick dash for it, just as he was about to make a jump for it he tripped over a protruding root. That was the moment the final shot came, and it came at him. He felt the whipping wind of the round as it skimmed past his ear. He stole a glance back the way he had come and saw the hooded figure approach and stop a few metres away.

"It looks as though I had the live round," the female voice cried, holding up her weapon. Barton stood up," it sure does, I'm glad you missed," she couldn't have heard him for she was well on her way back into the forest on the hunt for her pick-up point. It was then that another shot sounded in the distance. Barton dropped to the ground, feeling the wet mud on his clothing wondering, have I miss counted or was that an extra shot?

Although quite a distance away, sitting in the cabin of the truck. Damston was counting the shots as well. She was confused when she heard the extra shot," that didn't come from one of our weapons," she said to the driver "How can you be so sure? In this dense forest, sounds can distort through the trees.

"That," she held up a finger," came from a high velocity rifle."

"That being the case, what do you suggest we do about it?

"We go around and pick them up, see if anyone is missing. If there's another shooter in there, we better get out of here fast."

"Could it be that one of the members had a concealed weapon?"

"How could they conceal a bloody rifle?"

One more groom at his moustache with his fore finger and his thumb the driver starting up the engine.

Barton being the last to be dropped off was the first pick up. He sat in the same place as before and was able to help the next female aboard, thinking she might be the one who shot off the live round at him. She spoke only a few words of thanks, not enough to recognise her voice.

When the last of the members had been picked up, Damston and the driver got out of the cabin to see who was missing. Despite the number of rounds fired, there were still nine of them. "Hold on for five," she said to the driver, "she might turn up." When the minute ticked away, she ordered him to mount up and go.

It was a sad, wet dirty group that de-bused and made their way into the lecture room, Barton guessed it to be about three a.m. Their wet clothing stank in the heated lecture room. He was concerned about being caught off guard by that girl, could get him thrown off the course. His only hope was that she was the one who was missing. The only way to be certain is if he never heard that high pitched voice again. It was unmistakeable, sounding like a young schoolgirl, as if her voice box hadn't matured with her body. It was unfortunate for him that the two remaining females were keeping quiet, like the rest of the members.

Damston strutted in and took up her place at the lectern," okay," she began," put the weapons on the table, on your way out… to those of you who were paying attention, you would have counted an extra round was fired out there. My only hope is that the person who had the live round is responsible for the missing girl. At this point I don't know who that is, and I never want to know, I hope that, that person will be the only one to know, so until we find the missing member and get our doctor to examine her, we must assume that the exercise was a success." She fell silent for a while, looking into the eyes of each of them, as if by doing so she may detect who was the one with the live round. She gave up and with a deep sigh, "okay get some rest and be back here at zero seven hundred hours."

CHAPTER 4

The lectern was taken up by a tall gaunt man with watery blue eyes and an owl's beak shaped nose. He quickly glanced at the members sitting in front of him and announced," my name is Lumpy, well it's not my real name, but for security reasons, that's what you will refer to me as."

He stepped away from the lectern and walked around the room. It then became obvious, he had no left hand, the sleeves of his jacket were long, and the missing hand only showed when he stretched out his arms. "I'm an explosive expert," he held and up his stump," this is what it means to be mixed up in this kind of work. No matter how good you are, or how careful, things can so easily go wrong. Even the elements can make some mixtures volatile. This is what you must consider, when working with explosives.

Just as Barton was about to turn and face him, Lumpy moved on and returned to the lectern "Later today you will all be taken to an ex-army range, where you will witness an old car being bombed, after which you will learn how to disarm a bomb. I've no doubt, one or two of you will finish up like me," he held up his stump and chuckled," we don't use dummy explosives," this time he burst out with what Barton could only be described as a psychopathic giggle, which he continued with all the way out the door.

Taking the lesson learned yesterday from Miss nasty big boobs, Barton and the rest remained seated. They shuffled and stretched their legs a few times.

Damston pranced in all smiles and cheer, Barton grinned to himself wondering, maybe she had been with a lover. She shuffled the papers she had been carrying, placed them on the lectern and began." This morning we will be going back to that forest to search for that missing member, and to look for clues as to where that eleventh shot came from.

She spoke for over an hour before her lecture about tactics, weaponry, the most likely vehicles they would use on a job. She gathered up her papers and pointed to the door and shouted, "lets move."

It was no surprise to see walrus moustache and his bone shaker truck waiting at the same place as before. Barton climbed aboard behind the rest as he had done on the previous trip, Damston, a broad grin on her face got in and sat next to him, a bit too close, he could feel his face going red when the rest of the members glanced over and secretly grinned. Although there was ample room on the bench seats he made no attempt to move away.

This time the driver didn't use the dirt road, he pulled into a lay-bye and Damston ordered everybody out, as Barton rose to get out, she gripped his arm, "not you," she said," you're going to help me look for clues of that shooter."

The truck rolled on for a few minutes then stopped. She got up and jumped out, Barton, unsure what was expected of him, followed her. She waved the vehicle on and when it was out of sight, she said," I think that the shooter could have retreated to that old farm." She pointed to a cluster of old derelict buildings, at the other side of the field they were standing next to. "He or maybe she, would have driven here, there's a chance they could have pulled in there parked and crossed the field to the forest. There's a chance we might find tyre prints, if so, it will be a starting point. She ducked low behind the hedge, ducked her head down and at a slow trot made her way along the road back in the direction they had been driven.

Barton chased after her and almost stumbled over her when she stopped at the farm road end. He gripped her upper arm, "why are we sneaking along here?" he asked, "I don't think the shooter will be hanging around."

She pulled her arm free of his grip, "I'm not taking any chances."

Barton followed, stealthily making her way down the farm road, keeping close to the high hedge row. He kept as close to her as he could, all the while admiring her shapely buttocks. She made another sudden stop and turned around and jerked her head back when she found her face only a few inches away from his. They had arrived at the first of the old buildings. From somewhere under her tight jacket she pulled out a pistol. Barton was amazed wondering how she managed to conceal it.

"I'll check inside the buildings you stay out and keep watch." She made a dash for the nearest door and was inside before Barton could catch up. She reappeared minutes later, and darted to the next.

After checking the final building, she shrugged her shoulders and said, "no sign of anyone being here recently." Still holding the pistol at the ready, she led him around the back, "look for tyre tracks or footprints."

A half hour of checking around the buildings they found nothing of any significance. When Barton looked at her, the gun was gone, where he had no idea, never even noticed her putting it away.

"We'll cut across that field, head for the forest and see if the members have found that girl," she said pointing in the direction of the distant trees. She was about four or five paces ahead, before Barton began to follow.

"Why go to all this trouble?" He shouted after her and sprinted up close behind her.

She stopped, turned glared into his eyes," because we've got to know if it was a member who killed that girl, that's if she had been killed, or if it was a shooter and we can find any signs or traces, then we can eliminate our members being responsible." She turned and strutted on. Barton could quite easily answer that question, as could the girl that took the shot at him, if he did it would mean admitting he had been caught off guard, didn't want to take the risk of being put off the course. He started to wonder about that girl, the only way he would know if she had been the victim would be if he could hear the two remaining girls talk. So far that hadn't happened.

The long grass was wet and soon their combat trousers became sodden. That was the only obstacle they encountered crossing the field, until they reached the beginning of the trees. A neglected barbed wire fence separated the field from the wooded area. Barton had to help her release her jacket from the barbs by supporting her upper body, putting his arms around her. Now he discovered where she concealed her weapon, below her amplitude bosom. When she got free, He was expecting her to jerk herself away from his arms, this never happened, she gently walked away from him in amongst the trees.

They didn't have to walk far before they found a group of five members ambling about, "Well," she shouted after gathering them up enjoying the moment of shock on their faces," have you found the missing member?"

They shook their heads in unison, one of the girls stepped closer and said," we're waiting for the rest to join us, so far we have found no trace of her."

Barton had his ears pricked listening to her voice, but this was not her. He couldn't separate them by their physical appearance, they were all much the same size and build.

A sudden twig snapped close by, they all turned to see the other three members approach.

Damston put her hands to her ears and shouted," you lot sound like a heard of donkeys coming through there. Do I have to send you back to the first lesson, to teach you to move through the woods silently." She walked over to meet them," did you find the missing member?"

She got the same response as before, a tall gaunt young man put his hand up and said, "we searched the whole forest and found nothing."

"Right, spread out and head back to where we dropped you off, this time don't separate into groups. She took up the centre position and set them all off at a slow walk, heads bent eyes on the ground.

It was no surprise to Barton, when they all got back to the truck and found nothing of the missing girl. What made him wonder, was her casual response to it. She seemed more concerned about failing to find any trace of there being a shooter. She didn't ride in the back, with the rest of the members this time. She kept bald headed walrus moustache company in the cab. Barton was feeling a bit put out, but only just a little and he soon put it out of his head.

The ride back in the truck was like the last time very bumpy and uncomfortable. Only mumbled complaints, came from the rest of the members could be heard and not audible enough to hear a female voice.

When the truck stopped Barton being at the back looked out and was surprised to see they were out in the middle of a moorland. Lumpy stuck his head over the tailboard and ordered everybody out.

Barton found it quite amusing the way they walked in an orderly line behind Lumpy. A cold drizzly wind lashed at the side of their faces, their feet sank into the marshy ground, Barton estimated they had trudged for around half an hour before Lumpy call a halt at a depression, where they came to an old abandoned car. He held up his stumped arm and shouted, "far enough, now get down on the ground." Like most of the members, Barton only just got to the ground when the old vehicle exploded. Lumpy jumped to his feet and chortled. "That's a work of art, now let me show you how it's done." He led the members with Damston bringing up the rear along a sheep path, until they came to an old barn. He opened the metal doors to a well-equipped workshop.

Barton followed the rest of them in and was shocked at the amount of bomb making equipment he saw on the shelves and bench. His confidence soon flushed away when he thought that this idiot was about to make a bomb. He could feel the rest of the member thought the same. This was a mad man and didn't hide it. In his hands, they were all walking on a swinging rope. Barton glance over at Damston, she too wasn't brimming with confidence, she returned his glance with a nervous grin.

How could this one-handed man safely make bombs, Barton was thinking as he watched Lumpy with a screwdriver in his mouth and a set of pliers in his only hand.

"Gather round, boys and girls," he said," and pay attention."

Barton and the members gasped in amazement at how skilfully he worked and how well he instructed them as he assembled the timing device. How he managed to talk so clearly with tools in his mouth, was for them beyond belief.

CHAPTER 5

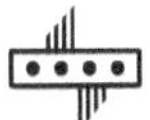

She entered his office; it only took a quick glance to know the big man was in a nasty mood. He didn't look up as she approached his desk but continued looking through papers, flipping them over in a deliberate manner. When he was finished, he gazed into her blue eyes and said," sit Damston." He waited until she was seated, "so did you find anything?"

"No Mr. Randell, we searched the farm buildings and found no clues in and around the place. Then searched the fields and the forest and found nothing."

"I take it you didn't find out if she was shot by one of your members?"

She flicked her hair back with her fingers and shook her head.

"Well get your arse back out there and find the weapon she had, find out if she had the live round or a blank. Get the members back out there and find out what went on, I'll arrange to get the body and the weapon disposed of. Can't have some poacher or farmer finding them and calling the law.

She jumped to her feet," yes Mr. Randell," she left him in the process of lighting one of his big cigars and had a collision with his tall black driver in the doorway, he stepped back to let her pass.

As soon as Nevil his driver, closed the office door, Randell manoeuvred his wheelchair around to look out the large window. The talk about the shooter with Damston had brought unwanted memories back, memories that had haunted him since the explosion almost six months ago, close to in his warehouse in Allotment street. He still sees the old door blown off its hinges by the blast and crushing the four men who were sat on the bench directly behind it. The only reason he and Nevil survived unscathed, was because they were sat off centre and at the top end of the bench, a bloody miracle.

He got into a panic when the explosion hit some of the newspapers, luckily one reporter suggested that it could have been a gas explosion and it soon died down. Although the police experts wouldn't rule out the possibility, that it could have been a bomb. The remains of a body had been found in the derelict house that blew up. He couldn't remember the name they had eventually identified him as. When he and Nevil got out of the warehouse, he had spotted another body lying on the street below. All those bodies had to disappear and soon before the emergency service arrived. A quick phone call sorted all that out.

Tom Barton paced his living room, several times he had combed his long fingers through his grey hair. He stopped behind the padded chair where his wife sat, put his hands on her shoulders and looked at his eldest son, now his only son, "your mum and I want closure on your younger brother. We know he was a petty crook, him and his pal Danny, up to all the dodges, but guns and bombs, no way."

"Dad, I've told you before, these things take time, I can't just rush in there asking all sorts of questions. I'll have to get inside the organisation, become a member, gain their trust, before I can learn anything." Barton reached forward from the sofa, lifted up his cup and took a sip of tea, "with the slightest bit of suspicion those people would kill me. Life doesn't mean a thing to them."

Jean Barton rose stiffly from her chair," I'll make some fresh tea," she said and lifted the cups from the small coffee table, she turned to her husband, "you're still determined to get our other son killed as well."

"It's okay, mum, I know what I'm doing," Barton assured her.

She turned around quickly on her way to the kitchen," are you sure about that?"

"Yes, I am,"

Her blue eyes were brimming with tears," they found what remained of poor Danny, D.N.A. Tests proved it was him, but no sign of Corrie."

With shaky hands Tom rolled himself a cigarette, "Jean, this is the only way we are ever going to find out what happened to him," he put his roll up in his mouth and lit it with a plastic lighter.

"Why can't you leave it to the police, it's their job to find out what happened," she replied."

Tom sucked at his cigarette, blew the smoke to the side, "it's been six months and still nothing."

"Don't worry mum," Barton cut in, "I'll get to the bottom of this, I'll dig and dig, I don't care how long it takes."

He was about to put his key in the lock to his flat when his mobile sounded, he snatched it from his hip pocket, saw her name on the screen, "hi Damston!" he shouted into it, "yes I can be there in half an hour." He turned around put his phone in his pocket and skipped down the steps into his car. She stood outside the building with the eight other members, all dressed in combat gear. as he approached, she stepped out to meet him.

"You've got five minutes to get changed and get back here," she barked at him.

Barton gave her one of his best smiles, "I've got my kit in the car, I could change in the truck." He folded his casual clothes, put them on the bench seat next to Damston when the truck stopped, she grinned at him and jumped out the back, ordered the rest to follow. She grouped them all together and said," we must find the gun that your classmate had, or any other clues that could lead us to it. I don't care, if we have to get down on our hands and knees, all the way through this forest to do it, now get moving." An hour of intensive searching revealed nothing. She demanded another search, this time on hands and knees.

Barton had had enough of crawling on his knees, the pains were starting to become unbearable, he stood up and went over to where Damston was searching, put his hand on her shoulder, "we are under the impression, that the shooter killed that girl," although he himself knew it to be more than just an impression, "that being the case, he would need a clear shot. Look around you, there's no way that a clear shot could be made amongst all these trees. He would have to have had a small clearing and possibly be elevated."

"So, what are you suggesting?" She said and stood up beside him, showing signs of pain in her knees.

"I'm suggesting that we look for a clearing, once we find that, we look for the tree he could have climbed to take the shot."

"What makes you so sure that there was a shooter," she chirped cockily, her hands on her hips, staring directly into his eyes. "It could have been one of you lot."

"That doesn't make sense, if it had been one of us, where did we find the time to move the body."

"Whoever it was, could have come back after we broke up. They would have had plenty of time before we returned the next day."

Barton stared back into her blue eyes and grinned, "that extra shot came from a high velocity rifle."

"What are you some kind of expert in firearms?"

"No, but I have had a few shots at a rifle in the past, I know they sound different from a pistol, you don't need to be an expert to know that."

She let out a deep sigh, held her arms out in mock submission, flicked a lock of blond hair out of her eyes," okay, let's go look for this clearing."

Damston walked away, heading into the heart of the forest. She turned without stopping and waved at him to join her.

He caught up to her walking at her side, his ego floating quite high because of his little victory over her. "would have a night sight on his weapon, a pro. More than likely, but why go to all that trouble to pick a random target?"

She stopped, turned and stared at him, "are you implying this shooter could have had a designated target?"

"To go to all that trouble, I think he must have."

She continued to walk, Barton paced alongside her in silence, detected she was deep in thought. They stumbled onto a clearing a lot sooner than he had expected. "This is ideal," he said.

She gripped his arm and held him back," don't take any chances, that shooter could be hanging around here."

Barton nodded, "you could be right if that girl was a mistake, he'll be back."

They crouched down behind a tree trunk, "how will we know if he's here or not?" Damston, whispered.

Barton smiled at her, "you step out, if he shoots you, I'll know."

She reached over and punched him on the arm, "I don't think that's funny."

"The only thing I can suggest, is we split up, you go that way," he pointed over her shoulder,"

I'll go this way. All being well we should meet up at the other side. Keep an eye up on the trees, he could be up one, look carefully at the trunks, see if you can find any signs that someone had climbed up one of them."

Damston hadn't gone far when she called him and waved him over. Barton didn't rush to her, thinking, if the shooter had returned, he must have heard her shout.

"What do you make of that?" She pointed out spike marks on the tree trunk, she was standing next to.

Barton had a close look at the holes in the bark of the tree and concluded," these were made with ankle spikes, worn by tree surgeons or telephone engineers. Whoever this shooter is, he is well organised. This wasn't a chance hit, this was planned."

"I would say that this proves there was a shooter," Damston said touching the spike holes with her finger tips.

"I was hoping that the girl had decided to do a runner, but it looks like she was shot. I get the feeling that she wasn't the intended target. We were all dressed in combat suits wearing ski masks. Although as I said earlier, he would be using night sights, it would have been difficult for the shooter to distinguish who was his intended target. He will realise this and eventually try again. Assuming he was a hired assassin he won't give up." Barton stepped back to look up the tree and pointed out a few broken branches, "that's where he would have perched himself. As you can see even from up there, he would have had a limited field of fire."

Damston looked up, followed his pointing hand and said, "you seem to know quite a bit of field craft ex-army, are you?"

Barton ignored her question, knowing full well she would be aware of his past, "another question pops up," he said lowering his arm and looking into her eyes, seeing that lock of blond hair had fallen over them again," how did this shooter know we were coming here?"

Nevil's favourite job was washing and polishing the limousine, had great pride in the condition he had kept it in. Mr. Randell had always praised him for it. Almost every day he was at it washing, polishing, vacuuming the interior. But this one wasn't quite as good at holding its shine as the previous one. He had been appalled at the damage the explosion had done to the last one. Flying debris had made huge ugly dent on the side of it, the windows were all smashed and the roof almost flattened. The escort car behind had been blown over onto its roof. Nevil had rushed over to see if he could rescue the man who had been inside it, but Mr. Randell had stopped him, saying just dump him beside the rest, in the cellar, the concrete lorry will be here in a few minutes to fill it in. Barton decided to take a stroll around the estate. Randell Storage was one of many businesses here, it seems the idea was to blend in with legitimate companies. Although Randell owned the largest complex. The thing that struck Barton as odd was the large windows were always blanked off with heavy curtains at the front of the building. At the rear where Randell had his office, they were left open. As he neared the end of the building, he caught sight of the big coloured man polishing a large black limousine. He casually approached, smiled and waved to the man and said," a fine job you're doing there, it must take some time to keep it in that condition?"

The tall broadly built coloured man stopped polishing, and returned the smile and exposed a set of pure white teeth with a large gap between the two front ones," that's what I get paid for," he replied and continued polishing.

"You get paid for polishing that car?" Barton approached grinning and scratched his designer stubble.

"I do a bit of driving as well," the other replied and continued with his task without looking up.

"You're a chauffeur?"

"Something like that."

"You must work for a very rich man?"

"I don't know about that, he pay's my wages, that's all I know."

"Good, you look after a good job like that, you're a lucky man."

"I do my best," he replied, packing his valeting equipment into a leather case and put it in the boot. He drew the remote control from his pocket and locked the car. After a sort of fair well gesture he bounded in through the office door.

Barton continued his casual walk to the end of the estate road, wondered if he was being watched. He delayed for a while and glanced back the way he had come, couldn't see any movement on the heavy curtains and decided to head back to his car.

He sat in his car for a while, thinking that the big chauffeur, if he was one of Randell's men could be the thin edge of the wedge in getting closure on where his brother's body lies. Getting on friendly terms with him might prove to be difficult and dangerous. He remembered a pub where Corrie used to frequent, surely somebody there will know something about what happened to him and his pal.

Wilma was on a stool leaning on the bar, staring into a half empty pint glass. Barton walked in and sat next to her, "you look deep in thought," he said.

She spared him a quick glance for a moment, her eyes lit up as she sparked out of her reverie, "Oh! High Richard, it's been a long time, where have you been hiding?"

"Down South working."

"What brings you back."

"Just visiting family, you know what it's like."

"I was really sorry to hear about your brother Corrie."

Barton nodded and pointed to her glass, "do you want a top up?"

She nodded, "okay,"

"You were one of his girlfriends?"

"One of the many."

"Any idea what happened?"

"Not really, he and his pal were in Hussey's club the night before that bomb exploded in Allotment Street. I was talking to him at a table, Danny was at the bar drinking with one of the other girls. Hussey came over, I got up and went to the bar, he and Corrie spoke for a while. The next thing I noticed was Hussey, Corrie and Danny leave together, that's all I can tell you."

Barton ordered the drinks and sat with her until closing time, had known Wilma for a long time. Never took much to do with her, even when she and Corrie were having a relationship, he hardly ever bumped into her. She seemed very laid back, easy to talk to with a ready smile. He could see why his younger brother would have liked her. Her wide staring brown eyes, long curly black hair that often slipped down in front of her eyes. There was never any mention about Corrie in the papers, but we all knew he was there, He and Danny were inseparable," she said as they entered her flat.

"You would have known Corrie better that most people?" Barton asked, as they sat on her sofa, "what was he in to?"

She got up, went into her kitchen and returned with two cans of beer, handed him one and re-seated herself next to him." You know we had a thing going, I'm not complaining, because it was good, but I started to get the feeling he was using me. I wanted to call it off, but just couldn't bring myself to do it. You could say I knew him better that most."

"Who is this guy Hussey, what is he, what does he do?"

She pulled the ring on her can, took a long drink and said, "He's bad news, into dealing in a big way, runs money lending scams, a bit of pimping, you name it he's into it."

"I would like to talk to this Hussey, as you say he had a long conversation with my brother, where do I find him?"

"You don't want to know, stay clear of him, he's got a team of goons that would kill you as easy as spitting on you."

"I just want to know what happened to my brother, I'm not out to harm him, just ask what he knows."

Wilma took another long drink of her beer and said," I'll ask around, see if anybody could arrange a meeting. The early morning sun shone through the window directly onto his face, Barton woke with a start and felt Wilma's arm across his chest. She stirred when he jumped but didn't waken, still she slept on when he gently moved her arm and got out of her bed. Barton gathered up his clothes and slipped out the room. Soon he sat in his car, wondering how it all came about. To spend the night with her wasn't in his plans and he hadn't learned anything of value from her. He pinned his hopes on her getting a meeting with this guy Hussey.

In the reference section of the local library, Barton found the newspapers with the bombing incident in Allotment Street, as Wilma said no mention of Corrie. One thing that did spark his attention was the two destroyed cars, one being a large black limousine that had been parked opposite the derelict building where the explosion had occurred. The charred remains of a man's body was found, buried in the rubble. Experts say he had been shot through the skull and must have been dead before the blast. That left him with the nagging question, did his brother meet the same ending? All these unanswered questions plagued him when he got back to his flat. In the shower Barton couldn't get it out of his mind that this guy Hussey was behind it all. surely Corrie and Danny weren't into bombs and guns? Above the sound of the running water he heard his mobile, he wrapped a towel around himself rushed into the lounge and picked it up off the table. Damston's number came up on the small screen, "Hi!" he said into it, he listened for a while and said," I'll be there soon as I can."

Barton was in the driving seat, "nice wheels you've got."

"Just drive," Damston snapped at him.

"Where to?"

"Just follow my directions."

The street she told him to turn into looked vaguely familiar to him, although he knew he had never been here before. The description that Wilma and the newspapers gave about the derelict houses on one side and the old warehouse on the other, fitted into the picture he had formed in his mind. He drove slowly, taking in his surroundings, until she told him to stop at the warehouse door, which looked to have been replaced, although not new.

"You stay here," she said, got out the car and pranced to the door, pulled out a key from her hip pocket and opened it, closing and locking up behind her.

So, this was where it all happened? Barton studied the derelict house opposite with the top floor and the roof missing. This was where his brother and his pal met their end. There would be little chance of Corrie's body lying in that rubble, not after all this time. Surely the police or the rescue squad must have discovered it. Damston appeared at the door scrambled to get it locked and rushed to the car, jumped in and cried, "get moving." She grabbed her mobile, "the guard's been killed," she yelled into it.

Barton guessed the street was a dead end and did a fast handbrake turn, the front wheels spun on the wet cobbles, a combination of smoke from the tyres and steam obscured his view until they took a grip, sending the vehicle forward with a jump. At that exact moment the passenger window next to Damston exploded in on them firing particles of glass at her. She screamed and threw herself onto his knees. Barton almost lost control, had difficulty steering the car with her on top of him.

At the end of the street he made a quick left turn, almost colliding with a truck, the truck driver blasting his horn at him. A short distance along the road he pulled up, Damston sat up and composed herself, wiping the glass from her lap and shoulders. She was doing a good job of hiding the shock, several beads of blood appeared on her cheek, she didn't seem to notice.

"Are you alright?" He asked placing his hand on her arm.

She dragged her arm away, "why have you stopped?" she demanded.

"To see if you had been hurt."

"Just get driving." She replied holding her phone at her ear, that was when she discovered the blood, for a moment she gazed at it on her mobile's facia, "someone has just shot at us from the back of the warehouse," she cried, "don't send the boys here in case the shots have been reported."

On the drive back she remained silent, her head turned looking out her side broken window. When he pulled up in the office carpark, she stepped out, stooped and eyed him through the shattered glass "get this to the garage and get this mess cleaned up."

Barton drove away watched her enter the building in the inside mirror. The nickname he had privately christened her came to mind, bloody appropriate he grinned as he pulled into the garage owned by the organisation, just around the corner. Barton was surprised to see Lumpy standing at the door. He stopped next to him, jumped out and said, "are you the mechanic?"

"Do you see anyone else here?"

Barton ignored the comment and handed him the keys, patted him on the cheeks and said, "we're in a nasty mood today."

Lumpy stepped back and sneered at him, "It's going to take a few days to replace that window."

Barton walked away, shouting back, "not my problem," he wondered how Lumpy managed to work on cars with only one hand? His experience in working with engines etc. Two hands were essential. He arrived at reception and was about to collect his phone and watch when the woman behind the desk pointed her finger down the corridor. He swung around to see Damston striding towards him.

"Where have you been?" She demanded with her hands on her hips.

He continued to strap on his watch and put his mobile in his pocket, "seeing to your car miss," he replied, like a schoolboy who had just been reprimanded by teacher.

She jabbed her thumb back the way she had come, "my office."

She was about to lead the way when Barton raised his arm, "please Miss may I go to the toilet?"

He got rewarded with the evil eyes and followed her along the corridor grinning to himself.

Her office was more like a large broom cupboard with a desk and a padded chair behind it, a wooden stool sat behind the door. She squeezed herself between the wall and the desk to get seated. A tubular light flickered a few times above her head, before settling to a steady glow. She looked at him for a moment, he could see behind that hard exterior, a glow of amusement in her eyes a slight grin playing on her lips. Maybe she was silently enjoying his banter.

"Get the coffees," she said, the expression changed a smile surfaced, but it was the smile of a zombie.

While he was carrying the two mugs of coffee along the corridor his mobile sounded, he perched the mugs on top of a radiator and snatched his phone from his pocket, "hi! Wilma," he listened for a while and learned that she was in hospital, having had a beating from a couple of goons." Sorry about that," he told her, "I'll try and get in to see you soon."

Damston nodded her thanks when he placed her mug on the desk in front of her. The only other seat was the wooden stool, like one that was used in a bar, only this had its legs cut. He parked himself on it and leaned back against the wall.

She tapped away at her keyboard, engrossed on the monitor, Barton couldn't help but admire her as every now and then she would stop to flick up a lock of her blond hair from her face. A face he decided was good looking, not what he would call pretty and doubtful to his taste. He stretched his legs out and accidently knocked her desk. She glanced up at him, at the same time taking a drink from her mug.

She put her mug down and asked, "who are you?"

"You've got my details on record."

She pointed at the monitor, "this only tells us what you want us to know."

"What else can I tell you?" He swallowed the last of his drink, leaned over and put the mug on the desk.

"You don't strike me as a run of the mill cons. We usually get here."

"Maybe I'm not your run of the mill cons, I'm ex services, did time in military prison, you look at your records you'll know why."

"Okay, we trust the man who recruited you to this firm, he has never let us down yet, but be sure I'll be keeping an eye on you."

As you have done with all the other members, Barton thought, He could tell by the slight quiver in her voice, that she hadn't got over the shock of being shot at earlier. "I've got a few things to clear up this evening, will you be okay for a few hours?"

Lora Damston was mildly intrigued with this man, his rugged looks appealed to her taste, his designer stubble, dark brown eyes, shoulder length black hair, his mocking smile. "do you have a girl you want to meet?"

Barton shook his head, "that would be wishful thinking," he grinned got up off the stool and left her sitting there wide eyed and open mouthed. Damston recalled an incident a few weeks back, when Mr. Randell's driver came into her office. They greeted each other with the usual pleasantries and chatted for a few moments. When the tall coloured man left, he didn't close her office door or his boss's whether this was deliberate, she wasn't sure. She overheard their conversation about the shooter, it was the driver's words that came across more graphic referring to the shooter, "a bloody mystery, Mr. Randell." The big man's voice boomed in response, "I can't afford mysteries, I want to know who this shooter is and soon."

All went silent, she wondered what next? The stillness went on, next the heavy footsteps, and the sound of Randell's office door getting closed. She had been with Randell for ten years, learned of his devious ways. Knew that within his organisation, if you heard anything, it was because you were meant to. She knew that their next meeting would be about the shooter.

The day she got out on parole, was a wet, windy, February day. She had got a black cab to her mother's house discovered she had sold up and moved. Three years she got for robbery with violence never got a visit, not even a few words on a piece of paper. After wandering the streets, wet and cold, also very hungry, she stepped into a café, ordered tea and a burger. Had no money to pay for it, as she ate, she planned her escape, when a five-pound note got slapped on the table in front of her. She gazed at it, looked up to see a dapper little man shifting the seat opposite her to sit down. "What do you want?" She had snapped at him.

"It's not what I want, it's what you want," the little man had said grinning at her, his blue eyes staring deep into hers.

"How do you fucking know what I want?"

"You want a home… you want money and a job?"

"What do you want in exchange for all that?" She had asked drinking down the last of her tea.

"Oh! Don't worry, I'll get well paid, if you meet the criteria."

"Hell, what the fuck have I got to lose." She had replied after a few minutes thought. The next thing she remembered was the dapper little man escorting her out the café into a waiting car.

As she stepped in behind the lectern, she wondered about the members sitting in front of her, this she had done every time a new group entered the course. Criminals every one of them, how many will pass the grade. How many have been killed trying to get this far? Only the dapper little man, known to her as Mr. Crow, could answer those questions, to ask him could mean a bullet in the head.

"Right then," she shouted, looking at them, "today some of you will be doing the job you have been trained for. This job will take five of you, I will hand you an envelope, inside you find your instructions. The person you will be protecting will be traveling in a limousine. One of you will be in there with the driver. The other four will follow in a normal car. She picked up the envelopes from the lectern and handed them out to preselected members.

She ordered the five selected members out, leaving Barton the two girls and the other member sitting, Barton shrugged his shoulders, wondering what next? Damston stood by the door, waved the girls over, whispered a few words to them, they left, then waved the remaining member out.

She returned to the lectern, Barton sat in silence, trying not to look in her direction. He lifted his arm to glance at his watch and remembered he didn't have it. One of the rules, no mobiles, no means of identification or time pieces, all had to be left at the reception and picked up at the finish of the day.

She gave a cough to get his attention, when he looked at her, he got one of her warmer smiles. She gathered up her papers and came and sat next to him. "You have been selected into the organisation, and have been given a special job as my minder. After what you pointed out in the forest, saying that the girl who was shot was a mistake by the shooter, could only mean that I was the intended target." She stood up and looked down at him, "go home get your clothes and things I've got a spare room at my house, you can move in, purely business, so don't get your hopes up."

Wilma showed no visible signs of the beating, but Barton could see she was in pain, must have taken it all in the body, "what's the extent of your injury?" he asked, sitting on the seat next to her bed.

"Badly bruised ribs and shoulder," she said and moved painfully round to face him. "I'm sorry Richard, I had to tell them you wanted to know about your brother. I'm sure they would have killed me, thought they were never going to stop kicking me."

"What's the big deal, I just wanted to inquire about my brother?"

She held out her hand and touched his, "You better watch you're back, now they know who you are."

"Don't worry about that, I'll watch by back. I just wondered what Corrie had got himself into."

"The word is that Hussey is trying to muscle in on the big time, the last thing he needs is you going about asking questions, might think your secret police or something."

"I knew he and Danny were into petty stuff, a bit of shop lifting, car theft, even bag snatching, I never thought he would get involved with people like Hussey."

"Corrie and Danny were regulars in Hussey's club. You've been away a long time, people change, he would have done anything for a price and that little black man had the means to buy anyone."

"Are you saying that Corrie and Danny were on his pay roll?"

"I don't know, all I know is, whatever Hussey and your brother talked about, must have been big, for that little shit to spend time with him."

A nurse appeared at the foot of Wilma's bed holding a small plastic container with pills in it and a glass of water. Barton stood up, bent over kissed her lightly on the lips and left.

Barton picked up what clothes he thought he would need for a few weeks, packed them into a few black bin liners. He locked up his flat and tossed the bag in the boot of his car, jumped in and drove off.

Damston was waiting at reception, looking very impatient when he got there, she took a deliberate glance at her watch. He received the evil eyes as she strutted towards him. Barton followed her as she rushed out the building, he caught up to her standing by his car, arms folded tapping her feet, "get a fucking move on, will you?" she shouted.

Half an hour's drive under her direction, they arrived at her house. Barton had been impressed by it, looked recently built, set at the end of a long drive with high hedges on both sides, well out of sight of the neighbouring bungalows. Young conifers surrounded the front courtyard and continued evenly spaced all the way around to the rear. A Double garage with white roller doors was detached to the side of the building. Two huge Bay windows looked out at both sides of a huge plate glassed porch.

"You don't spend much on your luggage equipment," she said with a giggle, as she helped him with his bin liners. "Your room is at the end of the corridor, on the right, toilets across from it. Get settled, I'll wait for you in the lounge."

Barton had tossed his bags on top of the double bed and joined her in the lounge, "nice to see you had a bit of a laugh, back there, considering what you've been through today," he said as he sat himself down on the sofa opposite her . She smiled and said, "let's talk about that."

"I would have thought you would want to forget about that?"

"On after thought," she said, "you acted very calmly, like a pro. You got us out of there fast not giving the shooter a chance of a second shot at us."

"I'm not sure I acted professional, I just wanted to get the hell out of there."

She got up, walked out the room and returned a few moments later with two cans of beer, handed him one, sat next to him on the sofa. "Most people would have panicked, You, kept your cool," She pulled the ring on her can and took a drink.

"Just pure amateur's luck."

"I don't think so, I know a pro. When I see one."

Barton took a long drink from his can, held it aloft, grinned and said," you sure know how to flatter a guy." He got no response from her and they both sat in thoughtful silence. Her assumption of him being a professional made him reflect to the night in the forest, when that girl caught him unawares. That was far from Damston's concept of him. He turned to face her, she stared at the beer can in her hand. He couldn't understand where that sudden feeling deep inside him came from and decided that was the last thing he needed, to become emotionally involved.

She placed her can on the small table in front of them, "I thought about going out for a meal and pointed to the small red wounds on her cheek," not looking like this, I'll make something."

CHAPTER 6

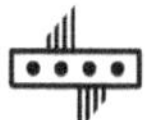

Cecil Hussey woke up feeling slightly hung over, from last night's booze orgy. He sat up in bed Looked at Jaco lying next to him, sound asleep. Every morning was the same, could never get a lie in, always had to go to the toilet. He cursed his lover and decided if I'm up you're up and this was Jaco's bed, so what the Hell. He stood up straddled his partner and urinated on his sleeping lovers face.

The hot fluid ran down Jaco's face and neck, for a moment he thought he was in the shower. But it dawned on him, he was still in bed, "what the fuck," he cried, sprang up bolt like knocking Cecil out the bottom of the bed. Jaco cursed when he saw the naked brown body lying on the carpet convulsed with laughter, "you rotten bastard," he roared," what did you do that for?"

Cecil got up, gazed into Jaco's face, "for a laugh."

"I don't think that was funny."

"Go and get a shower and dressed, we're going for a drive, we'll grab something to eat on the way."

As usual Jaco was driving, a job he hated and let Cecil know, this only resulted in him doing all the driving, knowing the little black man drew pleasure out of watching him suffer. After picking up two of Cecil's goons, they drove out into the country. Cecil directed him to a small cottage along a narrow bumpy lane. He was ordered to stop a few yards from the front door. Cecil reached over and blasted the horn a couple of times.

Two tall gaunt looking men appeared at the door. Cecil and the goons got out and went to meet them. They exchanged a few words and went inside. Half an hour lapsed before they reappeared, Cecil and his goons got in and Jaco was ordered to drive.

When the sound of the vehicle had faded in the distance, the Carter brothers re-entered the cottage and ripped open the envelope and divided the contents. Ben laughed held up the wad of notes that was his share and said to his brother," a nice little earner Tommy."

Tommy wasn't so jubilant, knowing the consequences if things go wrong. "let's look at this Ben, he gave us five hundred each and another five when the job is done?" He looked at his brother.

Ben nodded, "that's what the man said."

"We wait for him to call, he tells us where to meet, he hands us a bag, we take the bag to a place we don't know of, we brake in, leave the bag and bugger off."

Ben grinned held out his arms and said, "that's it."

"The bomb that's in this bag, he said he'll get it set to go off at a given time. What if we get held up or something. I don't like it Ben, I don't trust that little sleaze bag."

"You heard the man, we'll have plenty of time, all we have to do is follow his instructions, which he will give us when we meet."

"The big man will not be too pleased if he discovers we're doing a job for Hussey." Tommy complained and sat on the leather padded chair and switched on the television.

Ben sat on the sofa, "we better make sure he doesn't discover."

Tommy leaned forward and pointed his finger at his brother, "when he talked about a bomb it brought back the memory of the one that exploded in the old house on Allotment Street, across from the big man's warehouse, do you think that could be the place we have to plant this one?"

Ben chuckled, stumped out his cigarette," that got us a good bit of work, two hundred tons of ready mixed concrete to fill up the cellar," he shook his head, "I don't think so, that was an old house I don't think Hussey would pay a grand to blow it up again."

Jaco wanted to grab that chunky gold chain that hung around Hussey's neck and strangle him with it. His loathing for the man was well beyond committing murder. He had often considered suicide as the only way out of the relationship, the latter being his last resort. He had decided that the opportunity must come, sooner or later."

The two goons had jumped out of the car, leaving Cecil in the front passenger seat beside him. What Jaco thought might have been a kiss, when Cecil leaned over closer to him, was a dull punch on the mouth.

"I saw the way you looked at those two men, you bastard," Cecil cried.

Jaco felt the blood run down his chin and wiped it with his hand, could feel his lip begin to swell.

Through the tears he looked into Cecil's dark brown eyes and was horrified to see that familiar psychotic satanic jealousy in them.

"Don't ever let me catch you at it again," Cecil screamed, barged out the door and slammed it behind him. Jaco will always remember, with regret the night friends had taken him to the Hussey Club for a night out. He got introduced to Cecil and had bought some drugs from him. When he had taken the drugs and the effect started to work on him, he collapsed. That was the last thing he could remember until he woke up next morning in a strange bed and in unfamiliar surroundings. When he felt movement in the bed beside him, he swung his legs out. The little black man was lying there, wide awake smiling up at him holding his hand out, beaconing him to come back into bed. In that moment of weakness Jaco didn't resist. The first few weeks of their relationship was like a dream come true to Jaco, at last, he thought he had found his perfect partner. But that soon changed, he began to see the real Cecil. His mood swings became more frequent and more violent and he took the brunt of it. The grip Cecil had on him was the free cocaine, also the threat if he ever walked out, Cecil swore he would find him and inflict a slow painful death.

He grinned as he watched the Carter brothers carry the black holdall to their car and put it in the boot. Cecil Hussey's face was aglow with delight as he watched them drive away. He turned and entered his club, sat on his usual stool at the bar beside the two goons. They sat and chuckled together at their success, holding up their glasses, "that all went to plan," Cecil cried and downed his drink in one gulp.

The goons anticipated his next move, jumped to their feet and followed Cecil outside to the car.

Once again Jaco had to drive when Cecil ordered you obeyed or took the consequences. What worried Jaco, was the expression Cecil was wearing. That psychotic glow in his eyes, the wide grin, flashing his huge pure white piano key teeth. Jaco had seen it many times, knew something sinister was about to take place.

"Okay, drive and take your time," Cecil ordered.

Cecil's instructions took them back to the narrow driveway where they had previously been. This time they didn't go all the way to the cottage, he ordered Jaco to stop about halfway along the drive. He and the goons got out and walked a short way in front, stopped, had a few words and Cecil pulled what looked to Jaco like a television remote control from his jacket pocket, held it out in front of him. The explosion came from quite a long way from behind and not from the cottage where Jaco had expected it to come from.

Cecil and the goons ran towards the car and jumped in," get us to fuck out of here," Cecil shouted.

On the fast drive back, Cecil pulled the remote control from his pocket and tossed it out the window, turned to the two men in the back seat and said, "the Carters must have stopped somewhere close. That remote should have a range of about a mile."

"Maybe they stopped for a drink in a local pub," the man sitting behind Jaco said.

"Well," sighed Cecil turning around to face the front," if that's the case I hope that bomb has blown them to hell."

"That was what you planned," the same man said, "to get rid of some of the opposition, starting with the frontline thugs.

Jaco shivered at the devastation it must have caused, if as the goon suggested they had gone to a local pub. He heard it from inside the car, thought he felt a slight shock wave from it. How many people could have been killed or injured if the pub happened to be busy?

As happened on the previous return to Cecil's club, the goons got out first and went inside. Jaco could feel the little black man's eyes staring at the side of his head, turned to face him, bracing himself for another blow.

The punch never came, Cecil put his hand on Jaco's arm and said," I want you to give up your flat and move in with me."

Jaco was so relieved that the blow never came, he smiled. He realised Cecil must have taken it as a yes and watched him get out of the vehicle to join the two goons. Jaco knew that if he had reacted any other way what the results would have been. He was shocked at why after all times Cecil asked him to move now in, after all the months they had been in a relationship, mostly sleeping in his flat or one of Cecil's club rooms.

As Cecil's goons had predicted the Carter brothers, having been informed that the device in the bag wasn't set to go off for another twenty-four hours, they decided to stop in at a local pub for a drink. Being relative strangers to the area, none of the patrons conversed with them. All they got was the occasional nod or grin, even the bar staff were quite standoffish.

Ben felt like a smoke, told his brother his intent to go outside, Tommy gave him a wave and edged his way through the other drinkers to the bar.

The rain was now coming down in torrents, Ben, like the rest of the smokers, sheltered in the small porch. He only managed to get his cigarette lit when the bomb exploded. It seemed in that split second the world had stopped. A woman screamed and brought realisation back to everyone in and around the pub. The patrons rushed out, colliding with the stunned smokers in the doorway. Like a disturbed hornet's nest, the place was a hive of activity. Men and woman rushed from the building in threat of their lives, all shouting and screaming. A woman was knocked over and was trampled in the rush. A strong hand grabbed the stunned Ben and pulled him away to the side, he turned to see his brother, "come on and get to fuck out of here, "Tommy's voice sounded distant and hollow.

They had to clamber over broken glass, detour around overturned cars and fight their way past panic stricken onlookers. When they looked back at the carnage, their own car was on its roof, the back end was a tattered, twisted blackened mangled wreck. The rain had stopped, when they reached the cottage, Ben was still in a state of shock but was slowly recovering. Tommy had dragged him through fields, over fences, knee deep in a swamp, but were glad to have gotten clear without drawing attention.

After a shower and a change of clothing, they sat down to a cup of tea. Ben was back to his normal self and said, "we better get away from here as quick as possible, the law's going to trace that car back to us."

"That little creep told us that thing wouldn't explode for twenty-four hours, when he handed it to us, "said Tommy, he drank the last of his tea and stood up, "that bomb was meant to blow us up."

Ben stood up beside him," if we hadn't gone into that pub, it would have gone off when we brought it inside, remember he said to take it out of the car, until we decide to go and do the job. Don't let it get damp, leaving it in the vehicle, were his words, I think we should get that little bastard and blow his head off."

"How are we going to do that? He's well protected, he never goes anywhere without his morons to protect him."

"We just have to wait for a chance, it'll come, we need to think something up to catch him without his hoodlums."

CHAPTER 7

Damston never watched morning television, but because Barton was living with her it was on first thing. She almost dropped her coffee cup when the report came up on the news about the explosion in a village pub car park. It wasn't the explosion that shocked her, it was the part about the police wanting to talk to the owner of the car that exploded, registered to a man named Carter. She knew it had to be one of the brothers, because of the location of the incident. They lived in one of Mr. Randell's properties, not far from that pub.

Barton noticed the shocked expression on her face, "you look as though you have just seen a ghost."

"I wish that was all I had just seen," she said and picked up her mobile from the table. She thumbed a few digits and cried into it," have you seen the news?" She and went silent, listened to the reply. After a few nods she disconnected and put the phone in her pocket. She jumped up out of her seat nodded to Barton, "we're going for a drive, we'll have to use your car."

Barton got up, "as long as it's not going to be shot at."

"If anything happens to it, we'll fix it," she assured him, gathered up a few items and put them into a small duffle bag, slung it over her shoulder and led the way out the door.

Damston had glanced at her watch a few times and appeared to be getting impatient, they sat in Barton's car, parked in a motorway service station. She kept turning and twisting herself, looking in all directions. She stopped and grimaced, focused on the two tall thin men who appeared at the entrance to the shop.

Barton couldn't help but admire her shapely figure when she got out and walked towards the men. Got out himself and followed her and stood behind as she stopped to talk to the them.

She started arguing with them, looked fairly heated up, the duffle bag got tossed at the two men's feet. One of them stooped, picked it up and slung it over his shoulder. Damston turned on her heels and strutted back to the car.

Barton took a quick glance at the men, turned and paced after her aware of them walking close behind.

They dropped the two men off at a van hire company and watched them drive away in a white Citroen van. Barton started up his car and followed the van onto the main road. She had told him to head for the office, "and stop that infernal whistling and drumming your fingers on the steering wheel when you're driving, it's bloody annoying."

When he pulled up in the car park his mobile sounded. Damston was halfway out the car door, when she heard his phone, changed her mind and sat back down beside him looking very attentive.

Wilma's name came up on the small screen, "Hi!" he said, all the while looking at Damston. Wilma's message was short, but enough to start his adrenalin off, all he got was a nickname and enough to start him plotting a way of getting a break from Damston.

"Was that the girlfriend wanting to see you?" She asked. Barton shook his head," Don't have a girlfriend, just someone with a little advice about my flat, he knows someone who might rent it for a while. Will you be okay till I get back?"

She thought for a while and said," okay, be back here by four-o-clock."

Limping Lenny, Wilma had called him, said briefly that he lived rough in the old buildings on Allotment Street, Barton hoped that this character could be found and if so could tell him something about what went on that night.

With not much to go on, and not a lot of time, Barton pulled up a few streets away and walked to Allotment Street, looking for a down and out with a limp. He spotted a group of youths standing at the far end, smoking and drinking from bottles wrapped in newspaper. He Kept close to the walls of the old buildings, edged his way along, all the while keeping his eyes open for any of the boarded up windows that looked to have been prized open slightly. The youths turned as he approached, "I'm looking for Lenny?" He said.

One of the youths stepped forward, took a cigarette stump from his mouth, tossed it close to Barton's feet, "who wants to know?"

"I'm an old mate of his, from our army days, I was told he hangs about here,"

Another youth from behind shouted, "Lenny's always bragging about his time in the army."

That was one hell of a wild guess, Barton spared himself a grin, "any idea where I could find him?"

They looked at each other, most of them shrugged their shoulders or shaking their heads, the cigarette butt thrower said, "try the park, I've seen him sitting on one of the benches a few times."

That could create another problem, Barton decided as he stopped his car at the park entrance, if Lenny's sitting on a bench, how would he be able to identify him, if he's not walking about? There could be quite a few bums sitting about in the park. He spoke to quite a few people, asking the same question, always getting the same response. Barton decided time was running out on him, he headed back to the park gates, when he saw the limping figure, walking towards a bench and sitting down.

Barton sat next to him," hi! Lenny, how have you been?"

Lenny bent over and took a bottle of red wine from a plastic carrier bag at his feet, he scowled at Barton, "what the fuck's it got to do with you?"

"Just asking."

"Well mind your own business," Lenny growled at him and took a long drink from the bottle.

Barton notice the tattoo on Lenny's wrist, rolled up his own sleeve and exposed the identical art work. "Looks like we were in the same regiment."

Lenny grinned showing a set of smoke-stained teeth, "at different times, I was in when they were needing us not feeding us."

"You could be right pal," Barton smiled, "mind you, they were not all that good at feeding us."

"Do you have a fag?" Lenny held out a dirty hand.

Barton shook his head," don't smoke, but I could soon get you a pack."

Lenny shrank back on the bench, "what do you want?"

"Just want to talk to you."

"what about?"

"An explosion that happened six months ago in Allotment Street?"

"Don't know nothing about that."

Barton pulled out his wallet and drew two twenty-pound notes out, "you sure I can't jog your memory?"

"I can only tell you what I heard," Lenny replied his eyes staring at the notes.

"Well in that case you can only tell me what I've read in the papers," Barton tucked the notes back in his wallet, put it back in his pocket and stood up.

Lenny held up his hand and at the same time stooped down and grabbed his bottle." Are you the law or some sort of an enquiry agent, for some insurance company?"

"Nothing like that," Barton replied looking down at him.

Lenny swallowed a short drink from the bottle, "what's your interest in what went down in Allotment Street?"

"I'm willing to pay for answers, not to give them," he stared into Lenny's watery blue eye putting aside the body odour and the dirty hands, Lenny didn't come over as being down and out. Bright coloured trainers looked expensive. His jeans were spotless and fitted well, the old coat looked like it had seen better days, Barton decided this was where the odour was coming from, could've lifted it out of a garbage bin. He was beginning to think there was more to Lenny than the impression he was giving out. He sat back down beside him," did you injure your leg on active duty?" he asked.

Lenny grinned, "you're a crafty bastard, I'll give you that, change the subject, catch me off guard. Yes, in the early eighty's, got medical discharge, wounded in the Falklands war."

Barton would have liked to have listened to his war stories, got on his friendly side and probably learned more about the explosion. As it was, he had left himself short of time, "can we arrange to meet soon and talk?"

"Well I'm always around," Lenny laughed and took another drink.

Expecting Damston to be pacing about waiting for him, Barton didn't know if he felt disappointed or relieved when she was nowhere in sight. He asked the girl at reception and was informed that she had left with the rest of the group and that he had to wait in her office.

The time dragged as he sat uncomfortably on the wooden stool in the tiny box room-come office. Had he known that this was to happen he could have spent more time with Limping Lenny. Maybe got more information out of him. Without any warning the door swung open hitting him on the shoulder, Damston stood there, hands on her hips, glaring down at him.

"Glad you decided to come back," She snapped at him and glanced at her watch.

Barton stood up, their bodies only a few inches apart, she delayed there for a moment, they looked deep into each other's eyes, When, she moved away she did so, very slowly, Barton had to admit to himself, he savoured the moment. She squeezed herself between the desk and the wall and settled on the seat. She glanced at him as if about to say something and changed her mind, instead she reached behind her desk, opened a drawer, pulled a wad of papers and spread them out on the desk. Barton decided to stand would be more comfortable leaning against the wall. Without looking at him she said, "a girl's body has been found, had been dumped down a motorway embankment, about twenty miles away."

Barton shook his head slowly, "have they identified her?"

"Not yet, she had been stripped naked, no identifying features."

"You seem to think that it was that girl who was shot in that forest?"

She looked over at him, "How many young girls do you think gets shot with a high velocity round?"

Barton nodded, "I admit not many, but coincidences do happen."

She looked back down at her papers and said," take my word on it, it was her."

Now that he had been told that he had passed the course and detailed the job of minder, if the dead girl wasn't the one who almost shot him. It won't matter now, he was in a position to bluff his way out of it. He sat back on the stool, his back against the wall, arms behind his head, "now that I'm your minder, I think it would be a good idea if I had your mobile number."

She glanced up, looked through the lock of blond hair, she wore a slight grin that never reached her eyes, "yes! that would be a good idea, you can let me know when you have been held up, like you were earlier today. So, why were you late?" She demanded, sprung to her feet in such a sudden movement, that Barton almost fell off the stool.

"The people who were coming to view my flat got held up in traffic, as I did on the way here."

"Next time get back here when I tell you."

Barton jumped to his feet, stood to attention, gave her a mock salute, "yes mam will do mam."

He watched her squeeze herself around the desk. Was that a slight smile she was wearing when he reached over and opened the door for her? He followed her to reception, where she stopped to talk to the girl.

Damston stepped behind the desk to view a computer screen, looked at him and said, "wait in your car, I'll be a few minutes."

The few minutes turned out to be almost half an hour, before she opened the car door and got in beside him. Barton just couldn't resist it, had to get his two pence worth, "so why were you late getting back?"

She chose to ignore his comment, "we have to go back to the warehouse in Allotment Street. I didn't manage to do a check list the last time, also to make sure that dead guard's body has been moved. I need to know if the new guard is on the job."

The night was wearing on, but it was still daylight. Barton hoped that the youths he had spoken to earlier had gone, the last thing he needed was for them to see him and shout or wave. "Doesn't it put you off after the last visit we had there."

She shrugged her shoulders and shook her head, "you can come in with me, watch my back, but anything you see inside you don't talk about. Do I have your word on that?"

Barton nodded, "Okay you have my word."

The evening sun was behind the rooftops of the derelict buildings, when they pulled up at the warehouse doors casting long shadows across the street. Barton got out first, scanned the area and walked around the vehicle, opened the door for Damston. She held the Beretta M.9. In front of her, cocked it, walked towards the door, handed Barton the key, nodded for him to unlock it. When they heard the locking mechanism operate, she pushed past him and entered. Barton followed close behind, pulled his pistol from his waist band at his back. A small dim light shone from a small cubicle about halfway down the warehouse. Damston, darted towards it, kicked open the door and was confronted by tall heavy built man holding a steel bar aloft. Damston jumped back in surprise. Barton's reactions were finer tuned, he jumped at the man feet first, knocking the bar from his hand. At the same moment Damston rammed her weapon under his nose.

"Start talking," she shouted at him.

The man shot up his long arms, "I'm security."

Barton picked up the steel bar, pushed it into the man's chest and shouted," you better be or I'll break every bone in your body with this."

Damston stepped back pointed her pistol at the entrance and said, "right let's turn the lights on,"

Without hesitation the security man led them to the control panel at the side of the door and turned on the tubular lights. The old system flickered for a second or two, and when their eyes became accustomed to the brightness, Barton was amazed to see the large metal shipping containers, that lined the length of both the walls of the warehouse. He guessed about twenty on each side, leaving a passageway down the centre wide enough for a fork truck to manoeuvre the containers, broad side in and out the building. Damston went to the first container, checked the sealed lock. Satisfied it hadn't been tampered with, she asked the security man," who interviewed you for this job?"

"A little well-dressed man, I think he said his name was Crow."

"I wasn't informed of it, how long ago was that?"

The man shuffled his feet, held out his hands, "I've been with the organisation for over a year now, I was moved up here to look after this place until they got a permanent person for the job."

She nodded and moved to the next container, went through the same routine, again satisfied, carried on down the one side. At the last one she turned to Barton, take him to the toilet and lock him in. You'll find cable ties in the cubicle, secure his hands and feet, then come and help me."

The security man was co-operative held out his hands and feet and sat on the toilet seat. Barton found her halfway along the adjacent wall, at a container marked with the number, fifty-one stencilled on the door. This one she opened, stepped inside, "you stand there," she said.

Barton had seen a lot in his life and thought he had hardened himself enough to face anything, but what faced him now, shocked and sickened him. The container was crammed full of elephant tusks, leaving only a small space at the door, enough to let her step inside. Barton was relieved that she hadn't turned around to see his reaction, she was concentrating on jotting notes in a small note book, he had no idea where she produced it from. Maybe, he wondered, it was already inside the container.

She slapped the notebook shut and stepped out. Barton helped her to close the steel doors, watched her lock and seal it, with what looked like a small pair of nail clippers. Satisfied she turned and headed for the main door, "you release the guard I'll wait at the door."

Damston was standing at the door with her mobile at her ear, when Barton approached, walking close behind the man. "What's your name? She asked him. When the man told her, she repeated it into her phone. "Okay," she said to Barton, "let's go."

CHAPTER 8

$\mathcal{S}$he took the keys from him and locked the warehouse doors and they got into his car, Barton was taken by surprise when she put her hand on his, even more so when she said, "I think I'll take you up on that offer of a meal."

As the faint moonlight shone through the car window, he could see her smile as she gazed into his eyes. Sending that long, forgotten feeling of a schoolboy crush through him. He fought the urge to react. "Anywhere you recommend?" He asked and started up the car.

"Let's go home and change, then we can make up our minds," she said," get a shower and get rid of the stink of that old warehouse off us."

There were no doubts on Barton's mind, what brought on this sudden change in her. This was her way of making sure he could be trusted and be close enough to keep an eye on him. As he drove them back to her home, many confusing thoughts drifted through his mind. To get to the truth relating to his younger brother's demise, she could prove to be useful. To do that he must control his feelings, but also to let her think he was falling for her plans.

Damston took a shower first, while he went to his bedroom and stripped. Naked with only a towel wrapped around his waist, he padded his way on bare feet to her bathroom, opened the door as she was leaving. All she was wearing was a towel wrapped around her extensive breasts, that only just covered her sexuality. Barton reluctantly stepped back to let her pass, this she took her time doing, smiling at him all the way. He couldn't take his eyes off her as she swayed her way along the passageway to her room.

After a very cold shower Barton went to his room and dressed. When he entered the lounge, she was sat on the sofa, blow drying her hair, still only wearing the towel. The effect of the cold shower diminished fast, he took the dryer from her hand, left it on the sofa and lifted her. She didn't resist and put her arms around his neck, He was amazed at how light she was, as he carried her to her bedroom and stripped away the towel, laying her gently on top of her bed. It was the rattle of crockery that woke him, the morning sun was shining through the bedroom window, reflecting off the dressing table mirror dazzling him slightly. He got out of bed, quickly dressed and found her in the kitchen, busy cooking breakfast.

She looked at him as he entered, "I hope you like a cooked breakfast," she asked smiling.

"I'll tell you what I like better," he stepped over and put his arms around her waist.

"She shrugged him away smiling," no time for that now, we have to eat and get to work."

She lingered for a few moments, before getting out of the car, at the office block carpark, looked deep into his brown eyes, "as far as anybody else is concerned, last night never happened, now it's back to business."

Barton switched off the ignition, a broad grin dawned across his face, "a gentleman never reveals a lady's secrets, but you have been walking about the house this morning as if you had just jumped off a horse."

Damston returned his smile, stroked him stubbled cheek, jumped out the car and had opened the office doors before he had released his seat belt.

She was standing at the front of her desk when Barton pushed through the door. She ignored him, carried on shuffling through sheets of paper. He edged past her, failing to avoid brushing against her hips and took up his uncomfortable position on the wooden stool.

"Don't get settled," she said to him over her shoulder," you have a lecture this morning, you better be on your way."

The other members were already seated when Barton walked into the lecture room. He could feel all eyes on him as he strolled up between the seats to his place at the back. He wondered why this bothered him, never happened before, and he was always amongst the last to arrive. Could it be because he got a special job, or do they suspect him sleeping with Damston? He sat down and shrugged it off, enjoying his secret grin behind their backs.

A tall thin man with badly fitted glasses entered and made his way in behind the lectern, shuffled a few papers about on top of it, at the same time pushing his glasses up his thin hooked shaped nose. His lecture was about how to forge documents and passports and how to tell forgeries. Barton wondered if such a lecture was significant to the job they were being trained to do, until he began talking meetings with dignitaries and being able to spot someone who should not be there, just by glancing at their papers. He pushed his glasses up again, and handed sheets of paper to the member sitting closest to him. "Hand them around," he ordered and returned to the lectern, saying," you all have a document insert your number in the box at the top. Read through it carefully if you think it's a forgery, tick the appropriate box at the bottom, fold the sheet and hand it back."

Barton only had to read the first three lines to make up his mind. He decided to hold back, not wanting to stand out and have the other members thinking he was a smart arse. On the other hand he didn't want to be last and them thinking he was a dumb arse. When a group of them stood up, he did likewise and handed his folded sheet over. When the last member returned to his seat, the thin man gathered up all the papers and left.

The lectern stood vacant for a while, a few of the members started chatting quietly to each other. Barton didn't get involved but listened very carefully to what was being said. The two girls joined in when he heard that high pitched squeaky voice, the hairs on the back of his neck stood up. Not that it matters a great deal now, that he had been selected, it was that he had convinced himself that she was the victim. Over the past few days that voice had haunted him, now here it was. One consolation though she had kept her mouth shut about the shooting incident, or he would have been dropped from the course that night. Never-the-less, it was a cause for concern. She was a good looking girl, blue eyes, long blond hair tied up in a ponytail. Barton wondered if she had a boyfriend, and decided to make a point in finding out.

Lumpy skipped into the lecture room and was behind the lectern before any of the members realised it. He called them to attention, a twisted smile beaming over his face. The moment he caught sight of Barton, the smile vanished. He stooped behind the lectern and popped up with a slide camera, carried it to the back and set it up on a vacant chair behind Barton, found a socket and switched it on, bent over to Barton's ear and whispered," don't you be thieving that."

From behind the lectern, he lifted a screen, set it up at the front where all could see it. Stepping back admiring his work, he returned to the back to the projector, switched it on and the screen lit up. He shouted," I'm going to show you the wiring of a homemade bomb, remember I explained it to you, that day in my workshop. I will ask some of you to explain to me how you would deactivate the timing device."

The slide went in showing a digital clock, with four cables leading from it, one black, one red, and next to them, green and blue. The four wires led to a detonator, but were all taped off at the end, this making it difficult to decide which one to cut first. All had been taped to the sticks of explosives.

Lumpy strutted to the front of the screen," what wire would you cut first?" He pointed to a member at the front.

After a long puzzling moment, the member replied, "green."

"Well done that man," Lumpy cried, "you've just killed us all." He grinned and walked towards Barton clamped his good hand on his shoulder," you next he said, with a sneer.

Barton took a short while to study the wiring, "no need to cut any of the wires," he replied," the detonator's not been connected to the explosives."

"Ah!" Lumpy shouted with a satisfied smile on his face, walking back to the front, "that's what you're supposed to think. He pointed a finger at the detonator, "that's not connected, but the one behind it is, that's the reason for the tape, to blank the real one off..., Now Mr. Smart Arse, what wire, are you going to cut?

Barton's mind was racing, many years had passed since he had faced this problem. Green was out, red was too obvious, his choice was black or blue. Most bomb makers have a signature, this was strange to him, had never came across one with a false detonator, "black," he decided.

Lumpy's smug grin vanished, he looked around the room and said, "do you all agree?"

Two hours later Barton and the rest of the members left the room, after watching a few other slides and blowing the room up several times according to Lumpy. They all stood outside at the back entrance, for a brake and some fresh air. Some were smoking and quietly chatting. Barton approached the girl with the ponytail and the high-pitched voice. After a few words of greeting he decided she was a hard bitch, a typical ex-con. Do anything for a price. Strange what thoughts come to mind unexpectedly, a saying his mother often used, a little flame could melt an iceberg with persistence. Barton decided to carry on chatting her up. He learned that she had a boyfriend but he was inside doing time. Maybe in a few days if he could get away from Damston, he could try again.

CHAPTER 9

The evening sun shone through the window behind Randell's back reflecting off his bald head. He edged his wheelchair closer to the desk, leaned on both his elbows and gazed into Damston's eyes. "The experts say the bomb that exploded in the pub carpark, was made by the same person, as the one that blew the roof off that derelict house in Allotment Street."

"Are you thinking that it was Lumpy." Damston asked flicking her blond locks out of her eyes.

Randell shook his head, his ample cheeks and neck wobbled in unison, "I shouldn't think so, Lumpy, gave up making bombs when he lost his hand."

"Could it be one he made previous to his accident, one he has stored away somewhere?"

"That's a possibility, that I thought of, we will just have to keep an eye on him. On the other hand it could be someone he has trained."

"I can't think who that could be, certainly not one of the members or past members."

"What makes you say that?" the big man asked her, getting off his elbows and leaning back on his wheelchair. Nevil stepped forward and pushed his chair closer to the desk and handed him one of his huge cigars.

"He scares the shit out of them, come to that, he scares me as well."

"I'm informed that all bombmakers have a signature, if I can find out what that signature is, then we'll know for sure, even if it turns out to be someone Lumpy has trained." He put the cigar in his tight lipped mouth and Nevil using a plastic lighter with a huge flame lit it for him. Randell blew a cloud of smoke at her and said, "we will have to be careful we need him to be on our side and not opposing us, if he's anything like Lumpy he's mad enough to run up and throw one of his bombs in the front door," He took another long pull at his cigar, Damston got it on her face again." If I discover that they are his making I'll get him sorted out." He slapped his fat hand on a file, that lay on the desk in front of him, "this man Barton," he nodded at the file, "you say he is not the run of the mill ex. Con. What I've got on him, is he served in the forces, for several years was jailed for an assault on an officer in Northern Ireland. Seems just like the type of person we need; you say you want him for a personal bodyguard," he leaned on his elbows on the desk again and gazed into her eyes," why?"

Those sunken cold blue eyes, never failed to send a cold shiver through Damston, in the ten years she had been with him she could never get used to his gaze. "You did tell me to be careful, after that girl was shot in that forest."

"Is he living with you?"

"Yes, he's in the spare room, it's purely business."

"It could be a good idea to get intimate with him, that way you can keep an eye on him. How much do you think you can trust him?"

Damston shook her head, "I'm not sure yet, given a little more time and I'll be able to tell you."

"How much time do you need?"

Damston grinned flicked a lock of blond hair back from her eyes with her long fingers, "the more intimate I get with him the sooner I'll know.

"I don't give a shit if you married him, just let me know if he can be trusted."

"What will happen if I find he's not to be trusted?"

"You don't need to ask you know what happens to those who can't be."

Damston leaned over on his desk, "has a definite identity been made on that girl who was found on the motorway embankment?"

Bartell shook his head slowly," nobody's came forward to claim the body."

Sitting on his usual seat at the back, Barton noticed an empty seat that had always been taken up by a slim nervy young man. Including himself the body count should have been nine, now he only counted eight. He remembered the thin man with the badly fitted glasses saying that they would be whittled down even farther. What made him wonder was, why any of the other members never seemed to notice. Could this be one of the reasons they are still on the course? Every one of them, must have been closely observed, all their reactions recorded. He did sense a heavy silence among them, they all sat staring at the empty lectern. The two girls sat at the front, would normally be whispering to each other. The door burst open, the members jumped into life, as if a current of electricity had been shot at them. Damston dashed in and took up her place at the lectern. Barton felt his heart skip a beat as she looked directly at him and smiled. He felt as though the whole class had turned around to look at him. His attempt to return her smile failed, only a grimace was the best he could muster. He silently cursed himself for letting this woman get to him. Regretted letting his weaknesses take over him last night, just didn't know what the attraction was, had never in his whole life felt so vulnerable. Her attempt at keeping their relationship discrete, was deliberately washed aside. What had come about that brought on this sudden change in her? Barton realised, if he was going to get any answers to what happened to Corrie, he would have to fight against this. Play along with her but control his feelings.

Damston knocked on the lectern, this brought Barton out of his reverie. Her blue eyes wandered around the members, he could confidently admire her now as she took control. There were no doubts, she had a certain charisma about her. "You five I selected, as bodyguard, didn't do a very good job," she said, "so we are going to go through it all again, tomorrow."

The next half hour, she talked about how to walk with a person to give the most protection.

"Always wear dark glasses," she finished up saying, "so that nobody knows where you are looking, remember your body is a shield, you take the shot, that's why you're well paid."

Barton walked to the front of the lecture room behind the other members, he delayed at the lectern and watched them file out the door. Damston was busy collecting up her papers and he asked, "is that you finished for the day?"

She shook her head, smiled at him, tucked her paperwork under her arm, "I've a lot to do in the office, so if you have something you want to do, you have two hours. I'll wait for you here."

He left her at reception, talking to the girl and made his way to his car. He noticed a few of the other members mingling in the carpark as he got into his car. He got a smile and a wave from the blond haired girl as he drove out.

Limping Lenny was nowhere to be found in the park, which Barton thought unusual for a bum on such a nice evening. After an hour of wandering about, he phoned Wilma, she informed him that Lenny was in hospital. She gave him all the information on what ward he was in, but couldn't say what was wrong with him. He found Lenny in a side room watching television with other patients, Hi mate?" Barton greeted him with a slight wave and pulled a chair up next to him, pointed to the bandage on his head," what happened to you?"

"You're what happened, talking to you, now fuck off."

"Sorry mate I didn't think that talking to me was a reason for someone to give you a doing."

The rest of the patients had turned their attention from the television and looked at them, Lenny in a hoarse whisper said, "well it did, so fuck off."

"Who did it?" Barton asked in an equal whisper.

"A couple of yobs, told me not to talk to you again."

"Just answer one question and that will be the last time you'll see me."

Lenny glared at him through swollen blackened eyes, "just leave me alone."

"So! you're not going to help a mate from the same regiment, you know the score, never leave a mate behind, do all you can, go that extra mile."

"Look at the state of me, I think the regiment left me behind a long time ago. I don't see any mates going that extra mile.

Barton decided to fire ahead, "you help me, and I'll do more than go that extra mile for you. I was driving in Allotment Street a few days ago, somebody took a shot at my car, nearly killing a friend, do you know who that shooter could have been?"

Lenny struggled to his feet and limped out into the corridor. Barton helped him all the way. At the end Lenny stopped. "Since that explosion there last Christmas, there had been a lot of movement in that street. Cars and vans unloading and loading stuff from the warehouse, all happening at night. Guys with hood walking up and down while all this was going on. It could have been one of them."

Barton helped him back to the side room, thanked him and waved. On his long walk back to the hospital parking place, Barton couldn't quite understand what Lenny was all about, was he really the bum he made himself out to be. The first meeting when Lenny grinned, Barton noticed his teeth were brown stained, like a heavy smoker who never bothered to clean them. There in hospital when Lenny grimaced, his teeth were white and in perfect condition.

Damston was in her small office when Barton returned, this time looking a lot more relaxed. She glanced up as he entered and smiled, logged off from her computer and stood up.

"Are you finished?" He asked and drooled as she edged her shapely buttocks between her desk and the wall. She combed her hair back with her long fingers, drew up close to him, looked deep into his brown eyes, patted him fondly on the cheek.

"Let's go home," she said, took his hand and led him through the open door.

Barton was utterly disconcerted by this sudden change, just hours ago she wanted the relationship to be kept secret. Now she was practically advertising it. On the drive home they had stopped to picked up a carry out meal. Now sat at her table in her kitchen, they eat silently. They both knew the reason for the silence, Barton wanted an explanation, knew better than to ask. She wanted to explain but didn't know how to put it or how to begin. She dropped her fork and stood up, went to the fridge and brought out a bottle of white wine. Barton now, well disturbed out of his thoughts got up and lifted two glasses from a rack and placed them out on the table.

After the meal they went into the lounge with their glasses and the bottle. Still not much was said, both lost in their own thoughts. Damston could stand no more, put her glass down on the coffee table, looked at him and said," you don't even know my first name, do you?"

Barton taken by surprise, almost spilled his drink down the front of himself, shook his head and smiled," you never told me."

"You could have asked."

"One thing I've learned in this game, it's dangerous to ask questions, but if you insist, what is your first name?"

"Eva, Eva Damston, I know your first name is Richard, is that what you like to be called?"

"If that suits you," Barton replied, "while on the subject of asking questions. This morning you wanted our relationship to be discreet, now you're practically advertising it, why?"

"It's simple, if we have feeling for each other, then we will protect each other." She leaned back and tucked her legs under herself and put her head on his shoulder. She felt his arm slip around her and she kissed his neck and said," you saved my life that day in Allotment Street."

Barton and the rest of the members, stepped out of the office door the next morning to be greeted with torrential rain. They rushed over and scrambled into the vehicles. Damston drove the leading car, Barton got the job of driving the following vehicle and had a job keeping up with her, as she raced through narrow country lanes. His orders were to keep up close and not lose sight of her. With only the slightest flicker of her brake lights, she swung her car to the left, into a small rough track. Barton had only a split second of a warning and almost toppled his vehicle on its side. His passengers gasped in shock, the girl screamed and shouted a mouthful of curses that would have embarrassed a squad of building site workers.

About a hundred yards along the track Damston pulled up behind another vehicle, that had already been parked up close to a building that Barton soon recognised as Lumpy's workshop. He drew up behind her car, nobody made a move to get out, the rain was still relentlessly pounding the ground around them, drumming rigorously on the roofs of the vehicles. Barton thought she must be holding back until the weather improved, was soon proved to be wrong. Her door swung open and by the expression she wore on her face, she was back to being Miss Nasty.

She strode up to Barton's car jerked his door open and shouted, "everybody out, what the fuck are you all waiting for?"

The sound of a smallbore engine made them all turn to see a quad bike racing around the corner of the building, spraying water and bouncing almost out of control on the hardcore surface. It screeched to a halt next to her, making her jump back. The rider dismounted Barton recognised him as one of the men they met in the motorway services. Whoever it was that coined the fraise (Hell, hath no fury like a woman's scorn) must have been talking about a woman like Damston. She got ripped into that rider dressed in combat gear, the tall slim man looked down on Damston and if he had a mind to, lift her off her feet and tossed her to the side. Instead he just stood there and took it all. When she had said her piece, he handed her a clip board and walked to the car at the front, Damston followed him. They stood huddled close to the wall, which offered little shelter, but better than nothing, they all seemed to have accepted, Barton had decided, if they didn't return soon, he was back inside the car.

When she showed up again, she was on her own. She waved them all towards her as she stood looking at an open field. "That tree up there," she pointed to a solitary tall beech that was surrounded by long grass and shrubs, "a marksman is behind it, his job is to shoot the person you are to protect. All he needs is a ten second window in his sights to succeed. Your job is to make sure he doesn't get that chance."

Two hours, of constantly walking back and forth along the side of Lumpy's workshop. Every time they completed the walk Damston's phone would ring, informing her that the shooter had succeeded in getting a sight on his target. In the end she gave up when they all looked as if they had been pulled out a river.

Before they all got into their predesignated vehicle, Damston shouted," go home, get changed, we will come back here this afternoon and keep at it until you succeed."

When all the members had de-bused in the car park at the office. Damston got in beside Barton and he drove her home. They showered together; the idea was to save time. The idea failed and they had to rush to get dressed and dash out to the car. She sat in thoughtful silence, as Barton drove back to the car park. She secretly glanced at him a few times and became aware that this man was growing on her. Why resist, she settled back in the seat and smiled to herself, he's a big handsome brute, and Mr. Bartell doesn't mind and it's the quickest way to get to know if he can be trusted.

All the members seemed to be a lot happier now that they were dry and warm, they were sat in their usual seats in the lecture room when Barton entered, last again, he cursed and took up his seat at the back. A moment later Lumpy pranced in, supporting a black eye and a bandage around his head. Barton's first thought, one of his bombs have gone off unexpectedly, and could hear a slight chuckle from some of the members, what more could be expected from a group of ex-cons?

Lumpy deprived them of his toothless grin, mumbled to himself as he proceeded to set up his slide camera. The session went on for an hour, at the end he said, "I'm only trying to save your lives, homemade bombs are very unpredictable, the slightest thing could set them off.

Eva Damston arrived before Lumpy got out the door, they exchanged a few words, before he departed. She held the door open for him and his equipment, when he cleared the door, she pushed it, caused it to bang, giving Barton and the others quite a jolt. At the lectern she talked about the failings of the mornings exercise, "you were told where the assassin was and still you couldn't protect your assigned member. To your advantage you had a solid wall, that covered one side of the target and seven of you failed to cover his back, front and right side. You must keep briskly moving around the target, by doing this you foil the shooters chance at a definite aim.

The question that troubled Barton and he knew he would never get an answer until the last minute was, who were these people they were to protect? He could only suspect some big time criminal barons.

Damston collected up her papers and said, "it's too late now to go back and do it again, so be here sharp tomorrow morning, hope the weather improves."

Barton broke off from the rest of the members as they filed out the room, holding back until they were out the main door. He entered her office without knocking and sat himself on the hard stool. She spared him a quick glance, with a smile and returned to her paperwork. He fished out his mobile and amused himself playing games on it.

She had sprung up out of her seat and opened the door before Barton could get his mobile turned off and back in his pocket. He chased her down the corridor and caught her at the reception talking to the girl. She waved at him to go outside and continued her conversation.

It was a quiet balmy evening, with a consistent drizzle, that made him feel damp and uncomfortable. Damston seemed to be taking ages to come out, Barton wished he had been blessed with more patience and decided to wait in his car, maybe continue with his game on his mobile. He just got in and sat down behind the wheel when the huge black limousine pulled up at the office doors. The tall black driver got out and opened the rear passenger door when Damston appeared pushing the big man in his wheelchair. She and the driver handled him into the vehicle and afterwards folded the chair and put it in the boot, she and the tall man got in front and drove off.

Barton decided to follow, keeping at a safe distance, which was a simple enough task, considering the size of the limousine and it's distinction. It soon dawned on him where they were heading. When the big car pulled off the main road, Barton carried on for a few yards before pulling into a side street. He pulled his hood up and got out the car and walked to the corner of Allotment Street in time to see the driver push the big man in his wheelchair into the warehouse. Damston held the door open, glanced in both directions along the street before she closed and locked the door.

An hour dragged by, daylight was fading, there was no street lighting, Barton could barely see the limousine and considered this a waste of time. He rushed back to his parked vehicle, got in and phoned Wilma. "Can we meet somewhere?" he asked, "in about ten minutes?" After a bit of reluctance she agreed.

CHAPTER 10

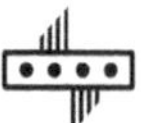

*H*e pulled into the deserted parking area and switched off the engine. She must have been close by when he phoned her. She walked towards him, her hands clutching the collar of her jacket to ward off the rain. Barton opened the passenger door for her.

"Did you visit Lenny?" She asked quickly.

Barton nodded, looked at her sodden hair clinging to her face, her eyes were puffed up as if she had been crying or had just woken from a sleep, but he knew that not to be the case. Knew this was drugs and selling herself on the street. "How well do you know Lenny?" he asked softly.

"Not very well," she replied lowering her head, "he's not a client, doesn't look as though he has enough money."

"Do you work Allotment Street?"

She turned on him and snarled, "I haven't stooped that low yet."

"I got the impression that he hangs about there a lot."

"He does, according to what I've been told, he walks up and down that street like a security guard, in and out of the old house. Some of the young guys that hang about there, say he lives there."

"When I spoke to him, I got the feeling, he does more than just bum about there, it's as if he was watching all that was going on, for someone."

Wilma smiled for the first time in the dim light of the car, "they say he's not right in the head, ex-army, maybe he thinks he's still on guard duty."

Barton reached over and held her hand, "I can assure you he is right in the head and you may not be far wrong when you say he's on guard duty."

She withdrew her hand, "he's just a down and out bum with nothing else to do with his time."

"I think the down and out bum part is an act."

"Well, all I can say, he's a bloody good actor."

"It's not hard to put on that act, just wear some dirty old clothes, show yourself about places like public parks and old houses."

She shrugged her shoulders and stepped out of the car, looked in at him and said," my advice to you

Richard is drop it," she closed the door and walked away, the way she had come, blending into the shadows of the surrounding buildings.

Barton had just got the car started when his mobile sounded, he grabbed it from his pocket and Damston's name came on the small screen. "Hi," he said into it. Her voice came through crisp and clear, sounding quite concerned, asking where he was," I'll explain when I get back.

Damston got the good day she wished for, sunshine and a blue sky, although things were still wet underfoot. No quad bike this time as Barton and the members stood in a group behind the first car. She briefed them and asked for a volunteer to act as the target," but this time," she reminded them, "the assassin will be using live rounds." She wasn't surprised at the response she got. The members looked at each other, some took a step back, none of them wanted any part of it. She grimaced at them, "I thought this would happen, so I've brought eight straws, the one who picks the short straw, gets the job."

Barton held back to the last, the other seven were looking jubilant, they all held up their straws, all were the same length. "Looks like I get the job," Barton announced and didn't bother to draw the last straw from her hand. He turned towards them, held up a hand, "you lot better get this right this time. We will walk briskly along the length of the wall, at no time must any of you be any farther away than two feet from me and you will keep changing position as we go."

As he got the group into position, he noticed Damston standing by her car, she smiled and waved as he and the members set off. They rushed to the end of the building in a matter of seconds and no shot had been fired. All of them gave a sigh of relief and laughed at each other, but it was short lived when Damston shouted and told them to do the same on the way back. One of the girls was leading as they all got started trying to get to the other side without running. She stumbled and fell, Barton like the rest of them, thought she had been shot, "don't stop he shouted, keep moving."

They stepped over her, she got up and scrambled to her feet and rushed to catch up.

Damston came towards them, applauded, "that went well if you had stopped to pick up that girl, you would have left the intended target vulnerable."

Barton sat on the sofa drinking coffee, Damston was stretched out with her head resting on his thighs watching television. His free hand was playing with her blond hair, he asked, "what would you have done if the members got it wrong today?"

She turned away from the television, looked up at him, with a stern expression," they did get it wrong."

"Well, why am I still here?"

"There was no marksman and what's more, there was no short straw."

"So, you had it all planned out, knowing that I would pick the last straw?"

She grinned and turned back to the television, "I assumed that with you as the target, a marksman would have a hard time getting a bead on you. I was right, the way you handled yourself inside that group was in my opinion, very professional."

"I'll take that as a compliment."

She sat up took his cup from his hand and drank what was left in it, "I'll make a fresh one," she said holding the cup up.

"In what area did you think the members failed?"

She got onto her feet, looked down at him, "you had to tell them what to do, they should have known."

That was only common sense, not professional."

Barton watched her carrying the empty cups into the kitchen, admiring the sway of her hips, the way her long blond hair rested on her shoulders," and anyway," he shouted after her, "I'm the oldest member, it's understandable, they would listen to what I said,"

CHAPTER 11

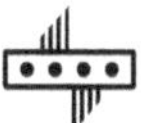

Six muscle bound, well-armed men, hoods drawn down almost over their eyes walked through the garage in single file. They barged into the small office, where Cecil Hussey sat behind a cluttered desk. Cecil stood up and welcomed them in, told them to sit, they remained standing. He offered them a drink, they refused. He grinned exposing his pure white perfectly set piano key teeth. "You did a good job on Limping Lenny," he commented, "Now let's hear what he had to say?" He directed his question to the man standing at the front, known to him only as Purdy. Purdy held out a big hand, "cash first."

Cecil drew a roll of notes from his jacket pocket and tossed it on the desk. "that's your price," he nodded at the money and sat back down on the seat.

Purdy snatched up the notes and pocketed them, "he told us about a man who approached him, asking about that bombing in Allotment Street last Christmas."

"Did you get this man's name?"

Purdy shook his head, "Lenny didn't get his name.

"Did you find out what Lenny told this man?"

Purdy recited Lenny's words, Cecil went silent for a while, in deep thought then said holding up a finger, "a whore I know was trying to arrange a meeting with me, on behalf of a man who wanted to know about his brother…, Barton's his name. You'll find this whore on the streets her name is Wilma. She's already been questioned about this you will have to watch how you approach her, or she'll do a runner."

"Who questioned her? Purdy asked.

I got a few of my boys to have a word," with both hands Cecil fluffed up his bush of tight curly black hair, that haloed his dark African features like a wreath. He sat back away from Purdy's bad breath. "I want to know what she knows about this man Barton, before you bring him here, I'll find out what he's about, then you can waste him and the whore."

The old chair creaked under protest of Purdy's weight when he sat down on it, "How about the Carter brother's, any idea where they are, now that your attempt to blow them up failed?"

"I've got someone working on that, I'll let you know as soon as I get word."

Purdy jumped up, the chair scuffed noisily as the back of his legs pushed it away, "I'll be expecting at least five big one for all this work."

Cecil rose, held out his small black hand dripping with gold rings. Purdy ignored it and turned for the door, He opened it and turned, "what about Lenny, do you want him wasted?"

Cecil shook his head, "No, Lenny's useful, but I want Barton here in twenty-four hours at the latest."

Cecil followed Purdy and his five thugs out the office, they walked through the garage, found Jaco in conversation with a young mechanic outside the main door. Cecil watched him rush over to the car and get in the driving seat. Without a backward glance Purdy and his gang boarded a white Range Rover. When the large vehicle drove away, Cecil and his two goons jumped in his own car next to Jaco, punched him on the side of face, "chatting up that young grease monkey? You bastard."

Jaco's head jerked side wards with the impact, could feel the hot blood oozing from his ear. The punch on its own didn't do the damage, it was the huge studded gold rings that caused the injurie. He wiped the blood with his hand, "he was only telling me about his job," Jaco whimpered, gazing at the blood on his fingers.

"Who are you?" Asked the paunchy bald man standing at the door wearing only a singlet vest and dirty jeans.

Ben Carter stuck his pistol on the man's bottom lip." Just back up pal,"

Tommy barged passed them and pulled the man by the back of his vest into the building, Ben closed the door and followed his brother and the paunchy figure into the small room and onto a wooden chair." Who, are you?" Ben shouted into his face and grabbed his fleshy tattooed arm.

"I'm looking after this place," the man screamed in agony.

"Where's the regular guy?" Tommy asked from behind.

"He's on nights this week."

Ben put more pressure in his arm," we weren't told about this."

The man roared in pain, it reminded Ben of a wildlife program on television about a male lion warning other male lions to keep away. He released his grip, the man buckled over nursing his arm.

Tommy was on his mobile, making enquiries about the situation, he was on it for two minutes, put his mobile back in his pocket, looked at his brother and said, "waste him."

Ben walked around the back of the man, jabbed his pistol into the back of the man's head, "who gave you this job?"

"No… no, please, the man pleaded holding his painful arms aloft, "it was a while ago, he never gave his name, he was a small, well-dressed man, had a southern accent, well spoken, looked like an ex-army officer or something."

"Why haven't we seen you here before?" Tommy asked.

"I'm on regular nights, the day man wanted to change over for a week, said he had something to attend to."

"What's your name?" Ben asked from behind.

"Archie."

Ben landed a painful kick on Archie's rump, knocking him to the floor, "get on your feet, we're going to inspect these containers, if we find any of the seals have been tampered with, you're dead."

By the back of his neck, Tommy lifted Archie onto his feet, Pushed him out the small security cubicle into the warehouse. He pulled a notebook from the inside of his jacket pocket and said "You have twenty-two containers in here, now let's all go and inspect them."

With Ben leading and Tommy behind Archie, they went down the line of metal containers, all of them huge forty feet long, ten feet high, eight feet wide. They stopped at every one carefully inspecting the seals. When satisfied all was in order, they returned Archie to his cubicle. Ben offered him a cigarette and said, "you, being on nights, you don't know the routine, your mate should have told you, that from time to time we arrive unexpectedly to check these containers, if we discover they have been tampered with, you're both dead."

"Have you ever wondered what's inside them?" Tommy asked.

Archie in the process of getting a light for his cigarette from Ben, shook his head," never even gave it a thought."

Tommy slapped him knocking the cigarette out of his mouth," you're a fucking liar, I bet you and your mate have often spoke about what you think might be inside them."

Archie, stunned by the force of the blow, fell onto the chair shaking his head, "okay," he cried," it's only human nature, but we never once mentioned anything about opening them up."

Ben bent down and retrieved his smoke, and handed it to him, "you know what will happen if you do."

They made sure Archie had no doubts what would happen to both him and his mate if they interfered, with the containers before they left. Ben was driving the hired van heading South on the motorway. He smoked cigarette after cigarette, while Tommy fed strips of chewing gum into his mouth. "Have you ever wondered why Randell has all his warehouses scattered all over the country?" Tommy asked, waving the smoke away.

"Well," Ben replied, coughing at the same time, "I would think for security reasons, he's onto a good earner storing all that contraband for dodgy foreign governments and cartels. There's got to be opposition for that racket."

"Tommy started to cough," for fucks sake Ben open your window, you're killing me as well as yourself."

Ben ignored the advice, "what has been puzzling me," another cough, "is why Damston never asked where the explosives came from, that day in the pub car park."

"Well, when she asks, just say someone must have put them under the car when we were in having a drink."

"She's not going to believe that," Ben assured him, laughed and said, "Poor Lumpy got a trouncing, Randell found out that the bomb was one of his making." He pulled the van onto the slipway of the first service station, drove into a vacant spot in the car park, for a while he stared into the side mirror, "I don't know if I'm being paranoid, but that white Rang Rover parked behind us, has been following us. Always a few cars behind, I change lane, it did too, been like that for about ten miles."

Tommy glanced in the mirror on his side as the vehicle in question pulled out the car park and onto the motorway, I think you're right, you are being paranoid."

"I wouldn't be too sure of that I think they suspect that we twigged on."

Tommy held up his arms," okay, if that's what you suspect, what do you propose we do?"

"Phone up this car hire company and ask for a replacement car, to be delivered here in the services."

Three cigarettes later a young woman tapped on their window, dangling a set of keys. They quickly exchanged vehicles and watched her drive off. "That was fast service," Ben commented, "they must have a depot close by."

Tommy nodded, "before we get into it, let's go and have that tea and something to eat."

They were back on the motorway, after eating sandwiches and two cups of (cat piss) tea. Ben called it. This time, Tommy took a turn at driving and only got a few miles when he had to slow down and stop at the end of a tailback." Now what's wrong?" he shouted. Ben turned up the radio and they discovered that a concrete block had been dropped from a bridge landing on a white Citroen van, owned by a car hire firm, killing the woman driver.

"Bloody Hell!" shouted Ben, "and you thought I was being paranoid."

"Might not be the same van, there could be other white Citroen vans on this motorway."

"A hired Citroen van with a woman driver, just a few miles from where we swapped it over, I don't think so Tommy."

The car in front started crawling forward, Tommy did the same," okay, I admit it is too much of a coincidence."

"Too bloody right it is, that concrete block was meant for us."

"That Range Rover you said was following us, do you think it could have been them?"

Ben stuck a cigarette in his mouth, lit it with a plastic lighter, took a long deep pull at it, blew out a cloud of smoke. He nodded, "yes and hired by the same little bastard who tried to blow us up."

Tommy again waving away the smoke said, "We should have gone straight over to that club and killed him that night,"

Ben opened the window, "The first chance we get, that's just what we'll do," he chuckled quietly and threw his cigarette end out the window.

CHAPTER 12

*B*arton had sat on the wooden stool for over an hour and a half, playing games on his phone. From time to time taking a glance at Damston working on her computer. He wondered if she was doing the same. Playing a psychology games with him, to see if he would get up off the stool to ease his discomfort. Words that rang in his ears, from years back, hammered into him, by his N.C.O. "It's all in the mind Barton." Was little comfort, difficult not to think of pain when the legs start to cramp up.

Damston's mobile sang out, jolting him out of his reverie. She snatched it from the desk and held It to her ear for only a second, she jumped up, put her phone in her pocket and said," we're going for a drive." She had squeezed her way to the door before Barton could get his game turned off.

Lumpy stood at the reception desk. They received a toothless grin from him, he tossed the keys at Barton. "car's ready," he said and handed Damston a small damaged shell," dug this out the steering column."

She held it in the palm of her hand examining it. Barton edged closer and saw that a fine hacksaw cut had been made at the point. "If that had hit you, it would have ripped you apart,".

She handed it back to Lumpy, "keep a hold of that, I might need later."

Lumpy gave her an inquisitive glance and pushed the shell into his oil stained Harris Tweed jacket pocket.

Damston grabbed him by the lapel, pushed her face close to his, "you're coming with us."

Lumpy pulled back from her, I can't I've got things to do."

"Get into the fucking car," she shouted and pushed him out the door, he stumbled, almost fell over, they followed him to the vehicle listening to his complaints and curses.

One thing that had mystified Barton, Damston always wore tight tops and trousers, yet she managed conceal that weapon and draw it out in less than a heartbeat. There it was in her hand, pushed it into Lumpy's back.

"Hands and stump on the roof," she ordered him, gave Barton the nod to open the doors. "open up the boot," she said, Barton complied, she grabbed Lumpy by the back of his neck, pulled him to the rear of the car, "get in," she shouted and tried to push him head-first into it.

Lumpy resisted, threw his arms up, tried to back kick her legs, cursed and swore. But all was in vain, he heard the pistol being cocked, he had no other option but to climbed in, he threw a barrage of curses at her. Barton stepped over and closed the boot door down on him.

"I think you've made an enemy in the last few minutes," Barton said as she got into the passenger's seat next to him.

"He's everybody's enemy that man, can't be trusted, sell his talent to anyone who is willing to pay."

Barton started up the car," where are we heading?" He asked.

"Just drive, I'll give you directions."

Her directions brought them to an abandoned council estate. All the windows and doors were blocked off with galvanised steel sheet. Toppled plastic wheelie bins lay dispersed all over the street, there contents scattered, from one end of the street to the other. She told him to stop at a house near the end. She got out walked to the rear and opened the boot. A very stiff Lumpy struggled out, flexing his arms and legs, to get his circulation going. "Go bang on that door," she told him and pointed to the house across the street. Noticing the weapon still in her hand, Lumpy had no option but to comply.

Damston got back in beside Barton, they watched Lumpy slowly walk towards the door, every few steps he would turn back and look at them. When he did this, she would wave him on," we must find out who's side he's on," she said thoughtfully," there are two men in there who will ask him."

Even from inside the car it sounded like the crack of a whip, Barton knew what it meant and rammed the vehicle into gear. The tyres screamed; the car fish tailed then jumped forward. Damston had lurched down cowering in the footwell. Barton took a moment to look back and saw Lumpy diving over a wheelie bin. A motorcyclist almost fell over when he swerved to avoid running into Barton as he swung onto the main drag. Damston got up, fastened her seat belt," what the fuck was that all about? She cried.

"This is getting to be a bit of a habit," Barton complained, and pulled the car to a halt a few streets away.

"Do you think Lumpy got hit?"

"I don't know, I noticed him diving over a wheelie bin."

"Well we're not going back to make sure."

"Not worth the risk, is he?"

Damston ignored his question, "did you notice where that shot came from?"

Barton let out a deep sigh, shook his head slowly, "I think it must have come from the bottom of the street, behind us."

"Lumpy must have been the target, I think somebody didn't want him to talk," she looked at him, "what do you think?"

"We must have been followed how else would the shooter know we were here? I think that he, or she took the shot from their car."

"Okay," Damston resigned herself to his theory, "let's get back to the office, be careful we could still be getting followed."

Barton made a few detours, using a double back tactic, kept glancing in the mirror, Damston constantly turned to look out the rear window."

Sat behind her desk in the small office, Damston decided if Barton's guess was right, then that shooter must have made a fast exit after taking the shot because they never detected any vehicles following them. He sat on that uncomfortable stool his long legs tucked up in the cramped space, his back leaning on the wall, playing with his phone. She couldn't help but admire him for his coolness and quick thinking under these circumstances.

She wondered was she developing a dependence on him, or was it more than that? She stood up as if by doing so would wipe these thoughts from her mind, picked up her note pad and edged her way between the wall and her desk. By the time she reached the door Barton was on his feet.

"The boss want's a word with you, we better go now," she said.

That sparked a momentary rush of adrenalin, Barton was struggling to contain himself. At long last to meet the top man, this was not a step in the right direction, this was a leap.

Coming from Damston's office to the boss's, was like stepping from a garden shed into a ballroom. This was more like a penthouse than an office. When has saw the big man behind his desk in a wheelchair, he decided that maybe this was an apartment come office. They stood at his desk looking down at him, Barton instantly thought, a snow man, the large white ball shaped bald head, deep sunken eyes stub nose and a narrow slit for a mouth.

Randell reached out a huge arm across the desk and picked up a thick smouldering cigar from a glass ashtray. He held it between his thumb and stumpy fat finger, gazed at it before pushing it into his narrow-lipped mouth. His deep sunken cold blue eyes turned on Damston, "what's this about Lumpy," he asked, blowing a cloud of smoke into her face.

Barton at this stage was standing there feeling like a piece of furniture, as he listened to Damston taking the big man through the details on the incident.

"Well I can tell you this," Randell assured her, "Lumpy is dead, shot though the skull. What you thought, was him diving for cover, was the impact of the of a high velocity round blowing him off his feet."

Barton felt a bit puzzled, on recall it must have been about ten seconds, from the time he heard the crack of the round to the time when he saw Lumpy falling over the wheelie bin.

"I know he was an idiot," Damston said, "but he had his uses, could be hard to find someone to take his place,"

"I don't think so," the big man replied shaking his head, he flashed his cold blue eyes at Barton for a second then returned to her, "I'm already working on that. He was as you say an idiot, too much of an idiot, too mouthy. I know he had to have someone to build his bombs, too risky for a man with only one hand. I want you both to find out who this character is, we need to know if he or she is on our side.

The office door opened, and the tall black chauffeur entered and walked in behind the big man. Randell and Damston took no notice of him, He grinned at Barton and rested a hand on the handle on the wheelchair. "Sit down," the big man invited them with a wave of his fat hand.

Damston sat on the chair already at the front of the desk, but Barton had to carry one from the other side of the office.

"How about this shooter," Damston asked, "do you have any clues who this can be?"

Randell waited until Barton was settled on his seat, "that's the reason I asked you to bring Mr. Barton here, I also want you both to find out who this person is and if someone is hiring him. But you must not make it obvious, do your investigations while doing your routine work."

Barton saw this as an opportunity to carry out his own enquiries, but knew he would still have to be careful. He cleared his throat and got the big man's attention, "When did this shooter first target your organisation?"

Randell ignored the question and pulled a fresh cigar from a drawer down the front of his desk, he put it between his thin lips, slightly turned his head to let his tall black driver light it. He turned his attention back to Barton, "it all began about six months ago, although the first person he shot from our syndicate was that girl in the forest, you were there when it happened." He blew a cloud of smoke, at Barton, "Damston here thinks you can be trusted, I hope she's right, for both your sakes."

Barton grimaced and held the big man's gaze, "trust is a two-way street, if I can trust you then you have my trust one hundred per cent." At his side he heard Damston catch her breath, saw she was about to interrupt, Randell held up his hand and stopped her, another cloud of smoke came Barton's way. His cold blue sunken eyes stared deep into Barton's, "oh, you can trust me, to make sure you're a dead man, if find I can't trust you."

CHAPTER 13

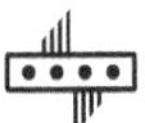

They had levered a bolt out of the galvanised sheet that blocked off the front window. It made a perfect peephole. Tommy gave his brother a running commentary on the events happening outside. Ben had been hunched on the floor smoking. Tommy jumped back. Ben dived flat on the floor when the shot rang out.

"What the fucks happening?" Ben shouted.

"I think somebody's took a shot at Damston's car, I heard it screech away up the street." Tommy replied, pulling his gun from his pocket.

"Did you see what happened to that idiot Lumpy?"

"The last I saw of him was when he jumped over one of those bins."

Ben picked himself up and recovered his half-smoked cigarette, "so do you think he got back into the car?"

"I don't think so, the car was already on the move when I saw him take a dive."

"We better wait here a while, make sure it's safe to go out and check."

They left the house the way they had entered, through a gap in the back window. The metal shutters had been left hanging, prized open by some squatters in the past. They found Lumpy's body lying behind the wheelie bin. Tommy pointed to the hole in his skull just above his ear. They had no doubts he was dead. "We better let Randell know," suggested Tommy fishing his phone from his pocket.

"We'll have to come back later when it's dark," Ben said, "get this cleaned up, hope nobody finds it first."

Tommy shut off his phone, "come on Ben, get out of here, we'll have to be vigilant on our way to the car in case the shooter is still hanging around.

Barton had guessed wrong on both cases, Damston and he hadn't been followed and the shot hadn't been fired from a car. The shot had been taken from a window on the second floor of one of the empty houses three block away on the opposite side of the street. The gunman had a good clear view of the house where the Carters had entered. But the brothers weren't his concern. His intel. Had always been good and the designated target was well described with photos and background information and always got the price he asked. The contracts were always fulfilled and the customers were happy. He carefully dismantled the rifle, placing all the parts into the padded compartments inside a specially adapted case. A quick, last minute glance out the window before closing the galvanised shutter and there they were, the Carter's with eyes all over, stealing they're way, down the street. Maybe one day he grinned, combing his long slim fingers through his premature white hair. The shutters slipped home silently, he wiped the dust from his clothing and shoes and made sure he had left no traces behind, he silently slipped away.

"Did you notice that steel sheet shutter on that upstairs window on the second floor of the second last house," Ben asked Tommy.

"No," his brother replied, shaking his head with a look of concern on his face.

"It had been sticking out a bit farther than the rest, when I took a quick look back from the end of the street it was back level with the rest of them. I didn't draw your attention to it in case you turned to have a look."

Tommy got into the driver's seat, but Ben delayed a moment longer listening for a car starting up and pulling away, only the rumble of a heavy diesel engine was audible from a nearby road." I think that shooter is still hanging about, "he said as he crouched in beside his brother in the passenger seat.

How much different life would have been for them, if only they realised, that the tall thin man with the white hair carrying a small black narrow case, crossing in front of them on the pedestrian crossing, as they waited for the lights to change, had their lives at his fingertips a few minutes ago. He waved at them as they drove away, thinking you stupid bastards if only you knew.

Damston strutted across the car park to the Carter's hired car, she jumped in the back seat and handed over a black holdall to them and said," you'll find all you need in this bag. The two girls will be with you in a minute or two. Like you, they have been briefed and know all there is to know. They have done the course and can be relied on to watch your backs, as you will do so with them."

Barton stood at the office entrance, Damston closed the door to the Carter's hired car and walked towards him. Two girls he recognised as the ones from the course crossed in front of her, she stopped them and exchanged a few words. He decided to go over and join them, maybe hear a few words of interest, but they had split up before he got near them.

Damston stopped in front of him, looked up into his eyes, "you guessed wrong about Lumpy's killer, I've been told that the shots came from one of the old houses." She strutted past him into the building.

"Can't be right all the time," he shouted after her and followed her into her office. "Did your informants see the shooter?" He asked as he sat down on the stool looking at her.

She shook her head and tapped keys on her computer, "they never saw the person, they saw movement on one of the steel shutters and guessed that was the firing point."

"Like me your informant could only guess that particular shutter could have been slack and got blown by the wind, one thing for sure I wasn't going to hang about there to find out."

She sat back on her seat and let out a deep sigh, looked into his brown eyes," how are we going to find out who this shooter is?"

"The first thing is to find out who the squealer is, has to be someone in the organisation. How else could he or she know our movements."

"How do we find this squealer then?"

"Who would know when we were going to that forest, when we were visiting that warehouse in Allotment Street and who knew about today?"

She stood up and squeezed herself around the desk, stood and looked down at him," any one of about six people in the organisation might have known."

"We could start at anyone you suspect the most, watch them closely, maybe set a trap or something to catch them out."

"We strongly suspect who is doing the hiring, the problem is the boss doesn't want a gang war and It would take that to get to him." She pulled the door open, but only got it half-way when Barton got up, shot his hand out and stopped it.

"Who do you strongly suspect?"

"That's not important," she said letting him close the door, "what we have to do is find this informer first."

"Can you think of anyone who that might be?"

She shook her head, "we'll just have to wait and see if they slip up."

"That could take some time," Barton replied, let her open the door and followed her out.

They walked in silence to the car, she skipped around and got in the driver's seat and sat for a while. Barton could see she was deep in thought, as she slipped the key into the ignition, she looked at him, unsure if she was doing the right thing by telling him. "I'll tell you this, but you must keep it a secret for a while."

"Oh kay" Barton said

"You've been to Allotment Street warehouse you must have noticed that one of the derelicts houses had the roof blown off, that was caused by a bomb that Mr Randell said was meant for the warehouse. He and a few others were in the building at the time. He and his driver were the only ones to survive. We're quite sure who arranged it, a little fly with an oversized ambition, we could have killed him but decided against it to see if we could catch this informer first." She started up the car and drove off

She pulled up at a vacant space in the car park, close to the metallic blue limousine. Barton followed her when she got out and headed towards the Victorian styled manor house hotel. She entered the arched doorway and spoke to a young man behind the reception desk. As he had been previously instructed, Barton stationed himself at the door. Soon he was joined by the two girls from the course, a slight grin and a nod was the only greeting he got. Two tall slim built men walked towards them, as they drew closer Barton recognised them as the two, they met in the motorway services. Barton hadn't paid much attention to them that day, but now as he studded them when they stood a short distance away he could see a resemblance in them. Could they be brothers?

Damston accompanied an oriental man and woman out of the hotel door. Barton got in step behind them, with the girls walking on either side of the couple. The two tall men led them to the limousine and opened the doors, the couple climbed in, Damston joined them. Barton got in front beside the driver, rammed the Baretta into the driver's ribs and said, "drive mate." This he had been instructed to do when the driver was a stranger.

Barton was expecting this man to get into a panic with a gun stuck in his ribs, but this white haired driver just grinned, started up the car, and drove off.

"I've got my instructions on what route to take," white hair said, "do you want to change it?"

"I'll tell you where to go," Barton said giving his gun an extra jab.

"If you want to make any changes, I'll have to inform my company."

"Just drive where your told."

To get to their destination, they had to drive along a single-track road, to a collection of farm buildings that had been converted into private houses, none of them looked occupied. Two men emerged from the largest building and approached the vehicles, both wore a black suit, white shirt and tie and as expected dark glasses. One stood at the front of the limousine, the other at the rear facing away from the vehicle. Barton got out and opened the rear door as the two girls approached. The two tall men stood a short distance away. The couple stepped out first, Damston got out the opposite side and quickly darted around to join them. They grouped together and escorted the couple into the largest building, Barton followed behind until they met Randell and the tall black driver in one of the rooms. The man and woman entered on their own, the door was closed and the two girls remained in the short corridor, Barton and Damston retreated to the front door.

He looked at Damston, she returned his look, held out her hands in confusion, the only vehicle parked in the courtyard was the limousine. The escort car was gone along with the two security guys and the white-haired driver was nowhere to be seen. "What the fucks going on here?" She shouted and pulled her gun out, ran towards the limousine. Barton was at her heals, when her mobile sounded, she snatched it out, held it to her ear, listened for a few seconds, Turned to Barton, "the limousine driver's done a runner, their chasing after him."

"We need to get that limousine out of here in case there's a bomb in it," Barton shouted to her. He jumped into the driver's seat, luckily the keys were still in it, got it started and reversed it out onto the single-track road with his foot flat on the accelerator. After about a hundred yards he stopped, noticed Damston running towards him, he got out and waved her back, but she ignored him and kept coming.

There was no time to listen to her protest and he said, "okay you check in the boot, if you find anything suspicious don't touch it, let me know." It didn't take Barton long to find what looked like a bomb, under the seat where he had sat. He lifted it out, "I think this is just a scare factor," he explained, "it looks like the real thing, but nothing is connected, the timer has stopped and that's not explosives, it's marzipan, has the same smell and looks similar." He tossed it to her.

Damston had no intentions of catching it and let it fall at her feet. She side stepped it and said, "why would anybody go to the trouble of planting a dummy bomb?"

"Scare tactics, to let you know how vulnerable you are, we can hope they catch that driver, get him to talk, we might find out who is behind it all."

"No such luck," a voice from behind said, "the bastard had a car waiting for him at the end of the road."

Damston turned, "did you get a look at the car?"

"I did," said his mate in the suit and dark glasses," it was a white Range Rover."

"Could be the same one that followed us on the motorway," said one of the tall men.

CHAPTER 14

*C*ecil jumped off his bar stool when Purdy and his thugs entered the club, "did you get Barton?" he shouted.

Purdy shook his head, "and whore has pissed off somewhere."

Cecil slapped his black hand down on the bar, the chunky gold rings making a metallic crack sound on the wooden surface, "and the Carter brothers, where are they?"

"We followed the Carter's to Darlington in a white van," Purdy explained. "They pulled into a warehouse on the outskirts, went inside with a bald-headed man who was already in there. When they came out we tailed them back to the motorway. We followed them into the services we decided to make their death look like an accident. We drove back onto the motorway to the nearest flyover. There was a village down the road, we found an abandoned builder's yard there, that's where picked up a slab of concrete. When we saw the van on the motorway, we dropped the concrete onto it from the flyover."

Cecil picked up his glass of gin, drank down the last of it, banged the glass on the bar and grimaced, "an incredibly good plan, the only thing that went wrong, the Carter's weren't in the fucking van."

"They must have changed vehicles."

"Well done Purdy," Cecil replied and clapped his hands, "you managed to work that one out."

Purdy's temper began to get out of control, wanted to smash his big fist into Cecil's face. But decided against it, the little shit was a good source of income for him and his boys. When the day came that it all stopped his little black face will be tangled among that bush of frizzy hair.

Cecil was enjoying himself, loved ridiculing people, this meant power, it was like a drug, couldn't live without it.

"This man Barton is proving to be difficult to get a hold of, always on the move," Purdy explained, "we found his rented flat and gave it a doing over. It seems he's moved out but not permanent, there's still some of his belongings there."

"Hope you haven't trashed the place," Cecil perked up sharply, "don't want him to know we're after him."

"The boys did get a bit careless."

"Well get back there and tidy the place up."

"As for the whore, as you said, she has pissed off, nobody knows where."

Cecil accepted that for the time being, "keep searching for her, I can't afford for her to be mouthing off."

"We need some cash up front," Purdy said.

"Well you're not getting it."

"How do you expect us to do all these jobs with no money?"

"I have already paid you upfront for a job you haven't done yet, so piss off."

Purdy lunged forward, banged his fist down on the bar, "fuck you," he shouted.

"Cecil grinned, when he saw three of his goons grab Purdy's arms, "you're not my type darling."

The goons forced Purdy to the door, one produced a pistol and pointed it at his three thugs, they stood back with hands held up and followed but before they threw him out, Purdy shouted back, "If we don't get paid when this job is done, you're fucking dead."

"If you don't do the job properly this time, you'll be fucking dead," Cecil shouted back. He grinned to see Purdy getting pushed out-side, he remembered being advised about Purdy and his mob, thick as shit, but never get on the wrong side of them. That was a while ago, now that he has six goons and money to pay them, Purdy's threats are like a grain of sand on the beach.

Jaco was behind the bar when he heard the disturbance, he stopped to look at what was going on, like the rest of the patrons. When Purdy got tossed out, he joined Cecil, jabbed his thumb at the exit," that's not a happy man."

"He's not entitled to be."

"Had a falling out, have you both?"

"What did it sound like?"

"I heard he's a nasty piece of work, him and his gang; thugs for hire, they say."

Cecil nodded, "you're not wrong, but they do have their uses," He pushed his glass at Jaco, "fill me up."

Jaco lifted the gin bottle from under the bar, Cecil's favourite brand, not for the customers, filled the glass up and pushed it back. He watched Cecil take a sip and thought, you wimpish little punk when you're on your own, always the tough guy when the goons are with you. With a little luck and some thoughts into a plot of some kind, Purdy could be the answer to his problems. It didn't take an expert to notice the revulsion between them, just a matter of waiting for the right opportunity to arrive.

Damston, two suited men, Barton and the Carter brothers, all sat on chairs around Randell's desk. The big man leaned back on his wheelchair and blew smoke from his cigar into their faces.

"You all did good out there today, our guests had no idea what was going on. I am though very disappointed that you didn't catch that driver. We could have made him talk, I'm sure what we could have got out of him, would have confirmed my suspicions. There's a local little fish trying to muscle in on our operation, we could wipe him out but that's not what I want, not yet. There's a third party involved and I'm sure this piece of shit is collaborating with them. In a matter of time he will get in over his head, that's when this third party will show face."

A long silence hung as the big man sucked away at his cigar. It was Damston who broke it, "are you saying this little fish planted that dummy bomb?"

Through the smoke Bartell gazed at her and grimaced, "If that little fish had planted that bomb it wouldn't have been a dummy."

Tommy Carter shuffled in his seat, cleared his throat, all eyes turned on him, "Do you think this third party is responsible for the shootings?"

The big man shrugged his massive shoulders, "that's what we have to find out." He stumped out his cigar in the ashtray, noticed Ben in the process of lighting up a cigarette, pointed a fat finger at it and snarled, "I'll not have you smoking in my office."

"You must have an informer in your organisation," Barton interrupted, "that's the only way, how else could they have known, where and when to shoot that girl and Lumpy?"

"That's a good point," Ben said, "how could they have known when we were leaving to go to Doncaster?"

Damston cocked her head to the side a little, this was one of Barton's observations, knew she was about to ask the brothers a serious question, "The day in that pub carpark a bomb exploded in your car how did it get there?"

The brothers did a bit of shuffling in their seat, looked at each other made it look obvious this was an unexpected attack. After some hesitations Tommy said, "It must have been put under the car."

A technique Barton had acquired over the years was to read body language, he spotted the lie with no effort. He decided not to pursue the subject but to change it, this way to keep them off guard, "This white Range Rover, you said, followed you on the motorway, you said it could have been the same one that this limousine driver jumped into?"

Ben nodded, at the same time trying to force his cigarette back into the packet," It could have been,"

"I don't expect any of you would have had time to take the registration number, but you might have noticed some abnormality about it, like a sticker on the back window, a dent, anything like that?"

"It had one of its rear lights broken," one of the suited men said," that was what caught my eye."

"Now that you mentioned it," Tommy burst in, "I noticed that when it drove off from the service carpark."

"My contact in the bomb squad informed me, the one that exploded in your car had a similar signature as the one that exploded in Allotment street," Randell said, withdrawing another cigar from his drawer. He pointed the big cigar at the brothers, "I was also informed that it exploded inside your car, it had to be, there were no damage to the tarmac under it.

"Somebody must have broken the window and tossed it in, when we were in the pub," Tommy burst in angrily."

Damston waited for the big man to light his smoke and asked, "Do you think this was Lumpy's making?"

Randell shook his head, "when Lumpy lost his hand he stopped making bombs, he trained someone in the art, I don't know who, but we had better find out, and soon. With Lumpy gone we have to get this person on our side." He turned to the brothers, blew a cloud of smoke at them, "that was your job, and by the look of it someone didn't want you to question him."

"We could watch Lumpy's workshop, if this person shows we nab him," Ben suggested.

"Okay," the big man replied, turned to Damston," you get that arranged."

Barton developed a strong urge to ask, knew the question was risky. It was in one of those moments when a hush came over everybody, "who is Limping Lenny working for?" He felt all eyes on him.

Randell choked on his cigar when he had recovered sufficiently, he stiffened in his wheelchair, glared at Barton, "never heard of him."

Damston and Barton took it in turn to watch Lumpy's work-shop from a small hide that had been built by the previous observers. Who had selected a copse about a hundred yards from the building. They each had binoculars and lay on their stomach. "Can't see much in this bloody rain,"

Damston complained.

"Lumpy was clever enough to block off all the windows, so the light won't show, the person that he was training, could be living in there we would never know, Barton said without taking the binoculars from his eyes, "But if you look very carefully, there's a small skylight at the far end of the roof. That should throw a slight beam upwards, even in this rain we should see it."

The next hour dragged in, Damston dropped her arms and put her binoculars on the ground, "we should do this in turns, that way we will have fresh eyes. You do a half hour I'll do the next."

She rolled over onto her back. For a while she lay silent, Barton could hear her soft breathing and thought she had dozed off. With a sudden turn of her head she asked," Richard Barton, who are you?"

Surprised by her unexpected question, he turned away from his binoculars and looked at her. In the fading light he couldn't read her expression, only the fine outline of her hair, neck and the slopping contour of her shoulders. "You know who I am," he replied and returned to observing the workshop.

"Sometimes I think I know you, and other times I'm not so sure."

"You know as much about me as I do about you, sometimes it's better that way. What I know about you I'm beginning to like, let's just leave it at that, for the time being." She returned to her soft breathing, Barton could tell, she was deep in thought. A few seconds after returning his full attention to the workshop, a very faint beam of light came from the skylight. He gave Damston a slight nudge with his elbow, "that light I was telling you about, if you look carefully at the end of the roof you can see it. The only reason I couldn't see it before was it wasn't dark enough."

She rolled over picked up her binoculars and followed his directions, "that light could have been on all day, let's get over there."

Barton caught her wrist, "not yet, I don't think that light has been on long, when I looked at you it wasn't on, a few seconds later when I looked back, there it was."

Not knowing who to expect or how many, Barton and Damston entered the workshop with guns in their hands, loaded and ready. The figure sitting on a stool at the workbench was quite a surprise for Barton. Damston with no hesitation, was at Lenny's head with her pistol. He screamed and almost fell off the stool, "who are you?" she shouted and grabbed him by the collar of his jacket.

"I'm a friend of Lumpy's, he cried and struggled to free himself, but Damston held him firm.

Barton stepped closer, "what are you doing here?"

When Lenny caught sight of Barton, his eyes almost popped out, "I could ask you the same question," he stammered, "Lumpy said I could kip here for a few days."

Damston pulled him off the stool, and pushed her weapon under his nose, "how did you get out here?"

"A mate gave me a lift."

"Where is this mate?" she slapped the back of the head.

"I don't know, he dropped me off at the end of the road and drove away."

"You're a fucking liar," she shouted at him and landed another slap.

"How long have you been kipping here?" Barton demanded.

"I just got here half an hour ago, I got the key from Lumpy last week."

"Your lying Lenny," Barton shouted at him and he also threw a slap to the back of Lenny's head with such force Damston had to let go her grip. He landed face down on the bench, Barton grabbed the back of his jacket and pulled him upright, "are you going to tell us where this mate is?"

"I'm telling you the truth."

"He's a lying bastard," Damston said, "Lumpy would never give anyone the keys to his work-shop, this was his loving domain."

"Honest he gave me the keys," Lenny whimpered.

"How long have you known Lumpy?" Barton asked.

"I've known him for a long time, a bit of a nut case but a good guy when you get to know him."

Damston pulled him around to face her, "has he been teaching you how to make bombs?"

"We know he had an assistant," Barton said, "we came here and found you working at his bench. Do you think we're stupid?"

Lenny shook his head, "I've often wondered how he managed with one hand, I've often seen him work with tools in his mouth, but never with explosives," he held up his hands, I've got the shakes. Do you think he would let me near bombs?" He emphatically shook his head, "I know what they can do," he patted his leg, "no way would I get involved with them."

"What were you working at when we walked in?" Damston shouted into his face.

Lenny pointed a finger at a wooden box on the bench," I was looking for a fuse."

When Barton had followed Damston into the warehouse, he left the door slightly ajar. Had he not done so they would never have heard the loose gravel crunching under the wheels of the approaching vehicle. In a heartbeat she swung Lenny around, using him as a shield. Barton ran to the door and stood behind it. He glanced back to see she had forced Lenny against the bench, and stood behind him for extra cover.

They listened to the vehicle pulled to a halt a few yards from the door, its engine ticking over, head light on full beam. Barton kept his eyes on the blade of light that shone through the narrow gab, he listened for the anticipated slamming of the car doors. When that never came, he began to think, this could be Lanny's mate back to pick him up. Still the silence of the early evening lingered on, a fox barked in the distance, the hush of the breeze as it swept through the nearby trees. Had it not been for the stillness, Barton would have missed hearing the creaking of the boards on the wooden step. The blade of light got broader as he watched the door open slowly. Lumpy must have kept the hinges well oiled, not even the slightest sound came from them.

When the door was fully opened a long black shadow cast along the warehouse floor. A dark figure appeared and halted just inside. Barton was tempted to jump on it, but held back guessing that this person was not alone.

The intruder must have spotted Lenny and holding a pickaxe handle aloft, rush at him but only got a few steps when the three shot came in quick succession, the figure slumped over, dropped his weapon and fell to the floor.

Barton heard footsteps and dived into the light, was about to fire a shot at the fleeing figure when three thundering cracks exploded next to his ear. The running figure fell. The engine of the vehicle revved up to a scream. The driver made a wild u turn in the narrow yard, bumped over the rough grassy edges and made his way back up the track. Barton fired a few shots, but the car continued into the darkness. Barton turned, Damston was at his shoulder, the pistol in her hand was still smoking.

"Who the fuck were they?" She shouted.

"You didn't give them much chance to tell us."

"I don't think they came charging in here armed with pickaxe handles to introduce themselves."

Simultaneously they turned to see Lenny, standing over the body on the floor of the workshop. Damston rushed over, pointed her weapon at him and asked. "who's he?"

Lenny shook his head, "I don't know."

Barton joined them, grabbed Lenny by the upper arm and pushed his pistol into the back of his head, "no more fucking lies Lenny, or you'll be joining those two."

"I don't know," Lenny yelped, "honest I've never seen them before."

CHAPTER 15

The evening staff were standing at the door waiting for it to be opened by the doorman. Purdy knew the routine. He would have to time it right he crossed the street and stood a few metres away from them in the shadow of the narrow lane that ran along the side of the building. He didn't have to wait long, heard the door lock mechanism operating, saw the staff begin to shuffle in. He charged at them, bulldozing the latter two in on front of him, shouldered the others to the side, knocking the doorman to the floor.

Cecil was at his usual post, sitting on his stool at the bar, chatting to his lover when Purdy barged in and launched himself at him landing a huge fist into the little black man's face. Cecil and his stool crashed to the floor. Purdy followed through, dived on top throwing punches wildly into Cecil's face. Women screamed, bottles smashed men roared, but the anarchy didn't last long before a team of goons jumped on Purdy, dragging him clear of Cecil. They punched kicked and gouged at him. Purdy fought back, but it was no use, they had him pinned to the floor, too many bodies holding him down.

A few staff members helped Cecil to his feet, his nose was bleeding profusely, eyes puffed up, blood trickled from his mouth. "Take that bastard down to the cellar and tie him up, I'll deal with him later," he screamed and staggered to the bar, picked up his empty glass and hurled it at Jaco, it missed by a fraction, "what the fuck are you gawking at?"

He got himself back onto his stool, elbows leaning on the bar, head in his hands drifting in and out of consciousness seeing himself at ten years old, playing cricket with his school pals. The ball hit him on the face, he had cried out for his only true friend. One of the very few white girls in his class. She was his sister, his mother, his protector, anything he needed her to be, always by his side. The club was almost filled up with regular patrons, by the time Cecil recovered. He waved a couple of his muscle men over," is that bastard well tied up down in the cellar?" They nodded in assurance, "Okay! let's get down there." He staggered to his feet and felt strong supporting hands holding his arms.

Purdy was well and truly tied to a chair, with ropes around his legs and body, hands behind his back secured with cable ties, broad bands of black duct tape covered his mouth. Cecil ripped the tape off and enjoyed hearing Purdy scream. "What the fuck are you playing at?" he shouted into Purdy's swollen face.

"You set us up, you fucker, we walked into a trap, they were waiting for us, I've lost two of my boys," Purdy shouted and struggled against his bindings.

Cecil stepped back and gasped, "what are you talking about, who was waiting for you?"

"Don't give me your crap," Purdy shouted, "you sent me a text, telling me where to find Barton."

Cecil shook his head and received excruciating pain from his jawbone, "I did no such thing," he protested, holding his face, "how could I have known where Barton was, if I had, I would have sent my own team to get him."

"It was a restricted number, I knew it had to be you, giving me all the details."

Randell lit his usual thick cigar, clouded the same audience who he had two days prior. He leaned back on his wheelchair, "do any of you know who these three men were?"

"I didn't recognise the two men we shot," Damston replied after a moment's thought, "I never saw the driver of the car."

"So, it could have been the police?" The big man growled.

"I don't think the police would have charged in, armed with a pickaxe handle," Barton said.

The big man glared at him, blew a cloud of smoke into his face, "so you caught your Limping Lenny in the workshop, what did he have to say?"

"We gave him a rough time," Barton replied, "we're sure he isn't Lumpy's apprentice, his hands were too shaky, probably the results of being in a war zone or too much booze."

"What did you do with him?" He turned his attention to Damston.

She gave Barton a quick glance, "we threw him in the boot of our car and dumped him on a layby miles from anywhere."

Randell's sunken blue eyes returned to Barton's penetrating into them like skewers. Barton stared back, determined not to be the first to look away or even blink. The big man's hand came up holding his cigar and his pencil line mouth opened to accept it. He took along pull at it and again clouded Barton in smoke, "so we still don't know who Lumpy's assistant is?"

"I don't think he will turn up there, not after what's been happening," Ben Carter butted in.

Before anyone could add to Ben's comment a knock came to the door. All eyes turned to see Nevil, the big man's driver step in, "it's time we should go Mr. Randell."

Randell nodded, stumped his cigar out in the glass ashtray on the desk. Barton had to conceal his humour as a vision of the big man's snowman shaped head came rolling off his shoulders, landed on his desk and rolled off onto the floor. Barton was the last to join the rest when they stood up as the big man manoeuvred his wheelchair around the desk.

"It's important we find this assistant of Lumpy's," Randell said over his shoulders as his driver pushed him out the door.

She sat behind her desk, twisting from side to side on her swivel padded chair. "That's us back to square one on finding out who this assistant of Lumpy's is."

Barton had realised the ice beneath his feet was getting thinner, he wondered why Lenny hadn't mentioned anything about the previous meetings that they had. "Lenny could have been lying when he denied any knowledge of this person," he replied leaning back against the wall with his hands behind his head.

She stopped swinging and leaned forward on her desk, "it's strange, how you mentioned Limping Lenny to the boss man, and suddenly he turns up at the workshop. I got the impression that you were quite familiar with him when we approached?"

"He's the local bum, I've seen him about town, I've tossed him a few coins at him said hi, to him."

"Why did you ask the boss who Lenny was working for, if you thought he was just a bum?"

"Rumour has it he hangs about Allotments street some say as if he was patrolling about like a security guard. I know he's ex-army, maybe he thinks he's still on duty, I just wondered."

She seemed uncertain of his explanation and sat back on her chair, "how did you know he was ex-army?"

Barton held up his arm, bared his wrist and pointed to the tattoo, "that's a regiment I was in, he has the same one on the same place. He was in a bit before my time."

"I think we should have a few more words with him, one way or another we have to get the truth out of him."

Barton nodded, but at the same time a wave of panic passed through him, couldn't let Lenny mouth off about the conversations they had, nor could he tell Damston about his younger brother. "I think he'll be keeping well out of sight after what went down in that workshop."

She got up out of her seat, "we need to try and find him," she squeezed past her desk, grinned when Barton opened the door for her, "he'll have found his way back by now from that layby, somebody must have seen him we'll go to his usual haunts and ask about, he witnessed us shooting those two goons, can't have him mouthing off about it and I don't want to bump him off, not just yet."

An hour and a half driving around the town, looking for Lenny and asking people if they had seen him, proved to be fruitless. "just go home," Damston said, "try again in the morning when it's daylight."

Barton turned the car, intending to head for her house, she caught his arm, "I would like you to move in with me permanently,"

"Are you proposing to me?"

She ignored his comment and said, "go to your flat and collect what belongings you have left."

"Can I ask you why, you want me to move in with you permanently?"

"Don't get any sloppy ideas…, so I can keep an eye on you?"

The moment Barton opened his flat door, he knew someone had been there, "I've had a visitor," he told her."

She walked around him into his lounge, "thing looks fine to me, there's nothing smashed or anything."

"Whoever it was has tried to tidy up behind them, but they haven't put things back in the right place."

"Anything missing?" she asked.

"I don't see anything missing in here, not at a quick glance, I'll have to check."

She followed him around the flat helping to search, after a while he gave up and they sat on the sofa. "there's nothing missing." Barton concluded, "I don't know what they were after,"

"Are you certain someone has been here?"

Barton pointed to the television remote," I never leave that on the mantlepiece. "You see that ornament on the table?" He pointed, "it's turned the wrong way, there's quite a few things out of place." He placed his forefinger on her lips and shook his head, could see she got the message and silently they got up and packed his belongings, again into bin liners and left.

"Do you think your flat has been bugged?" Damston asked as he started up the car."

"Not taking any chances," he replied and drove away.

"They could be watching your place for you to return."

"In that case we better watch we're not being followed."

Barton had made a few diversions and a few stops on the way, but never detected any following vehicles. He asked for her key and told her to wait in the car, while he opened her house door. She was right behind him when he entered, her gun in hand ready. As he quietly closed the door a dark figure burst in knocking Barton backwards, he bumped into Damston sent her stumbling forward, Barton quickly recovered and dived at the attacker.

The three of them grappled on the floor of the small corridor. Damston managed to get free and brought her pistol down on the assailant's head, Barton heard the bone crack and the figure went limp.

Barton struggled to his feet, was about to hit the assailant again, when the handle of the door to Damston's lounge sounded, the mechanism was faulty, something she had meant to get repaired, but never got around to it. This fault gave her time to point her pistol at the door and fire three shots through it. The door handle stopped turning, a man's voice roared in pain, the sound of her glass topped coffee table smashed they knew that she had hit whoever it was behind the door.

Barton shouldered through the door and discovered a man lying on the broken coffee table, he put a finger to the man's jugular vein, felt no pulse. He searched the man for weapons and wallet or any kind of I.D. Found nothing. The other man from the corridor staggered in holding his face, Damston was behind him, her gun at his back. They both followed Barton's eye, looked at the body lying amongst the broken glass. "Your mate's dead," Barton said to the man holding his face, "and if you don't start talking, you'll be joining him."

Damston hit him again with her weapon, this time on the back of his shoulder and pushed him onto the sofa, jabbed her gun under his nose, "start talking you bastard," she shouted.

"Fuck off," the man mumbled through an obvious broken jaw.

Damston's gun exploded, three time, putting three .45 rounds from her Glock 21, into his left foot, the blood splattered all over her sofa and carpet. The man let out a deafening scream, tried to roll away from her, but the sofa fell over backwards hitting his head against the wall behind.

Barton rushed over and grabbed his long greasy hair, jerked his head up, "are you going to talk or loose the other foot?"

"You lot are fucking mad," the man shouted.

Barton jerked his head back farther, "now that you know that, are you going to talk?"

Damston aimed at his other foot.

"Oh kay, oh kay!" he shouted.

Jaco searched through Cecil's mobiles and found the text that had been sent to Purdy, he pushed it over the bar Cecil, picked it up and read the message. He stared at Jaco, his brown eyes blazing, saliva dripping from his mouth," did you send this?"

"No," Jaco protested, "how could I have known where this Barton was, I've never ever heard of him, and I've no idea where that place is, how could I have sent it?"

He thumped the mobile on the bar, "find out who sent that," he demanded.

"How am I supposed to do that?" Jaco whimpered, "it could have been anybody, you leave your mobiles lying on the bar unattended."

"Can you think of any strangers who might have come into the club," Cecil asked, "someone who was standing close to me, that could have sent that text when I was in the toilet or something?"

Jaco shrugged his shoulders, shook his head, "It could have been anyone, not necessarily a stranger." He reached under the bar and brought out Cecil's gin bottle, poured some into his glass, "what's all the fuss about, with this man Barton?" He asked and returned the bottle.

"You mind your own fucking business." Cecil shouted, "get me the keys to the cellar."

Purdy lifted his head when Cecil and two of his goons stood around his chair. Cecil leaned close to Purdy's ear, "I've decided to give you a second chance," give me the number of one of your gang, I'll punch it into my phone, you can tell him to get his mates and go and grab Barton. I want him here tonight, if that doesn't happen, you are dead meat."

"How am I supposed to do that, they'll want to know where he is?"

Cecil chortled, "That's your problem, now give me a number."

"I'm not good at remembering numbers, I've got them all on my phone," Purdy mumbled through swollen lips.

"Where is your phone?"

"One of your goons took it out my pocket and stamped his heel to it, should be lying on the floor somewhere."

Cecil glanced around the f loor; the shattered remains of Purdy's mobile lay behind the chair he was tied to. "You better start remembering the number, or I'll get my boys down here to give you another going over."

Three or four times, Purdy's guess at a number failed," that's it," Cecil cried and strutted towards the cellar steps the two goons behind him. They collided with Jaco at the door, "where are you going?" Cecil demanded.

Jaco hastily stepped out of their way, "just letting you know customers are coming in."

Cecil let the goons barge past and said, "go down there and put the tape back on that piece of shit's mouth."

Jaco descended the stairs, waited to hear the door close before he approached Purdy. "I bet I know what you would like to do with him," he pointed his thumb at the door.

"You would win that bet."

"His goons won't be down until the club's closed I'm going to loosen the ropes enough to let you work yourself free. I'll have to lock the door for he will check, shouldn't be hard for a man of your expertise, to open it. Sneak out when the place is busy, go out the fire door, I'll create a distraction."

Purdy wasn't sure he was hearing right, "why are you helping me, you know what will happen to you if Cecil finds out?"

"That's why I'm helping you, to make sure he doesn't live long enough to find out."

"How about the thugs who stand at that door?"

"As I said I'll create a distraction."

CHAPTER 16

*B*arton was impressed by how quick Randell's people got Damston's house cleaned up. The door had been replaced, the coffee table renewed, carpets cleaned of blood stains. He was tempted to ask where the dead body and the injured man were? But decided against it. Damston was in a nasty mood, after a sleepless night. They had been so wound up when they got back to his flat, they knew sleep would never come, sat up all night, watched television, not paying much attention to it, drinking coffee and tea. He stood at her lounge door, watched her pace back and forth looking at her belongings but not touching them, as if everything were strange to her, like a child in a toy shop, wanting, but frightened to lay a finger on things.

She stopped, slumped down on the sofa, bent her head over and cupped her face in her hands, he sat beside her and put his arms around her shoulder. She wrapped herself around him and cried like a child. Barton was quite disconcerted by her behaviour, was he seeing another side of her, or could this just be the lack of sleep?

She broke away from him and jumped to her feet, "we're going to have to move from here," she said, "there was nothing missing, nothing damaged, just the table, the carpet and the door. It's obvious it was me they were after."

"Do you have any idea who they were?" Barton asked and followed her out the door.

"It could be any of a thousand people, you know what it's like in this game," she replied as they got in the car, "if they keep trying, they're going to get me, that's why I need you, they only need to get lucky once, I need to be lucky all the time."

On the drive back to the office, she spoke on her mobile all the way, Barton assumed she was conversing with Randell. When he pulled up in the carpark, she put her phone in her pocket and told him to wait in the car. He watched her walk into the building, not her normal confident strut, more like a timid school pupil heading into a class she didn't like.

Expecting a long wait, Barton was surprised when she reappeared at the door in less than two minutes. This time the strut had returned, and she was wearing a grin as she got in beside him. He wondered how a person could change so quickly, was this a learning process, starting to notice all her sudden mood-swings?

"Mr. Randell has given me another of his properties to live in," she said, "we should go and view it, if it's okay, he will get our belongings moved there. He thinks it's too risky for us to go back there."

"What are you going to do with your house, sell it or what?"

Damston looked at him for a long moment with a puzzled expression, a grin slowly dawned across her face, "I forgot you didn't know, Mr. Randell owns all the properties that the organisation's members live in. A sound investment he has said, and it is, in many ways."

Barton started up the car," are we going to this other house now?"

She shook her head, "first we have to find out who those two guys were and who they work for. The Carter brothers are questioning the one who's still alive, we'll have to go and see if they have got some answers."

Before driving off, Barton grimaced and looked at her, "you shot the foot off that guy and threatened to shoot off the other, I don't think he's going to talk to these Carter brothers."

Barton assumed she was referring to the two gaunt looking tall men, referred to as the brothers. He put the vehicle into gear and drove off, "where are we going?" He asked.

The two men Cecil had sent down to the cellar to give Purdy a farther beating, were lying on the floor unconscious. Thanks to Jaco's help, he had succeeded to get free. The wooden chair he had been tied to, he pulled it apart, using one of the legs as a club. Now he had to get out quickly before Cecil decided to send more goons down to see what the delay was.

Except for the lights above the beer pumps the place was in darkness. Three figures were stood at the near side of the bar, all the patrons stood clear of them others sat at the tables chatting to the girls. Purdy could only see their silhouettes, there was no mistaking that of Cecil's, his slight frame sitting on his stool, the bush of frizzy hair catching the dim light, bobbing up and down in self-assured conversation.

Jaco was behind the bar carrying a tray of empty glasses, Purdy caught his eye as he was about to close the cellar door, a sudden crash of broken glass got the attention of the three figures. The goons rushed over from the fire door. This gave Purdy time to sneak over to the fire escape, which had been left slightly open.

Purdy got out the door and ran up the dark narrow lane that separated the club with it's neighbouring building. Luck was once again on his side a taxi came cruising down the main street he stepped out, waved it down and jumped in.

Purdy's taxi would have been almost a mile away before Cecil realised what had happened. The two men he had sent down to the cellar to give Purdy another going over, had staggered over to him and reported what had happened. Cecil screamed with rage, slapped his hand down on the bar and shouted, "I want that bastard back here, every one of you to get out there and find him, don't come back until you do."

The four goons cursed and protested at him as they filled out the fire exit. When only he and Jaco were left standing at the bar, Cecil called Jaco closer, "do you think I'm stupid?"

Jaco shrugged his shoulders and shook his head, "no I don't," he replied cowering back.

"You deliberately let that tray of glasses fall to distract my attention, while that bastard sneaked out that door," Cecil's rage was well above boiling point, he picked up the heavy wooden tray and smashed it down on Jaco's head. He watched Jaco stagger back, fall against the metal sink and slither to the floor. "I hope you're dead you piece of shit," he shouted, wiped the saliva from his lips and downed the remains of his drink. He turned to see all the remaining patrons looking at him. "What the fuck are you lot looking at." He stared at them until they all turned away and pretended to continue with their conversations.

They caught the tail end of the early morning traffic, Damston was driving. It had taken them nearly an hour to arrive at the metal roller doors of a fairly-new unit, in an industrial estate.

"What's this place?" Barton asked.

"Another of the boss's properties," she replied getting out of the car, Barton followed her to the doors, she banged them with her fist, a moment later, they rolled up to about half-way. She ducked under, he followed and came face to face with the Carter's

The brothers led the way to a small office as the roller doors closed behind them. Damston almost slipped on the laminate flooring, Ben gripped her elbow to steady her.

"You were meant to come here last night," Tommy complained as they took their seats in the small office.

"Well we're here now," Damston snapped back at him, "did you get anything out of that goon?"

Ben lit a cigarette, creaked his chair as he sat back blowing the smoke upwards, "he was in no state to answer questions, was delirious when we got him here, he couldn't understand a word we said, now he's dead," Tommy tilted back the skip of his baseball cap, at the same time waving away the smoke from his brother's cigarette, "if you lot hadn't shot his foot off, he wouldn't have bled out."

"What were we supposed to have done, made them a coffee, and say thanks for wrecking my home?" Damston shouted into his face.

Barton looked from one to the other and began to wonder where all these bodies were being disposed of?

"Have you informed Mr. Randell?" Damston asked.

The brothers looked at each other and shook their heads.

"Get that done now," she ordered and jumped out of her seat.

She stormed out of the small office, Barton was left looking at the brothers, Ben with his cigarette in his mouth began talking into his mobile. Tommy stood up, looked at Barton, "you better follow your master," he said with a sneer, pointing towards the door.

Barton stood up and looked into Tommy's grey eyes, they gazed at each other, like boxers about to begin a championship fight. Barton smiled, took a step back, gave him a mock salute, about turned and marched out the office.

Tommy held up his hand with a pointed index finger, aimed it at Barton's back and pretended to shoot, his hand jerked up with the simulated kick from the shot. He grinned when Barton was on his way down the warehouse and said, "one of those days mate."

Like the other warehouses, Barton found himself walking between two rows of steel shipping containers. Damston was nearing the bottom of one side, checking all the seals. He waited at the roller doors until she had completed her task.

Damston didn't seem too disgruntled with her new accommodations, Barton on the other hand didn't like the idea of living in a block of flats, especially ten floors up. The place was fully furnished and all their personal belongings were on the floor of the living room. They settled down on the padded leather sofa. She rummaged in one of her plastic bags and pulled out her iPad while he picked up the remote for the television. He switched from channel to channel but couldn't find anything to concentrate on. She slapped the ipad on the coffee table and stood up," let's go out for a meal."

Barton grinned, got onto his feet, "where do you want to go?"

Damston drove to the town center public car park, from there they walked onto the high street. She led him to a small Indian restaurant, "hope you like Indian?" She asked as they sat down close the window, she had her back to it and Barton could see the flashing lights of the club across the street. It was the name that caught his attention, it sent chilling flutter in his stomach.

"What are you looking at?" she asked and handed him a menu.

Barton shook his head, "nothing much, it's the flashing lights that keeps drawing my attention,"

"Do you want to change seats?"

He shook his head and took the menu from her, held it up to his face and from behind it asked, "when you asked the Carter brother's where the bomb came from that exploded in their car…,"

Her hand shot over and pulled the menu down, looked into his brown eyes," what about it?" She snapped.

"I don't think they were telling the truth."

She grinned and relaxed back on her seat, "let's order."

Through the meal Barton's mind was preoccupied with the question, what has happened to the bodies, where are they, who is responsible for the disposal of them, could the answers leed him to discover where his younger brother lay?

"You seem to be full of thought?" She asked, looking over the rim of her wine glass.

Barton sparked out of reverie and smiled, "just some passing thoughts, nothing important." He looked over her shoulder at the f lickering lights. Convinced this was the place that Wilma had described, the place where the demise of his brother and his pal began.

"I don't think you like Indian food," Damson interrupted, "you've hardly touched it," she pointed to his plate.

"The food is good," he assured her, "I just don't feel hungry."

She finished drinking her wine and put the glass on the table, "if you're finished, let's go home."

They walked up the narrow sparsely lit lane to the car park, three hooded youths stepped out of the shadows. One approached Damson and said in a drunken slur, "give us a kiss darling."

"Okay," she replied and stepped towards him, but it wasn't the kiss he expected, it was the butt of her pistol on the bridge of his nose. The youth screamed and staggered back nursing his bleeding broken nose. Barton jumped at the other two of his mates and pushed them back, they stumbled over each other, regained their balance and ran off.

They watched the injured youth stagger off behind his mates still holding his broken nose, blood seeping between his fingers. "Are you alright?" Barton asked her.

She grinned and tucked the Glock into the back of her trousers, "what a lovely way to end a good meal," she giggled and walked on.

Barton strode along beside her, "what was that all about?" he asked her and wondered if this was the kind of harassment his brother and his pal would have been involved in?

She shook her head, "just the normal pranks these kids get up to, high on drugs and booze, been there myself."

At about a yard from the car, Barton took hold of her arm, turned her around and walked her away to a safe distance. "stay here he told her, maybe I'm being paranoid, but those youths could have been a delaying tactic. I'll go and check the car, remember what happened to the Carter's He walked towards the vehicle and stopped a few yards away, pressed the remote, the hazard lights came on as normal. A short interval lapsed before Barton continued, gently he opened the rear nearside passenger door, took a deep sigh when nothing happened, he closed that door and repeated this procedure on the other three. He reached in and located the catch and released the bonnet. It was a simple device, but an untrained eye would have missed it. Sealed in a plastic bag and cable tied to the battery frame, wired to the ignition box. It only took him a few minutes to make it safe. He lifted it out and waved Damston over, "It's not powerful enough to cause a great deal of damage," he assured her, "but we could have been injured."

Damston looked at plastic explosive in Barton's hand it was shaped and looked about the size of a cholate bar, "are you sure it's safe? She said.

"I'm sure," he replied, handed it to her and opened the car door and waved her in.

She sat in the front seat and sniffed the package, "it smells the same as the one you found in that limousine."

"It does," Barton explained, "like marzipan, it's dynamite, solid plastic, consists of nitro-glycerine and kieselguhr," he started up the car, "at least they haven't messed up the ignition." He noticed she still held the package in her hand, looking down at it.

"I hate that smell," she said, "reminds me of when I was about nine, at a wedding, I was given a piece of cake. The moment I got the taste of marzipan, I spat it out all over the table. That got me a slap on the head from my mother and dragged into the lady's toilet. There I got another good hiding. we need to dump this package somewhere."

Barton nodded, "dump it in the canal, let's go there now and be done with it."

Their heads were on the same pillow, Barton lay on his back, wide awake, he could feel her breath on the side of his face with the lingering odor of the wine she drank earlier. His attempt to move away failed, her arm came across his shoulder and pulled him back. "can you not sleep?" he asked.

"Take's me a while to get used to a strange bed."

He knew it wasn't the strange bed that kept her awake, it was the same thoughts he was having. Had that bomb exploded, they would be lying in a hospital bed, and a lot of awkward questions would have to be answered. It would have been useless pleading ignorance, her with a Glock 21 in her bra and him with his Heckler & Koch P9S. Pedestrians don't go about carrying this kind of metal work on them.

She withdrew her arm and sat up, "what made you suspect there was a bomb in the car?"

"I can't explain, a warning light flashed in my head the moment I saw the car, I just knew something wasn't right."

"Do you get these warnings often?" She asked and lay back down. "None that I can think of."

"Well we can be thankful you had one at the time," she turned dragged the duvet with her leaving him naked on the bed. It wasn't long before the nightly ritual of snoring began. He wondered how long she had been with the Randell syndicate had she been recruited by the same little dapper man as he had been? "Mr. Crow," he had introduced himself, Barton had doubted that was his real name. Thought he looked more like an ex-high-ranking army officer with a double barrelled one. Barton had come across many of his types in his years in the army, chests full of medals and never fired a shot, did most of their fighting in the officer's mess drinking brandy. He had met Crow while on his early morning jog in the park, a habit he had gotten into since his dishonorable discharge for assault on a senior officer. The dapper little man had approached while Barton had stopped to do stretches. They had talked about army life sitting on one of the benches. Their conversation lasted about ten minutes, Barton stood up, the little man joined him and they parted company.

The next morning, Crow was stood at the park gate at the end of Barton's run, "would you like to go into that café for a coffee?" He asked and pointed across the street.

Barton selected a table while Crow got the coffee's, how are you today?" he asked as he placed the mugs on the table and sat opposite.

Barton shrugged his shoulders, "same old same old," he picked up the mug and took a sip.

"That doesn't sound very enthusiastic," Crow had replied and grinned.

"That's the way life is in a place like this, every day's the same, the only thing that changes, is the weather."

"Do you have a job?"

Barton nodded, "it's a bit boring but it pays the rent and keeps the Sheriff Officers away."

Crow took a sip from his mug and frowned at it, "if you want a job more suited to your way of life, give me a call," he stood up pulled a card from his top pocket and placed it down in front of Barton. He turned on his heels and strode out the door, his head held high shoulders down and back in military style.

Barton remembered sitting there wondering, what did this little man know about his way of life? Later that same day, his boss had called him into his office and told him, due to loss of a contract he no longer had a job.

CHAPTER 17

Damston led the way into the lecture room. All the seats had been occupied. Barton followed her to the back of the room, where they had no other choice but to lean against the wall. "What's going on?" he whispered.

"We have a meeting every month, with all the members of the syndicate, "she whispered back.

The tall coloured driver pushed Randell in his wheelchair up to the lectern, and as usual, blasted cigar smoke in his wake. When his chair was positioned facing his audience, he held up a huge arm and shouted, "I'll have none of you smoking in my lecture room."

Barton searched the room for anyone who might be or have been smoking, as did all the others, but the only person smoking was Randell. They all listened as he went on about how bad business was and how opposition gangs were trying to muscle in. He pointed out that his intentions were to recruit more people and eliminate these opposing gangs and to build up more security in all his warehouses. There was a stir amongst the audience when he mentioned about having to sell off some of their luxury homes to pay for it. An hour later he called the meeting to a close and left. This was when the eruptions started. Barton felt inwardly amused to hear all the arguments from the group. Damston pranced up to the lectern waved her arms and brought them to order.

"If extra security must be brought into the warehouses, you will have to pay for it. So, you better make sure it's not required," she shouted at them, "also if Mr. Randell recruits more people to eliminate these syndicates, he may have to sell off some of his properties to pay for them, my advice to you is to help get rid of them."

The room burst into chaos again, everybody was on their feet shouting. Barton rushed to the lectern and stood in front of Damston thinking somebody might attack her.

"What properties are you talking about?" A woman's voice sounded above the rest bringing total silence. All eyes turned on Damston.

"All your big fancy houses, with your heated swimming pools, and all the other luxuries you have been enjoying," she shouted.

Barton was expecting another riot, it never happened, the silence continued, they all sat down. One by one, with shocked expressions, they got up left the room, Damston and Barton was left on their own, watching them file out. She sat on the nearest seat and exhaled a deep sigh of relief.

Barton sat next to her as she flicked a wave of blond hair from her eyes, "not a happy bunch," he said.

"They don't want to get off their arses to help deal with rival gangs…, well they're going to or the high living will come to an end. That's where the boss has them stitched up; he owns all their big houses, big fancy cars, pays for expensive holidays, children's education, private medical care. When he says jump they ask, how high?"

"I take it, you come under the same category?"

She slowly got to her feet, "yes, and soon you will."

Purdy got out the taxi at one of his mate's house, phoned his girlfriend and told her to get out of their home. She protested and ranted on about having nowhere to go, how much she had to pack and carry their baby as well. "Fuck packing," he shouted, just pick up the baby and get out."

He cut her off, had he held on a moment longer, he would have heard her scream.

"Problems?" His mate Bloch asked.

Purdy put his mobile back in his pocket, "I've got Hussey's mob on my tail. I need to get some of our mates together, I need you to arrange it."

Bloch grinned showing a set of twisted smoke-stained teeth, "sounds like we're going to have some fun."

Purdy pointed to his swollen lips and blackened eye," nobody does this to me and gets away with It."

"It might take a few hours to get a decent size gang," Bloch replied scratching his stubble with his dirty little hand.

Reluctantly Purdy sat on the cluttered sofa, moving piles of unwashed clothing, "I've got an idea," he said and waited until Bloch was seated on the chair opposite, also covered with dirty laundry, Bloch sat on top of it, "I need to get somebody inside Hussey's club, for a night and leave the place last. There's a sofa against the left wall as you enter, it's old and won't be fire resistant. Remember the days when paper match boxes were common? I know where I can get some, this is a simple incendiary device. Light a cigarette until it's about halfway smoked, fold it into the match box, leaving about half an inch for it to smolder. Place it on the sofa out of sight."

Bloch chuckled, "I think I know the right person for that job…, the trouble is, it's not really guaranteed to work, it would be better to sprinkle some lighter fuel on the sofa first."

"The smell of petrol might be a give-a-way, better to use whiskey, also so, don't send a guy in on his own, get a girl to go in with him as a couple, it won't look so suspicious."

"This is beginning to look like fun," Bloch replied clapping his hands.

"This couple first have to knock off an old van, drive it along that narrow lane, right up to the fire door and block it off."

"Why?" Bloch became serious.

"To block off Hussey's escape."

"What about the front door?"

"That'll be locked," Purdy assured him, "Hussy locks it against any late-night raids, anyone left inside the goons let them out and lock up. When the barman leaves, they give him the keys, he locks up from the outside. He takes the key home so he can open up in the morning."

"I might do that myself," Bloch said, scratching the back of his neck and reached over, lifted a lager can from a small table in front, drank the dregs from it and dropped it on the floor.

Purdy wondered how Bloch knew which can among the multitude of open ones already there, "no you can't do it, Hussey knows you're one of my mates, his goons would be over you like fies to shit."

CHAPTER 18

Ben and Tommy Carter, decided to pay Cecil Hussey a visit, "time to kill that little shit before he kills us," Ben said.

"Have you any plans on how we are going to do it?" His brother asked.

Ben stretched himself out on his seat with his hands behind his neck, "that narrow lane that runs between his club and the neighbouring building."

Tommy nodded. "what about it?"

"There's a fire door down at the end of it, we go down that lane make a bit of noise, when one of the goons come out to investigate, we bump him, dive in and blast everybody that's inside."

"Tommy grinned," that's the dumbest idea I've ever heard, so dumb that it could work. That little shit won't be expecting it."

Ben lit a cigarette, "we will have to watch the place for a few days, see if we can discover how many goons he's got protecting him."

Tommy went into the kitchen and returned with a can of beer on each hand, he handed one to his brother and suggested, "or we could follow Hussey to his home, bump him off there."

Ben pulled the ring on his can, took a long drink," does he have a home? He seems to spend a lot of time in his club."

"He must have, or he has a flat upstairs, as we know that is where his girls take their punters, he could have a pad up there somewhere."

"We can only hope that Randell doesn't need us for the next day or two," Ben said taking another drink from his can.

"I don't think there's much chance of getting time away from the big man, with all this extra security he wants," Tommy advised and pulled the ring from his can, sat down on the seat opposite his brother and took a long drink and afterwards made a noisy burp. As he was about to take anther drink his mobile sounded. He grabbed the device from his pocket and seeing it was a restricted number, he shouted," Hi! Who's calling?" The message was short, confused Tommy shook his head and gazed at his phone.

"Who was that?" Ben asked dropping his cigarette butt into the empty can.

"I don't know, something about a guy called Jaco was in hospital."

Ben sat up, "who the fucks Jaco?"

"I think it could be that tall thin bag of bones with the large earrings, who serves behind the bar and drives Hussey about."

"I think we should pay him a hospital visit, find out for sure, might be able to get some info. From him."

Tommy wasn't sharing his brother's confidence, "that's not going to be easy, we don't know his full name, what ward he's in, when he was admitted…, that's a big hospital, we could be wandering about for hours."

A wide grin dawned across Ben's features his droopy moustache almost straited across his cheeks," I've just thought about that, we go to reception as policemen, tell them we need to interview a recent admission, we only know him as Jaco."

"That could take a lot of time, they must be getting lots of admissions in every day…, and what if they ask for I.D.?

These are chances we must take, if we get our hands on him and make him sing, could save us a lot of time in the long run, he should know Hussey better than anyone."

Barton woke up with a start, for a moment he was confused by his unfamiliar surroundings. Noises from upstairs, footsteps, faint voices, doors opening and closing. He sat up, expecting the cold water and the guard shouting. The touch of her warm soft hand on his shoulder, gently pulled him back down, brought him back to reality, shrugged him out of his recurring nightmare.

"What's wrong?" Damson asked in a sleepy voice, "had a bad dream?"

His head sank back onto the pillow, "something like that, "he replied reached for a tissue from the bed side table and wiped sweat from his forehead.

"It must have been a very bad dream," she said and reached over for another tissue and wiped the perspiration from his bare chest .

"I think it was hearing the neighbours moving about, I'm not used to living in these high flats."

"Well get used to it, we might be here for a while," she replied and swung her legs out of the bed, "we might as well get up the alarm will be going off in an hour."

Barton took hold of her arm, pulled her back down beside him, "let's make it an hour to remember."

"That's fine by me," she giggled and let herself be pull back in beside him. They lay contented in each other's arms, waiting for her alarm to go off. "what's to happen now?"

Barton asked.

"We will find out when we go in." she replied, "there seems to be a panic, Mr Randell doesn't like it when things get out of his control. All these bombs going off isn't good for his business. We've got to find who's making them," this time she was out of bed and out of reach and rushed out the room into the toilet.

"How do we do that?" Barton called after her, but all the response he got was the sound of the door closing. He lay for a while staring at the ceiling, was beginning to regret not haven made an effort to develop a closer relationship with his younger brother. Corrie was a toddler fouling his nappy and sucking on a dummy tit when Barton left home and joined the army. Visits were few and short, he never witnessed his brother growing up. The shrill of Damston's alarm clock and the flushing of the toilet, abruptly pulled him out of his semi-dream.

She walked in drying her hair with a towel, fully dressed, "get out of that bed, lazy oaf," she cried.

Barton obeyed instantly and ran past her naked. He was glad of the interruption, took his mind off his brother for a while. After completing his toilet, he met her at the door holding his clothes.

He got dressed quickly, "you never answered my question," he asked, "how do we find out who's making these bombs, when Lumpy's no longer with us. She shrugged her shoulders, threw him the car keys, "maybe Mr. Randell could answer that question."

"I think we should find Lenny, I'm sure he knows more than he has been telling us," Barton suggested as they descended the stairs. Damston had a fear of lifts, she never explained why, he decided she had spent so much time in a cell, didn't like being enclosed in a place where she couldn't open the doors. He followed her down the steps, breathing in the pungent odour of disinfectant and was glad when they reached the bottom and outside to the fresh air.

She stopped a few yards from the car, "do you think we should check it first?"

Barton nodded, operated the remote, the lights flashed, and he went through the same procedure as before, "seems okay!" he cried and waved her over.

Randell shook his head, his jowls wobbling in unison, "I don't know this Limping Lenny, but from what you both have told me. I don't think Lumpy would let him handle explosives or let him anywhere near his workshop."

"He had the keys," Damston assured him, "he claimed that Lumpy said he could kip there."

Barton shifted in his chair and said, "I don't think finding him is going to be simple, after what has happened he'll be staying out of sight."

The big man nodded, "I'll get a few of the team to help you find him."

Barton followed her out the office, leaving Nevil busy lighting the big man's cigar. The daylight was fading as they headed for the car. He got in the driver's seat and said, "we're going to have a hard time finding Lenny in the dark."

"Well we've spent most of the day with Mr. Randell organising the team, giving them areas to search, maybe when we get there, one of them have found him."

"So now we go to the town centre car park and wait for one of them to phone you?" Barton put the car in motion and headed out.

"If we don't get a call soon," Damston said, "we'll have to join in the search, you heard what Mr. Randell's final words were, find him tonight."

Barton steered the car to the darkest part of the parking area, close to the overgrown shrubs that surrounded it. The ratchet sounded when he pulled up the hand brake, he cut the lights, "how long do we wait for a call?"

In the dim light she shrugged her shoulders, "give it about an hour, if we hear nothing, then we start to search and don't dare start drumming your fingers on the steering wheel."

"So, we sit here and just twiddle our thumbs?"

She grabbed his jacket, "it's nice and dark here, let's make it another hour to remember," she giggled and pulled him over on top of her.

Barton put up no fight, had no resistance from this woman, he fumbled for the lever and the rear of the seat fell back. Damston glanced at her watch, "oh kay! Richard, let's go and help find Lenny."

After an hour's driving and locating the searching team members, with negative results. She was about to call Randell to get permission to halt the search for the night when she cried, pointing her finger, "that looks like him standing in that bus shelter with those girls."

Barton swung the car over, hit the brakes and they both jumped out. The girls screamed when Barton jumped on Lenny, they ran off in different directions.

Barton had him in an armlock, Damston stood in front with her pistol under his nose.

"What the fucks going on? Lenny screamed.

"Hands behind your back," she ordered, and handed Barton a cable tie.

Barton released his grip from Lenny's neck and secured his hands behind his back. Grabbed the back of his neck and pushed him towards the car. They bundled him into the boot and drove off.

"Where are we going?" Barton asked.

"Just follow my directions."

Barton soon found himself driving along a narrow country lane that snaked between high banked grass verges and tall hedges on both sides. He could only manage a top speed of around twenty.

"Stop!" Damston cried and gripped his arm.

Barton hit the brakes and turned off the lights, "what's wrong?" He got no reply and watched her get out the door and crouched behind the rear wheel at her side. he quickly joined her, "what is it? He asked when he noticed the gun in her hand. This time he didn't need a reply. The vehicle came around the bend. The driver hit the bakes; the tyres screamed the vehicle fish tailed but managed to stop a few inches from the rear of their car. A second later another vehicle came around the bend, this one failed to stop and rammed into the rear of the first.

"Get in the car and drive like fuck," she screamed.

Barton had left the engine ticking over, they hadn't closed their doors. This gained them valuable seconds to get in and speed off.

He hadn't gone far before he saw the headlights of the pursuing cars, in his rear-view mirror.

"Turn left here," she shouted.

It was a last-minute call, Barton almost rolled the vehicle and had to fight to get it under control.

"In about a hundred-yard turn left again and switch off the lights, keep your foot off the brake pedal, we don't want them to see the brake lights in the dark.

Barton noticed the rough road and turned in, decided this was a farm entrance, was narrower than the lane they had turned off, with a steep decline, making it difficult to keep his foot off the brake. Even with his foot clear of the accelerator the car began to pick up speed, it bumped and bounced on the deep potholes. Barton was almost feeling sorry for Lenny in the boot, could hear him shouting and screaming.

"We should have taped that bastard's mouth," Damston complained.

All Barton could do was hope there were no sharp turns on this track, could only see a few feet in front. The steep banking on both sides were his only guidelines. The speed was now approaching forty miles an hour, the engine was screaming in the low gears, "how much farther?" He shouted.

"Not very far now,"

"How am I supposed to stop if I can't use the brakes?"

"Well if you don't manage to stop, we'll hit a solid wall."

The words had hardly passed her lips when the dark shadow of the farm buildings appeared. It took all his willpower not to stamp on the brakes. He grasped the hand brake and pulled it up, the vehicle fish tailed violently but it didn't slow down much, "fuck this," He shouted and rammed his foot on the brake. The car fish tailed more violently and began to slow down. The solid wall was now about ten feet away. All they could do was close their eyes and brace themselves for the impact.

It never happened all they could do for the next few minutes, was sit in silence until the shock dissipated. Barton got out first, went to the front of the car and judged he couldn't have been able to push his flattened hand between the front bumper and the wall.

CHAPTER 19

Cecil decided, Purdy was a waste of time for the moment, convinced he will turn up soon enough, he had plenty of eyes out there looking for him, knew where his flat was, also he had learned Purdy had a family there. If he didn't turn up, it would just be a matter of kidnapping them. He knocked his empty glass on the bar, for the barman to refill it, never needed to do this when Jaco was on the job. He shrugged his thoughts away from that subject, didn't want to think of that bone bag of a traitor. The bald barman with the hound-dog expression, filled his glass up and returned to dealing with customers. According to Purdy and his thugs, the whore Wilma had convinced them that Barton was Corrie's older brother. Cecil couldn't remember Corrie mentioning about having a brother. He and his pal Danny had been regular patrons, but they were becoming a a bit of a pain, causing trouble, drawing attention to his club. He decided to deal with them and at the same time, deal with Randell.

"How's Jaco?" The tall red-haired girl shouted from the other end of the bar. Cecil felt all eyes on him, could feel his uncontrolled temper boil up, "none of your business," he shouted back. He hated being disturbed out of important thoughts and made a mental note to have her dealt with, teach her not to disturb him again.

The club was beginning to fill up with regular patrons and a few strangers, the girls dressed in bikini tops and tight shorts began mingling. This was when a close eye had to be kept on them, when they received cash from the customers, this money had to be handed to the barman, if caught trying to keep it, he would derive personal pleasure dealing with them. This was his world, he made the laws and if need be, only he could change them. The laws of the rest of the world stopped at the door. Patrons could smoke, could take drugs, drink as much as they could take, have sex with any of the girls or boys, gamble in the back room. The cash flow was enormous, but it wasn't enough, Cecil wanted more.

Two of his most recent thugs, recruited by his business associates, Mr. Crow. Came over and stood on either side of him. Cecil glanced from side to side at them. "What do you two want?"

"The guy standing at the door's, complaining he got a dose from one of your girls," the thug on his right said.

Cecil took a sip from his glass, "get him to point out the girl, deal with her, then deal with him, make sure he doesn't open his gob about it." The girls were a good earner and he didn't want to lose that part of the business. Upstairs he had five bedrooms where the girls took their Johns, earning around five grand a night. The thugs headed for the door. Cecil watched them edge their way through the patrons stood at the bar, couldn't help that lustful feeling, but guessed it was a waste of time, they didn't portray the signs. Cecil knew it would be wishful thinking, but hoped the the whore who contaminated the man was the mouthy bitch with the red hair.

He was proud of what he had achieved with his club, in the three years since he had taken it over. Admittedly, it wasn't in the same class as the night clubs in the city, but they were far too expensive for his clientele. The tables and chairs needed replacing, all looking well used with wabbly legs. The carpets were full of cigarette burns and beer stains, the pile at the bar worn bare, the walls were dark brown with a cream patch where a picture once hung. Above, the ceiling was stained almost black from years of nicotine. The lighting was inadequate, but in Cecil's opinion it was all this that added to the atmosphere of discretion. None of his patrons wanted to advertise their indulgences, and the girls weren't the best of lookers. The bar was his design, with mirrors behind, glass shelving displaying bottles of assorted drinks. But all this was small time, Cecil wanted the Randell enterprise, and that was just a beginning.

He swallowed the last of the gin from his glass and knocked it on the bar for a refill. The barman instantly stopped what he was doing and poured his drink. At the same time the two thugs escorted the red-haired mouthy girl over to him.

"That punter pointed this one out," said the shortest of the two and pushed her against the bar.

"Take her down to the cellar," Cecil pointed his thumb at the door," tie her to a chair, I'll deal with her later." The whores were easy to replace, just a matter of contacting Mr. Crow, tell him a customer beat her up so bad, she died, for a price, he will replace her and arrange for the disposal of her body.

The red light behind the bar flashed, this was a warning from the doorman that a stranger had entered. Cecil gave a nod to a couple of thugs who were sitting at the fire exit talking and smoking. The thugs acknowledged his signal, got up and strolled over to the door. Cecil followed, always prided himself at reading strangers, could tell a policeman immediately, or what he decided was a troublemaker. The thugs searched the man, handed his wallet to Cecil, who discovered the man had little cash on him was about to toss it back when he noticed the name on the elderly man's driver's license. The name jumped out at him, Cecil couldn't believe his luck, but this man was surely too old. Cecil smiled, held back the wallet, "Mr. Thomas Barton, welcome to my little club," He ushered the old man to a nearby table and sat him down, "can I call you Thomas?"

The oldster shook his head and grinned back, "Tom will do fine."

"Get Tom a drink, on the house," Cecil told one of the thugs, he drew the other to the side, "Go down the cellar and bring that pox ridden whore up to me. Make sure she tidies herself up first."

Cecil returned to his seat at the bar, checked his three mobile phones, he was in the habit of placing out in front of him on the bar. The bald-headed barman noticed Cecil downing the last of his drink and skipped over and gave him a refill.

"Here we are boss," the thug said pushing the girl over against the bar.

"That man's a liar," she protested, "honest Cecil I'm clean, was checked yesterday."

Cecil held up a hand, "never mind that just now, I've a job for you, if you do it well, you can go back to work." He waited for a response. When she gave him a nod, he continued," the old man sitting on his own at the table behind us, I want you to entertain him, ask him about his family," he handed her a pill, "slip that into his drink, loosen his tongue."

One of his mobiles sounded, Cecil checked the small screen and smiled," I hope this is good news," he barked into it. It was good news, so good he nearly jumped out of his chair. "hold onto them until the club closes before you bring them here." The goons had lost Purdy, but managed to get his family. He pushed his drink away, needed a clear head for the fun later. The red headed whore was getting chatty with the old man. Things were working out very well this evening, he whispered to his reflection in the mirror behind the bar. Over his shoulder he caught red hair's eye, she winked and gave him the thumbs up. Stupid whore thinks she's off the hook, you're in for a shock.

Purdy paced Bloch's littered floor he had tried all day to get his partner on her mobile with no results. Now Bloch was telling him that the couple, they had planned to go into Hussey club couldn't find a suitable van.

"It has to be one that isn't boxed in, at the back, because when the van gets parked on that narrow lane, their only way out of it would be through the rear doors." Bloch explained.

"Well couldn't they have jumped out and pushed it down?"

Bloch shook his head, "there's no way of stopping it at that fire door, and anyway, a couple would stand out, that's a whore's club, men seldom take girlfriends in there, most of the regulars are coloured, a white man and a girl would stand out like a Christmas tree in July."

"You don't happen to know any of the girls who work there?"

Bloch shook his head, "I could ask about, maybe one of the boy's knows one."

"Get on the blower now, I've got a feeling that little shit bag Hussey's got my family."

Bloch sat on the littered sofa and got his mobile out, at the same time trying to light a cigarette with a plastic lighter that refused to work. He gave up with it and tossed in amongst the rest of the litter on the floor. Six calls later he spoke to a mate who was familiar with one of the girls. He arranged to meet, disconnected and grinned up at Purdy exposing his mouth full of smoke stained teeth. "Got it sorted, Jason's sister works there, but he's not sure she would do anything to cross Hussey, says she's shit scared of him."

"How soon can this be set up?"

"Jason's on his way here now, and for fucks sake sit down."

Purdy ignored Bloch's advice and continued wading through the rubbish kicking some of it aside. He made another attempt at calling his girlfriend, this time he got a reply, she sounded scared her voice trembled, "two thugs have got me and our baby in the back of a van, they say if you don't go back to the Hussey Club, you won't see us again," the signal got cut off. Purdy roared in rage and punched a hole in Bloch's wall.

"Did that make you feel any better?" Bloch asked, had picked up another lighter from the cluttered table and got his smoke going.

Purdy repeated his girlfriend's message, "how long will it take for this Jason to get here? We're going to have to move quick before they decide to take her and the baby to the club. I don't think Hussey's stupid enough to drag a woman and baby in there with all those customers watching. We'll have to get Jason in before it closes. This girl he knows is she in there tonight?"

Bloch shrugged his shoulders and picked up his phone again, "I'll ask him."

Purdy stopped pacing and tried to read Bloch's reactions as he spoke to Jason. When Bloch grinned and stuck up his thumb, he began pacing again, "tell him to give her a call, ask her how many goons Hussey has in his club with him. Where there are stationed if they're armed etc."

Bloch replaced his phone back in his pocket, "he'll be here in a minute, you can tell him yourself."

He got up off the sofa, cigarette held between his lips with a half inch of ash ready to drop off. Went into his kitchen and returned with a can of beer in each hand, handed one to Purdy when a loud knock came from the outside door. "that'll be him now," Bloch dumped his unopened can beside the discarded ones on the table and rushed to the door.

Purdy stopped pacing when Bloch led the red-haired Jason through the door, He explained the situation to the young Jason, invited him to sit but the young man refused, complaining that he didn't want his new jean dirty. "If you phone that girl now," Purdy said, "we could get things started."

"That girl is my older sister, her name is Carmel," Jason pointed out, "the reason I'm helping you is to get her away from that place and that way of life. She never answers her mobile, not allowed to have it with her in that club."

"Do you have a mate who would go with you into that club?" Purdy asked, Jason thought for a moment and nodded. Purdy explained the simple incendiary device to him, "but don't go into the place until it's near closing, you'll see an old sofa placed on the back wall. That's where to hide it, spill some whiskey to help the flames catch. You and your sister will have plenty of time to get out with the rest of the customers."

Barton grabbed the shoulders of his jacket and pulled Lenny out of the boot. Damtson rammed her pistol under his nose and backed him through the farmhouse door into the empty living room.

"Get down on your knees," she shouted at him and located the light switch, turned on a bare bulb hanging from a long cable.

Barton leaned over and pulled the black duct tape from his mouth. Not having shaved for a while made this extra painful. Lenny howled, tears streaming from his eyes, "what the fuck do you two think you're doing?"

"We're looking for some honest answers," Barton snarled at him.

"Honest answers to what?"

Damtson stooped down beside him, pushed her gun against his ear, "to what we are about to ask you."

With all his weight on his knees, Lenny showed signs of being in agony, his bad leg gave way under him a few times. "I've answered all your questions honestly, what the fuck else do you want?"

Barton grabbed what little hair he had and forced his head back, "don't give us the poor pathetic bum act."

Damston now with her weapon under his chin, "you can start by telling us the name of Lumpy's assistant?"

"I've seen him with a lot of people anyone could have been his assistant, I don't know all they're names."

"Give us the names you know?" Barton asked releasing his head.

"I can't remember, I've got a bad memory for names."

"Right Lenny you ask for it," Damston shouted, put the barrel of her pistol to his ear and fired. The explosion reverberated around the empty room blood splattered the white wall behind Lenny, his scream seemed to resonate through the whole area.

Barton cringed at the sight of what was his ear, now resembled a bloody piece of raw meat. Couldn't imagine the pain Lenny will have to suffer in a few minutes when the shock dies.

"You could have saved yourself all this pain by talking."

Damston moved her gun to his other ear, "Tell us what we want to know, or the other ear gets it."

"I can't remember any names, honest," Lenny mumbled, the blood from his injury was running into his mouth almost choking him. With his hands still bound behind his back, he had no way of wiping it away.

"Who is paying you?" Barton quickly asked before Damston had a chance to shoot off his other ear.

Lenny coughed out the blood from his mouth, "a well-dressed little man, I think his name is Crow."

Damston got to her feet, took a few steps back and nodded for Barton to join her, "what do you think, is he telling the truth?"

"Under that threat I think I would, rather than get my other ear shot off."

She nodded, "patch him up we'll dump him on the steps at the hospital," she returned to Lenny now curled into a tighter ball on the floor, "how long have you known Lumpy?"

Lenny was now holding his head to the side, so that the blood wouldn't run into his mouth, "not long," he admitted," I found him lying on the street of a derelict estate, I think he had been shot, I found keys on him and some money. I knew where his workshop was and got a pal to run me out there."

"How did you know where his workshop was?" She snapped at him.

"He told me, he told everybody, he wasn't one for keeping secrets, very mouthy."

CHAPTER 20

Two strangers approached Jaco's bed. One stood on the left side the other on the right, He gazed from one to the other, "who are you, what do you want?"

"Your friend sent us, we're here to take you home," the stranger on the right said.

Jaco sat up alerted, "what friend?"

"Never mind," said the one on the left, "just get your clothes on and come with us," he opened his jacket and exposed the gun in his waist band.

Jaco sneered at them, "I don't think you would be stupid enough to use that thing in here."

"Don't bet on that," the gunman said.

"Get dressed or we'll drag you out like that," the other man said and grabbed Jaco's arm.

"Let go you bastard," Jaco shouted, tried to pull his arm free but the grip was too strong.

"If that's the way you want it," was the last words Jaco heard, saw the big clenched fist coming towards him, was too slow to avoid it. With only a flimsy hospital gown to ward off the cold frosty wind, Jaco woke from unconsciousness felt himself being pushed into the back of a boxed in van. The vehicle rocked as the two men got in with him, pinned him down and bound his hands, feet and mouth with duct tape. Satisfied with their work they got out, slammed the door leaving him in total darkness. The engine started and the van was soon on the move. The fear of what was going to happen to him grew to the extent that he could no longer control his bowels.

When the rear doors of the van opened, the daylight stabbed at his eyes, he realised he must have slipped back into unconsciousness. It seemed like only minutes since he had been abducted from hospital bound and tossed into this vehicle. He gagged at the smell of his own excretion, as did the two figures stood at the door. With hands at their mouth, they grabbed Jaco by the ankles and pulled him out. He landed heavily on a slabbed surface, hitting his head and again he passed out.

They lifted Lenny out of the boot, dumped him at the side of the road close to the hospital entrance, untied him, Damston ripped the tape from his mouth, Lenny supressed his yell this time.

"You can walk the rest," she said.

They got in the car and watched Lenny stagger in the direction of the hospital gates. "we're too bloody soft," Damston remarked.

Barton put the car into gear and drove off, "what good would it have done killing him?"

"The hospital will want to know what happened to his ear, if he says it's a gunshot wound the police will be involved." She gazed out her side window as they drove past shuttered up shop windows and doors, late night dog walkers, drunks standing outside pubs smoking. "He's going to have to tell them something."

"I don't think Lenny would want the cops asking him questions, I'm sure he'll come up with a convincing story."

Barton pulled the car into the block of flats carpark, pulled up the hand brake and switched the engine off, "you looked surprised when he mentioned Crow's name?"

She ignored his question, "what's bothering me is, who were in those cars that were behind us on that small country lane? It was obvious they were following us."

"Are you sure you're not being a bit paranoid?"

She half opened her door and turned to him, in the dim interior light, noticed a concerned expression on his face, "I wish I were," she stepped out and slammed the door.

Drinking coffee on the sofa after dining on a microwave meal, she said, "we are no farther forward in finding out who Lumpy's assistant is," she kicked off her shoes and put her feet on the small table in front of them.

Barton placed his mug next to her feet, picked up the remote and turned on the television, "I did learn something, Mr. Crow, if that's his real name, seems to be keeping a close-eyes on everything."

She grinned, flicked a lock of blond hair from her eyes, sipped her coffee, "I don't know if that's his real name, we use him, he's good at finding the right kind of people we need."

"It seems he is paying Lenny as some kind of informant."

"It looks like it, I thought at first Lenny was just a bum, until you pointed a few things out about him."

"Then there's a possibility that Crow recruited Lumpy's apprentice?"

"That's just a possibility, and there's no way of finding out, either way."

"We could ask Crow?"

She shook her head, "that's one thing we must never do." She swung her legs off the table, stood up and tied her blond hair up into a bun, "I need a shower, care to join me?"

Barton grinned, pointed his thumb in the direction of the toilet, "that shower is too small, if we went in it together, we would need the fire service to get us out."

"Now there's a thought, in that shower with you and a team of firemen," she walked away laughing, still trying to secure her hair.

The carter brothers were getting impatient waiting at the hospital reception area. They had repeated their rehearsed lie a few times to different people. Ben was pacing about in desperate need of a smoke, Tommy was sat on one of the many seats, reading an out of date magazine. A young man dressed in a green hospital jacket approached Ben.

"Are you the police who were enquiring about an admission?" the young man smiled at them.

Ben nodded, Tommy dropped his magazine and joined them.

"Working on the information," the young man said, "we're not sure who it is you're looking for, all I can suggest is, that we go around all the male admissions we have had in the last twenty-four hours. We have had fourteen male admissions, we can eliminate six of those as they are too old, if you would like to get started, follow me."

Fortune was with them, on the third visitation they discovered a group of nurses and doctors having a heated conversation around an empty bed. The young man approached them, exchanged a few words and returned," it seems that this patient has gone," he said.

"Was he discharged?" Ben asked.

"No," said the young man, "he just got up and left, without telling anyone."

Ben turned to his brother, "I bet that's Jaco."

Not wanting to be subjected to more questions, the brothers made a quick exit. "Do you think Hussey might have sent some of his goons in to get Jaco? Tommy asked.

"You would think in a busy place like this someone would have noticed him leaving," said Ben, holding the door open for his brother, ignoring Tommy's question.

Tommy got in the driver's seat, Ben busy fastening his seat belt said, "let's go to the Hussey club, see what's going down."

Tommy glanced at his watch, "we're too early, the place won't be open for another two hours."

"I know, but we can have a good look around the place in daylight."

"I don't think it's going to be that simple," Tommy said and started up the car, "that place will have C.C.T.V. All over that area, we will have to pull our hoods down to hide our faces. That's going to look suspicious to any pedestrians walking about. Somebody might call the cops."

"Anytime I've went past there, I've noticed a few hoody's hanging about, we're not going to look out of place. I don't think that lane is private, the shopkeepers next to the club have to haul their wheelie bins up there, we could grab one and push it about for a while."

"Are you suggesting we walk up and down, hauling a ruddy great wheelie bin?" Tommy asked as he got the car in motion.

Ben laughed, wound down his window and lit up a cigarette, "if we have to," he coughed in his laughter.

"Those fags are killing you." Tommy said and wound down his side window.

"In this game I'll be dead before the fags have a chance to."

They parked the car on a side street and with other pedestrians walked past the Hussey Club, spent a short time there before crossing to the opposite side of the road, where they had a view of the lane.

"Not much going on there," Tommy said nodding his head at the club.

"That's good," Ben replied and pulled his hood up, "let's take a walk along it and have a look at what's at the back, see if we could find a suitable place to take a shot."

They took a casual stroll the length of the lane, finding the club fire exit on their left, just a few feet from the end of the building. "That's not good," Tommy said, "we won't be able to take a shot from the rear, without being spotted first," he looked around," look at the security light, all over the, place."

Ben grinned widely, "remember when we were kids, all our pals used to call you Hawkeye because you were good with a sling shot?"

Tommy anticipated his brother's next words and quickly interrupted, "that was a long time ago, I don't think I'll be much good at it now."

"I think we better go somewhere and let you get some practice

Purdy parked his car in the same place that the Carter brothers had done, an hour earlier. Bloch was in the passenger seat with Jason and his mate in the back. Like the brothers they walked towards the Hussey Club, blending in with other pedestrians. Purdy called a halt at the top of the narrow lane. Purdy and the two others stood watch as Bloch made his way down to the fire exit, delayed a moment, but couldn't see or hear any signs of life and continued to the end of the building. Two large green wheelie bins blocked his way from going any farther, he lifted the lid of the nearest one, was about to look inside, just a thoughtless moment a short distraction, Bloch never knew what had hit him. He got the sensation of a blinding flash striking his inner eyes, from above he could see himself falling from the bin, this lasted no more than a heartbeat before blackness engulfed him.

The sound of buses and taxis constantly traveling along the street, failed to blank out the muffled sound of the shot, it sounded like the slap of a hand on the back of someone wearing a leather jacket. Purdy had heard it before, knew it was from a hand weapon using a silencer and wasted no time, with the two mates he rushed towards his car.

"What was that?" One of the men asked when they got into the vehicle.

"I don't know," Purdy lied, "I'm not hanging about to find out." One experience with Hussey's goons is enough he decided and drove the car away the tyres screaming in protest.

Purdy pulled up at the gates of an abandoned building site, he turned to the two men in the back, "I'm not sure what Bloch has told you, the reason I'm trying to get to Hussey is because he's got my family. When I get them out of there, I would love to see that place burn down with that little psychopathic shit bag inside."

"They must have cameras at the bottom of that lane and spotted Bloch snooping about," Jason said.

Purdy engaged the gears and pulled away, "they would have recognised him, he was with me in there a few weeks ago."

He stopped the car outside Bloch's house," we'll wait in here until near closing time, but be warned, the place stinks, beware of the rats and cockroaches and wipe your feet on the way out."

"I know," said Jason," I've been in there."

The path to Bloch's house was like an obstacle course, the grass had never been cut, an old cooker lay on top of a mattress, a box style television lay close to the door. At the side of the house lay an abandoned car that was sat on blocks of wood, the wheels were nowhere in sight. Purdy pushed the door and it creaked open.

"Does Bloch never lock his door?" Jason's mate asked.

"Only the bravest would enter in here," Purdy replied and stepped inside, "to say Bloch was a hoarder would be the understatement of the century," Purdy went on, as the two men followed him along a short passageway cluttered with junk mail and unopened letters. "In truth I think he was too lazy to throw the garbage out."

Jason's mate cleared a space on the sofa of half eaten sandwiches, dirty dishes and soiled underwear, reluctantly he sat down, "I think I'm going to be sick," he declared.

Purdy cleared the padded chair and sat down, "be sick if you have to, it won't look out of place."

"I think I'll just stand," Jason said.

Purdy glanced up at him, nodded his head towards the kitchen, "see if there's any beer in the fridge."

Jason made his way into the kitchen, but soon returned, "the fridge is lying open," he cried.

"there's lots of fury little things in there, I think it's moulded food, it fuckin stinks."

"Is there any beer?" Purdy asked, at the same time trying to get his girlfriend on her mobile.

"I can't find any beer," Jason stepped into the living room, "where's the toilet, I feel sick?"

Purdy returned his phone to his pocket, "you don't want to go there."

CHAPTER 21

amston had to ride in the back beside Randell, Barton was in the front of the limousine, beside Nevil. The glass partition had been closed he couldn't hear what was being said in the back and decided to take the chance at starting a conversation with the driver, maybe slip in a few questions, "this is a beautiful car, a good job you have driving it?"

Nevil gave him a quick glance, with a wide grin, showing off his white teeth with a wide space between the two front ones.

"Been doing it for long?"

The driver nodded.

"A man of a few words, are you?" No response came, Barton decided to try the irritation tactic and started to whistle and slap his hands on his knees in time with the unmelodic tune. He continued doing this until Nevil turned up the radio.

It was a no-win situation and Barton gave up and concentrated on where they were heading. After a time of cruising smoothly North on the M6, Nevil slipped the big car onto the M25, leaving for the sign of Ellesmere Port. Nevil wasn't a happy driver when he had to pull off the main road onto a narrow gravel track. The ruts were deep from years of truck use, even Barton cringed when he heard the bottom of the vehicle scraping the high crown on the centre. All the way down the mile and a half track, the big coloured driver used every swear word that was ever invented, plus a few that were new to Barton.

The big car came to a crunching halt, on a gravel courtyard a few yards from a red bricked building. Behind this on all three sides was the high face of rock that was once a quarry. A tall gaunt man wearing a yellow high vis. Jacket appeared at the door of the building. He closed the door behind him and stood looking at them. Barton wondered why nobody had made a move. The answer came shortly after, when a red car came bouncing down the drive and pulled up behind them.

The bodyguard team jumped out and surrounded the limousine, Randell didn't move until he got a nod from one of them.

"You stay here," Nevil ordered, "guard the cars," he got out, lifted the wheelchair out of the boot and he and Damston manoeuvred the big man into it.

While all this was going on, something caught Barton's eye at the other side of the building, was it a piece of litter blowing in the breeze, a wild animal, or a person darting back out of sight? He couldn't be sure. The man at the door stretched out his arm in their direction. Barton jumped out the limousine and shouted just as the shot hit the red car's door. Although Randell panicked the bodyguard did what they were trained to do, surrounded him and got him back into the vehicle.

Nevil crouched behind the limousine, got in through the passenger's door and drove the vehicle a safe distance up the drive.

Barton made his way over to Damston and the others behind the red car, "if we're to get in there, we'll have to split up."

"How do we do that?" Damston replied, "we're stuck out here behind this car if we make a move we could get shot we don't know how many there are in there."

Barton pointed to an abandoned digger, a short distance from the building, "if we could get to that old machine, get behind it, we will be on their blind side, use the quarry sides for cover."

"That's too far we would be mowed down before we got halfway," Damston said

"We push this car over to it staying behind it for cover." Barton opened the passenger's door reached over and released the hand brake.

Four men and two women had no problems pushing the car, leaving it tight against the rusted tracks of the digger. After they had all caught their breath, Damston asked, "why didn't you shoot that man at the door when you had the chance?"

"From that distance, I wasn't sure I would hit him."

"Well at least," she let out a deep sigh, "Mr Randell safe."

Barton led the way from behind the digger to the quarry face, from there they soon reached the corner of the building. He was quite surprised at the length of the building, the early morning Sun created an optical illusion, casting a dark shadow from the steep rock face. His plan was to get around the back and come up to the door on their blind side. That looked out of the question now, it would take too long.

He used hand signals to split the group up, sent three of them the long way around. He, Damston and one of the girls waited there giving them time to cover the distance.

Barton's timing was spot on, they all met at the door at the same time. He and one of the men gave the door a kick and they charged in, guns cocked and ready.

They met no resistance, could see nobody in the dim light, stacks of cardboard boxes were built up along one of the walls, wooden crates and pallets occupied the other side. At Damston's signal they spread out and began to search. They hadn't gone far when three men stepped out of a door at the back, holding up their hand.

"We're unarmed," one of them shouted. Damston accompanied by another girl rushed over, pistols aimed at their heads," you fuckin better be," she shouted.

The rest of the team soon surrounded them, Barton stepped forward, "Who stood at the door and took a shot at us?"

The three men gave him a dumb look and shook their heads, "it wasn't one of us," the tallest of them said."

"One of you was standing at the door in a high vis. Jacket holding a gun," Barton said.

One of the other men said, "that was me, but it wasn't a gun I was holding, it was a screwdriver."

"So that bullet that hit the car came from a screwdriver," Damston roared, a few of the group laughed softly but soon stopped when she gave them a stern look.

"Who are you, what are you doing here?" Barton asked.

"We're here representing the owner of this property, to survey and negotiate the value with a Mr. Randell, the youngest man with a bald head stepped forward holding out an I.D. card.

"Sit down on those crates," Damston ordered, directing them with her pistol. Without hesitation, the three men stepped over and got seated. She turned to Barton, nodded at the door they had came from, "see what's in there."

The door was partially concealed with cardboard boxes. Barton approached it expecting a broom cupboard or a toilet, and was surprised when he opened the door to discover a well-equipped office, with modern computers, a huge desk and several padded swivel chairs. The walls were panelled with dark Oak, the lighting was from a long tubular system on the ceiling. There were no windows, which to Barton thinking was essential, with this place being a quarry and dynamite was the main tool for shattering the rock face and would also help in soundproofing. On the wall in front of the desk was three C.C.TV. Monitors all in working order and operating. The place was warm with the smell of percolated coffee. He returned to the door and waved Damston in.

Her eyes widened, she gasped and flicked back that infuriating lock of hair, "this is a bit of a surprised."

Makes you wonder what's going on," Barton said, walking around the office, looking at the monitors, opening cabinets and drawers, "an ongoing thing whatever it is."

She came over beside him and examined the screen of one of the computers, "I've no doubt Mr. Randell will know all about this."

"Should we call him in?"

She followed Barton's eyes, looking at the C.C. TV. Monitors. They seem to cover the whole building, all the way around, if there has been anyone else out there, we should be able to see them on the tape. Until we find who it was that fired that shot, we better not call him in."

They scanned the recordings, dated for that day, in case they missed anything, they did this a few times. All that was on the tape was the arrival of the three men and the one wearing the high vis. Jacket standing at the door at the time of their arrival. "Stop it there," Barton told her and pointed to the picture," where did that jacket go to?"

"We'll soon find out," Damston said and stormed out the door. Barton followed her out wondering who was going to lose a foot an ear or maybe a hand. Before he could reach her she had whipped her gun out and held to the head of the screwdriver man.

"Where's your high vis. Jacket?" she demanded.

"It's over there," the man shouted with a tremble in his voice and pointed at the exit.

"Why did you take it off?" Damston asked.

"When I heard that shot, I soon got rid, thinking I would make an easy target."

She slapped him on the mouth with the barrel of her pistol, "you're a fucking liar, you tried to kill one of us, when you missed you ran back in here discarded the jacket, so we wouldn't know who the shooter was."

"That's not true," he screamed, blood running out of his mouth, "I don't have a gun."

She turned to the bodyguards, standing around the men, "tie them up and bundle them into those wooden crates, nail them down until they decide to tell the truth, but first search them for that gun."

Barton helped to secure the three men and bundle them into the crates. Damston insisted that the gunman was packed into the smallest one, although he was the tallest of the three. They had trouble nailing it down, his legs were too long, but with two guards sitting on the lid, they managed.

She told two of the guards to stand at the exit, the others to stand by at the crates, in case they tried to get out. She gave Barton a nod to follow her back into office, where she phoned the big man giving him the all clear. When the big man was wheeled in a few things had to be moved, to get his chair into the office, even then the tall Nevil had to manoeuvre him in backwards.

He got settled behind the desk, got a big cigar going, "what's been happening?" His sunken blue eyes staring at Damston.

"We got into the building," she explained, "discovered three men, they must have been hiding in here, they came out, we asked them who the shooter was, and what they were doing here. We got little response so we have them tied up and bundled into those wooden crates."

Randell took a long drag at his cigar, blew the smoke at them, grinned, "better to be safe eh. I am to meet three men here to negotiate a price on this property, if they are the genuine people, why fire a shot at us?" He nodded at Nevil, "get me that company on the phone, I'll soon find out if they are the real agents."

CHAPTER 22

*J*ason's pal Franky, knew where he could nick a van that wasn't boxed in, as Purdy had explained would have been a problem to get out of when it was jammed up that narrow lane. They drove it to the entrance, switched off the engine and Franky pushed it with Jason steering. At the fire exit Jason pulled up the hand brake, jammed it in gear and climbed out the back door. At the end of the lane they delayed for a while to see if there had been any reactions. When satisfied that they hadn't been noticed on the security cameras, they headed for the club door.

They walked in behind other patrons who were held up at the door by a tall man standing there checking they were not bringing in any of their own booze or drugs. Jason began to have doubts if they would get admitted when Franky walked over and shook the door man's hand. "This is an old work mate of mine," he declared with a grin, "done a few jobs in the past." The door man laughed and waved them on in.

"I take it that's our target," Franky said, nodding towards the sofa on the far wall as they stood at the bar waiting to get served.

"Looks like it," Jason said, "I don't see any sign of my sister."

"We'll have a few pints she might turn up."

Three pints later, still no sign of Jason's sister, "do you think we should ask for her?" Franky said.

"Oh no, we can't do that, one thing I have learned in a place like this, you never ask for a girl by name, they never use their own name and I don't know what she calls herself in here."

Franky drank the last of his pint, "what do we do if she doesn't show?"

"I'm not going to set this place on fire, if my sister's still in here."

"Maybe she's not in tonight."

"I'm not going to take that chance."

Franky waved the barman over and ordered two more pints, "what do you want to do?"

"Let's take our drinks over and sit on that old sofa."

A disturbance at the fire exit drew their attention, three of club thugs had opened it and started arguing.

A little coloured man appeared on the scene, Jason instantly recognised him, "that's the boss man," he whispered, "an evil little shit,"

"Looks like they've discovered the van."

Jason nodded, "if we get up and rush out, someone going to notice and get suspicious, we'll sit for a while, have a few more drinks, it looks like the plan's fucked up anyway."

"Any sign of your sister?" Franky asked glancing around the place, finding it difficult to distinguish one girl from the other in the dim lit, smoke filled crowded room.

Some of the patrons had got up out of their seats to see what the commotion was all about. Two thugs ushered them back. Jason took advantage of the turmoil, signalled to Franky to get up and slip out. They placed their empty pint glasses on the bar and headed for the door. Three thugs blocked their way, "Excuse us gentlemen please," Franky said and tried to edge between them. That was as far as he got when a huge fist slammed into his face.

Jason attempted to run past them, but was knocked to the floor and struggled under the weight of two heavy bodies on top of him.

"Who let those two in?" Cecil shouted, as he pushed his way between the goons who stood over the two men on the floor.

"I did," came the deep voice of the thug, nick named King Kong, because of his bulk and size, he pointed a huge finger at his own chest. Cecil could see the challenge in the giant's demeaner and backed down, knew what he was like when riled. "take them down to the cellar and tie them up. Did you see the red flashing light?" He turned and shouted to the barman, when he got a negative reply. "that means you recognised them?" He said to King Kong.

The giant nodded.

Cecil was losing patients, with the big man, but knew better than push him, "who are they? He asked in a gentle voice.

"I did a few jobs with the skinny one, a few years ago."

He returned to his seat at the bar and watched the thugs scramble the two men to the cellar door. By the gasps and sighs of the patrons, he knew the scenario was the topic of the conversations. He knocked his glass on the bar for a top up. The barman skipped over with the bottle of his special gin, hidden under a shelf by the sink, so the patrons wouldn't ask for it. He was confident that the incident wouldn't get reported, his regulars had too much to hide, and where else could they get drugs and cheap booze, a whore for the night and feel comfortable that their dirty little secrets won't get revealed outside these doors.

The patrons who could walk, started trickling out, some went upstairs with the girls, others slept where they fell. The goons appeared from the cellar and assisted the sleepers onto their feet. Cecil felt light-headed, from the effects of the gin, normally this made him blithe, but with so much going on, he wanted blood, needed to vent his anger out on someone. He couldn't wait to see the last of the customers out the door to get down the cellar, but he most wanted to see Purdy's girlfriend and her baby, being dragged through the door and down below.

Cecil got great pleasure watching the goons ravish and rape the woman, while he held the toddler up by the arm. "Tie her up and gag her," he ordered the goons, after they had finished," get me a kettle of boiling water."

He ordered two of the goons to hold her legs open and they cringed as they watched Cecil pour the boiling water into the woman's vagina. She struggled and screamed for a while and finally passed out with the pain. He picked up the child and placed it between her legs and burst into a fit of laughter.

His next victim was the red headed whore. She had been tied to a beer barrel and gaged with duct tape, he ripped the tape off, and smiled as she screamed, "now tell me what you discovered from that old man?" He pointed his thumb at Tom Barton who had been secured to another barrel close to the staircase. He grabbed her red hair and jerked her head back, "this better be everything I want to know, or you'll get the same as she got."

With her head pressed hard against the top of the barrel, all she could do was make chocking sounds as she tried to speak, he let her hair go and slapped her on the head," what was that?" he screamed into her ear.

"I've told you all I've learned, I don't know what else I can to tell you," she whimpered.

Cecil gave her another slap on the head, "I'm going to talk to that old man, if he tells me something that you haven't, you know what to expect."

Cecil pushed his face close to Tom's, ripped the tape from his mouth, the older man's eyes watered but he made no sound, "tell me about your family?" Cecil demanded, pulled himself back from the smell of cigarettes from Tom's breath.

"Fuck off."

This earned him a stinging slap across his face, "if that's the way you're going to act," Cecil said, grinning, "you're going to have to watch me give the same treatment to the child…, get me another kettle of boiling water," he cried, to the goons behind him.

"I've got two sons," Tom lowered his head, the fight in him had diminished.

"What's their names and ages?"

"The oldest is Richard, he's thirty-six, his younger brother is Corrie, twenty-one."

Cecil turned to the redhaired girl, pointed his finger at her like a simulated pistol, smiled widely before returning his attention to the older man. "Give me the mobile number of the oldest?"

"It's in my phone."

"Get it," Cecil ordered the nearest thug.

Cecil soon found the number and pressed the call button, he held it close to the older man's face, "tell him where you are and to get here soon or else."

The tall coloured driver escorted the three inspectors out of the office, closing the door softly behind him. Damston and Barton remained in their seats in front of the desk facing the big man. A cloud of thick blue smoke hovered above their heads. They watched Randell shuffle papers with his fat fingers. Out of the corner of his eye, Barton noticed Damston fidgeting impatiently in her chair and felt the same way. He had been warned by her a few times in the past, never to let your eyes wander away from the big man, he demands to be the focus of all your attention.

Through the boredom a sudden thought hit Barton at first, he considered it not worth mentioning, but the more he dwelled on it, the more urgent it became. He couldn't hold back any longer, was forced to interrupt the big man, "Those three inspectors," he sat bolt upright in his seat, "how did they get here, I didn't see any other cars parked when we drove in."

Randell raised his head, the deep sunken eyes widened, his mouth dropped, the normal white countenance turning scarlet, "you're a bit late in bringing that observation up," he shouted, banged the palm of his hand on the desk.

Damston jumped, "maybe they got dropped off," she stammered.

"Get out there and see what's going on."

Barton followed her as she rushed out the office and bumped into Nevil in a rush to get into the big man. The inspectors were panting behind him, "another shot has been fired," Nevil exclaimed, "the guards have moved the cars up the drive, to a safe distance."

Damston made to rush for the main exit, Barton caught hold of her arm, "let's not rush, we don't know what's out there."

She stepped in front of Nevil, "has anybody been hit?"

The tall driver shook his head, "don't think so," he edged around her, through the open office door, the inspectors followed him.

The main exit was ajar, when they reached it, Barton led the way cautiously out. He could hear her breathing at his back, heard the click of the safety catch on her Glock 21 being released. As Nevil had said, the vehicles were nowhere in sight. The September sun was low in the sky and shone into they're eyes, making it difficult to see beyond the abandoned crane, which was casting long shadows that reached close to their feet. To his left, huge rocks lay close to the quarry sides, if the shooter was still here, that would be his best place to take a shot. Or from the top of the quarry face, where long grass and shrubs grew, offering good cover. He had to make a choice soon, not wanting to be standing on the same spot too long, giving the marksman time to get a bead on them.

"You go inside," he told Damston, "stay with the big man, I'm not convinced those three are genuine inspectors, "I'm going to have a look about, see if I can find any trace of that shooter."

She was about to protest, but could see in his eye there was no compromise, "you be careful out there," she backed in through warehouse door, turned and trotted towards the office.

When he heard the office door close, Barton made his move, taking advantage of the blinding, sunshine on the rock face, he knew the shooter would have problems spotting him stepping away from the building. His first stop was the bucket of the old crane, after bounding from the exit. Barton's first observation was the top of quarry face, nothing moved, only the shrubs swayed in the gentle breeze. He soon realised that a platoon of shooter could be concealed up there, and decided to retreat to the edge of the building, using it as cover to get a better view behind the loose boulders at the far side. The space between the rock face and the wall was only a few feet and was cast in the shadows. Although confident he couldn't be seen, he still took it slowly to the top corner. He edged his way around to the back wall, where he discovered he was more exposed and crawled the rest of the way. When he reached the front wall, no shots had been fired and decided to risk standing up.

He felt he had been slapped across the face with a wet cloth, the crack of the round hitting the wall fired shards of brick at him. Barton felt himself falling, couldn't stop himself, the world was spinning around, getting faster, until only blackness and blissful unconsciousness.

CHAPTER 23

*P*urdy had suffered the dirt and stench of Bloch's house long enough, he decided it would be safe to go back to his flat. The two men were glad to be out as well, but showed signs of reluctance, about returning, fearing the goons would be there waiting for them.

Purdy led the way into his flat, gun in his hand, the two men shocked at the sight of the weapon, followed close behind. A sigh of relief came from them all when they discovered the place was void of goons. The relief was short lived for Purdy when he spotted the child's Teddy Bear, on the floor, he picked it up sniffed it and placed it on the child's chair, "if that little shit has harmed them in any way, I'll tear his head off."

The two men watch Purdy pacing the living room and decided to sit on the sofa, they glanced at each other, shrugged their shoulders, didn't know what to say for the best. The sound of a mobile disturbed the moment. Purdy stopped, grabbed it from his pocket, saw his girlfriend's number on the screen, he never got a chance to ask where she was. She screamed as if in pain, informed him where she was and he had to get there soon. Before he could react, the phone went dead.

"The little bastard's, got them in his cellar," he told the two men, "I've got to get over there soon or else."

"You go there, and you are dead meat," the youngest man said and got a nod of agreement from his mate.

Purdy checked his watch, "the place will be closed now, only Barker, his goons and maybe a few whores with their clients, will be in the building," again he started pacing.

The youngster stood up held out his arm and stopped Purdy pacing, "I've got an idea that might work."

Purdy gave him a doubtful glance and stepped around him. "okay, let's hear it?"

"We call Hussey, restrict the number, tell him the law is on their way, to make a raid on his place, that should cause a panic, he'll be too busy hiding all his illegal booze and drugs. Him and his goons will be running all over the place. That should give us a chance to catch them off guard, we could gun ourselves up and blast them away."

The taller, older man interrupted, "if he's holding your girlfriend and the child, plus Bloch and Jason and his mate, he'll have to hide them as well."

Purdy sat down on a padded chair, pulled out his mobile and scowled through it for a while, "I've found it," he pressed the call icon, handed it to the older youth, "you know what to say, he might recognise my voice."

"We need to get guns," the youngster said.

"That not a problem," Purdy jumped up, I know where to get them, a bit of a drive from here so we need to get moving."

Barton woke up to see dark clouds racing past a full moon. A shadow appeared and blocked out the faint light. "Richard can you hear me?" the familiar female voice asked.

He struggled to get up, but the effort sent a shooting pain through his head, at the same time the side of his face started to sting as if it had been burned. He felt hands on his shoulders restricting his movement. It felt he had been there for an age, unable to move, before the hands moved from his shoulders to his arms. The pain intensified when he felt himself being lifted, he wanted to break free, to lie back down again and drift back into tranquillity.

A tubular light replaced the moon, white polystyrene tiles, instead of the night sky was the background. He realised once again he had passed out. That all too familiar female face, smiled down at him and said, "sleeping on the job again?"

Barton found himself lying on a carpeted floor, Damston was knelt beside him and behind her a few more figures towered over him. He tried to get up, but she held him down, "what the hell's going on?" He asked.

"We heard the rounds hit the building," she explained," we all took cover, after a while, we heard an off the road bike or a quad bike start up and leave, from the top of the rockface. We decided it was safe and came looking for you."

Damston's face was replaced by Nevil's, Barton felt a wad of cotton wool being placed on his wound, he winced when it stung.

"It's okay," the tall black man grinned, "just cleaning some of the dirt from your wound, have to use disinfectant, before I bandage it up."

"You're going to have a nasty black eye," Damston said looking over Nevil's shoulder.

Nevil was having trouble with the bandages, after a few attempts gave up, and used sticking plaster. Barton heard the big man's voice from across the room, but couldn't make out what he was saying. The next moment, he felt himself being lifted off the floor and placed on a chair, looking at Randell across the desk.

The big man leaned forward on the desk, extracted a fat cigar from his mouth, blew the smoke at Barton, "that was a brave but stupid thing you did out there."

"Had to find out where the shots were coming from."

"And did you?"

"They must have come from the top of the quarry, from a rifle."

The big man took another pull at his cigar, "that would explain the latter two shots, but not the first one that hit the car, that must have been fired close to this building, to make you think that, that inspector fired it."

"Then there must have been two shooters," Barton said, "no way could a single shooter be able to climb up that face in such a short time, without being spotted." He glanced around the room, the plaster pulled at his wound, "where are those inspectors?"

"A car came and picked them up, while we were attending to you," Damston interrupted.

"That's an unusual place to park a van," Ben Carter said to his brother.

"I don't think it has been parked, more like it has been, planted there for a reason."

"Let's get to fuck out of here," Ben said and started to walk away, "that thing could be full of explosives."

"Do you think somebody else is having a go at Hussey? Tommy asked as they got in the car

"That wouldn't surprise me, with that little shit."

Tommy started up the car, "I wonder who it could be?"

"Anybody in the whole world, take your pick," Ben replied and light up a cigarette. Driving along the main road, Tommy's mobile sounded, he pulled it out his pocket and handed it to Ben, "who could that be at this time in the morning?"

Ben instantly recognised the number, "it's Randell," he put the phone to his ear, "what can I do for you Mr' Randell?"

Tommy had driven a mile or two before his brother handed him his phone back, "what's happening now?"

"We've got a job to do, just outside Ellesmere Port."

"When?"

"Now."

"At this bloody time in the morning?"

"It's only half an hour's drive on the motorway."

Although the traffic was sparse, at that time in the morning, Ben's estimated timing was wrong and daylight was braking as they drove into the quarry. "keep your eyes peeled," Ben advised his brother, "Randell say's that a few shots had been fired at them, yesterday."

Tommy pulled the car up close to the old crane, "this machine will give us a bit of cover, if that shooter is still about."

Using the crane as cover, the brothers made their way to the door of the building, found the key where Randell said it would be hidden. "What are we supposed to do here?" Tommy asked.

"Clean this place out, get rid of the boxes and crates etc. And wait for some trucks to arrive with the shipping containers."

"I think the first thing to do, would be to make sure that shooter isn't hanging around, before we start carting this junk outside."

At the top of the quarry face, they found tracks of a quad bike, and flattened grass where a cover had spread out, "this is where they took the shots from," Ben pointed out, "Randell thought there could've been two of them, one up here, by the look of it, the other down there," he pointed down to the courtyard sixty feet below.

"It looks as though they left on that quad bike," Tommy replied, staying clear of the cliff edge.

Ben grinned at his brother, knowing he suffered from vertigo," have a look down see if you can spot where the other shooter was positioned?"

"Fuck off, Ben, we can have a look when we get down there."

Ben was still grinning to himself when they reached the quarry base, "you search over there, I'll go this way and meet up at the door."

Tommy found himself stumbling over loose gravel, squeezing between huge cut off rocks, sometimes having to climb over them. Ben was at the door waiting when he arrived, "find anything?" he asked.

Tommy shook his head and was about to step inside before his brother, when a slight movement caught his eye. He stopped and turned in the direction.

"What is it?" Ben asked, almost bumped into his back.

"Thought I saw something move, behind that old crane."

"Right," said Ben, "just carry on into the building and watch from behind the door, if it is that other shooter, we'll rush out and nab him."

A half hour later at the point where they were about to give up, they heard the cabin door of the old crane creek open. Where the old machine lay, the door was on their blind side. A moment later a figure appeared behind the tracks, stooped over so they could only see the top of his head. Tommy gave his brother the signal, too rush out, the door was wide enough and they both charged out together. The figure raised slightly and open fired at them, all they could do was retreat, back inside.

"Are you okay? Ben asked, when they got behind the door.

"I'm fine," Tommy replied, when the sound of a small-bore engine came rushing into the courtyard.

More shots were fired forcing the brothers to stay behind the doors. An engine revved up, the wheels of the vehicle spun, still shots were coming at them. The shooting stopped, and they heard the vehicle rush away.

Ben chased out, fired a few shots after them, with no results.

Tommy walked up behind, "who the fuck are those people?"

CHAPTER 24

When Cecil took possession of the building and converted it into a club, one of his jobs was to split the cellar into two compartments. The best thing he ever did and often praised himself on his brainchild. The sliding wall was in his eyes a work of art, even a building expert couldn't tell there was a separate compartment behind when it was closed. Only two other people knew about it and they were dead. One killed on his instructions, the other, hell knows who shot him, both wasted before they had a chance to mouth off about it.

The false wall was controlled by a small button on the skirting, which was almost invisible unless you knew where to look, nobody else in this world knew. When trouble came this was Cecil's escape, he would rush down to the cellar, and according to some of his thugs and staff disappeared, as if he had some supernatural powers. The voice Tom Barton heard on his mobile was the pre-recorded message informing him that person you are calling is unavailable, "he's not answering or has his phone switched off," he told Cecil.

Cecil snatched the mobile, tried the call again and got the same results, "we'll try again later, if that fails, you know what will happen." He slapped the tape back on the oldster's mouth and returned his attention to Purdy's girlfriend. He lifted the child by the arm, away from between it's mother's legs and threw it across the floor. The mothers scream could be heard through the duct tape, when he kicked her, on the same place where he had scalded her earlier. "Your fucking boyfriend better come soon, or the baby gets it next."

The red headed Carmel, sighed in relief, when Cecil walked past her towards the two men who had been bundled in last. They had black bags over their heads, tied with hands behind their backs, lying face down on the floor, a rope around their necks attached to their ankles, legs folded over so that if they struggled, the rope would tighten and choke them. Her relief was cut short when Cecil drew the hood away from the one closest to her. The shock of seeing her younger brother lying there, sent a chill through her entire body, her head began to spin and had to fight to stop from passing out.

Although the cellar was dimly lit, Jason eyes still took time to accustom. The first thing he focused on was the black face, haloed by a bush of tight curly hair, a smiling mouth full of pure white teeth, cold brown eyes that didn't reach the smile.

"So, you and your pal, pushed that van up against my fire door, why?" Cecil asked in a soft friendly voice. He ripped the tape from Jason's mouth, chuckled at the sight of the young man's eyes watering with the pain.

"We didn't push a van anywhere," Jason managed to say.

Cecil slapped him across the face, "you fuckin liar, I recognised your pal's jacket on C.C.TV."

Jason remembered the studded pattern on the back of Franky's leather jacket, and cursed himself for this oversight, "piss off," he said, and braised himself for another slap.

"One of your phones is ringing," a voice called from the cellar door, Cecil glanced up at the little man, waving his arms. He bounded up the steps, barged past the barman to the bar where his three mobiles lay. Noticed the number was restricted, and reluctantly answered.

Cecil cut the message short, grinned, could spot a hoax call in an instant, had hundreds of them. But to be on the safe side, he operated a system he had perfected, to remove all illegal substances in a matter of minutes. All were kept in a revolving cabinet, when a threat from the law came, he just turned it around and huge mirror took its place. Often it wouldn't come to that, a phone call to one of his patrons and the raid would be called off. He made the call and was informed that no such raid had been planned.

He sat in his usual seat, elbows resting on the bar, staring at his three mobiles, willing her to call, she always did when he had a problem, she would soon advise him what to do with all these people he had in his cellar. Couldn't let them go after torturing them, but what would he do with all the bodies? He had promised never to call her, always to wait for her to call, this was one promise he would never break. Some would say it was telepathy, he wasn't sure, she always called when he needed her.

The wounded Bloch, came to mind, Cecil wondered if he was still alive, had him hidden behind a stack of barrels, had been bleeding badly from the shot in the head and wondered if he had bled out? He gathered up his mobiles and headed back down to the cellar.

The goons were standing around the victims smoking when Cecil slipped past them unseen. Bloch was barely alive, a mixture of blood and saliva oozed from his mouth. Cecil knew he would get no response from him and put his foot on Bloch's throat, pressed with all his weight until the rasping breathing stopped. "Good riddance you stinking bastard," he said, turned to see all the goons had witnessed what he had just done. He grinned and waved his hand at Bloch's body, "just a piece of shit that could put us in the nick for a long time." Seeing the goons talking among themselves and showing signs of approval, he continued, "once all this mess is cleaned up, I'll be paying you all an extra bonus. Now gag them up again," he pointed to the other victims," and get upstairs, we might be getting some unwanted visitors."

CHAPTER 25

Purdy could picture Hussey in a panic running all over his club, ordering his goons to do this, that and whatever, to hide all the contraband, from the police raid. How the little shit was going to hide his girlfriend, his child, Bloch, Jason and his pal, would be imposable. The two yobs had managed to get three more pals to help, all were more than willing to trash the place and get their hands on the booze and drugs. They all mingled separately in small groups on the main street, where they could see each other and observe the club's entrance and the lane.

The yob standing with Purdy asked, "what's the plan?"

"Just get ready to move," Purdy said and waved to the rest of the yobs to move towards the door. Purdy kicked the door in, the yobs rushed in ahead, but came to a sudden halt when they were faced with six goons all armed and ready to fire. They stumbled over each other trying to retreat, shots were fired at them, two were hit but never fell. Purdy and the two original pals got to the car, where the other three were? Purdy wasn't going to hang around to wait for them and drove off.

"That little shit was expecting us," Purdy said as he pulled the car into a parking place on the outskirts of Wigan.

"Or maybe he was expecting the law," the youth said, sitting next to him.

Purdy turned on him, "don't be so fucking stupid," he roared, "if he'd been expecting the law, he would have just got rid of all his illegal booze and drugs, he's not stupid enough to have a shootout with the police force."

Ben Carter was stood at the office front door smoking, when Damston and Barton walked up, they gave him a nod and entered, found Tommy chatting to the girl at reception. Barton didn't know whether to take it personal or if Tommy looked at everybody, like something he had just scraped off his shoes.

Tommy jabbed a finger at Randell's office door, "we've been waiting for you two to go in and see the boss."

Ben walked in, still blowing smoke from his mouth and followed behind them.

Nevil stood at the back of the big man's wheelchair, indicating with a big hand for them to be seated. Randell with his head down shuffling through papers and sending clowds of smoke out from the big cigar between his thin lips, ignored them. Barton decided to risk a glance at his mobile, holding it below the level of the desktop. Discovered he had a few miscalls and scrawled through them, He stopped when he noticed a number he recognised as his father's, knew it must be urgent for his father would never call him unless it was. A grunt from the big man clearing his throat, drew his attention. Barton put his phone away, hoping to get an opportunity to call back later.

Randell looked disgruntled and drew fiercely on his cigar, pushed his wheelchair away from the desk, "it cost me a lot of cash training you lot up as bodyguards. I'm told that the other shooter was hiding in the cabin of the old crane. How the fuck did you manage to miss that?" He roared at Barton.

"I was intending to search that area, when I got fired on," Barton replied placing his hand on the plaster on his cheek.

The big man took the cigar from his mouth and turned his deep sunken blue cold eyes on the Carter brother's, "any clues who these people were?"

The brother shook their heads, "the guy who was driving the quad bike had white hair, we thought it could be the same guy who was driver of that limousine, the day Barton found the dummy bomb, if you remember, he did a runner and got away in a car that must have been waiting at the end of that road." Ben said, while Tommy nodded in agreement.

On recall, Barton had to agree, but thought, why did this man display such a distinguished feature? Was it thoughtlessness, or deliberate? He decided not to bring the subject up in case he got ridiculed.

"I'm planning to start up another group of members," Randell came forward to his desk again, "train them as extra security guards on my warehouses, you lot will have the job of training them."

Out of the corner of his eyes, Barton could see signs of disapproval from Damston, the big man must have noticed and turned his full attention on her.

"Any objections?" he asked.

"I think we had better find out who this shooter is and who he's working for," she said.

"You can do that as well."

"When do you plan to start training these guards?" Tommy asked.

"Early in the new year."

"We might be able to dig something up before then," Ben said, but showed obvious signs of doubt.

The big man stumped his cigar in the glass ashtray, stared at Barton, "any advance in finding who Lumpy's assistant is?"

Barton shook his head, "never had much time to work on it."

Randell turned his snowman shaped head to Damston, "we can't have someone making bombs and selling them to whoever wants to buy them. Make it your priority the last thing I want is my properties being the target if that happens, we're out of business, nobody will trust us with they're goods." He returned his attention to his paperwork.

Damston knew that was the signal to leave, she rose from her seat and headed for the door, Barton followed her, with the brothers trailing behind.

"How are we going to find out who this assistant of Lumpy's is?" She asked as she sat on the chair behind her desk, staring at Barton as he tried to get settled on the hard stool.

"Whoever shot him was making sure he couldn't tell us," Barton replied, "it looks as though there could be a connection with this shooter, Lumpy's trainee, and whoever is doing the hiring."

"They're very well informed whoever they are."

A loud knock came from the door, Ben Carter stuck his head in and was pushed from behind by his brother, "we need to find this Mr. Crow," Tommy shouted and edged his way in.

"We think you're the only person who knows how to get in contact him," Ben added.

Damston stood up, still quite startled by the interruption, "Mr. Randell won't allow us to do that."

"We could ask him," Barton said getting up off the chair.

Damston swung around on him, "we could, but I know what he will tell us."

"We need to get to Crow, if we're to find out who this shooter is and who is hiring him, and he will know who Lumpy's apprentice is." Ben said.

"Even if we did get permission to ask Crow, do you think he'll tell us?"

"We could make him," Ben replied.

Damston sat back down and sighed, "one of the reasons the organisations hire him to get the right people, is because they know you would have to kill him, before he would give out information on his recruits, and the syndicates he sends them to."

"So, how do we find out who is hiring those shooters?" Tommy asked.

"You'll have to go about it in the same way as we have to, to find this apprentice."

"There's got to be an informant in this organisation, for them to know our every move," Barton said, "if we can find who it is, we could get the answers."

All eyes turned on him and a long minute of thoughtful silence followed. "How the fuck do we do that?" Tommy asked in a heated voice.

"Who do we know who is closest to Mr. Randell?"

Another period of silence followed, before Damston broke it, "as far as I know, only us and his driver."

Barton sat down again, "how about the receptionists, what information is she privy to?"

A grin dawned across Tommy's face, "I'll soon find out."

Damston held up a hand and got out of her seat, "no, the last thing we want is to go charging in, if she is the informant. Let's just set trap, give her some false information, if it gets results, then you can do what you can to get it out of her. But bare-in-mind, she is also one of Crow's recruits, if he learns that we suspect her, he will dispose of her before we get to interrogate her, we will have to be careful, Mr. Randell mustn't know we are setting this trap, until we are certain it is her, if we are lucky we should be able to nab this shooter."

Tommy steered his brother to the door, "we'll let you work out something, let us know what we have to do."

Barton stood up, "have to go to the toilet," he informed Damston and followed the brothers out. The staff W.C. was behind the receptionist desk, Tommy was back chatting to the girl, Barton guessed his brother would be outside smoking. When Barton approached, Tommy abruptly stopped talking and walked out the main door. This aroused a slight spark of suspicion after the conversation they had just had. Maybe Tommy fancied this girl and was just chatting, on the other hand, could be warning her . As he pushed open the toilet door his mobile sounded, He managed to get the door locked as he pressed the reply icon, "what's wrong?" Was all he managed to say, his father's voice trembled, the words flushed at him so fast he could barely understand them. It was a while after the contact got cut off, before Barton got the gist of what his father had told him.

Damston was talking to the receptionist, when he walked out and told him to meet her outside. The Carter's were standing there talking, Ben as usual smoking, leaning against the wall, Tommy saw Barton, stepped over and gripped his upper arm, "you stay out of my road."

Barton jerked his arm free, "what's your problem?"

Ben stepped in between them, pushed his brother back, pointed a finger at Barton, "I'd take that advice seriously pal if I were you."

"Yeh yeh… I'm pissing myself," Barton grinned at them and watched Ben pushing Tommy towards the carpark.

"What was that all about?" Damston asked coming up behind him.

"I don't think Tommy likes me," Barton said, putting on a childish act.

She shook her head and strutted over to the brother's car as they were getting in, Barton couldn't hear what was being said, but knew they were doing a bit of arguing and she was pointed a threatening finger at them.

She stepped back as the brother's car screeched away, Tommy doing the driving, Ben giving her the two fingered gesture from the passenger's window. Damston returned the compliment, but with one finger. "be careful Richard, they don't normally make idle threats," she warned when she walked up beside him.

"What's their problem?"

"It's a long story, I'll explain it to you some time."

"I can't wait."

"You're going to have to, those two are on their way back to the quarry. I've told the girl in reception, we're all heading up there later this morning, if she is the informant, those shooters will turn up and the Carter's will nab them."

"That's a bit optimistic."

"Do you have a better idea?"

"Not at the moment," Barton replied, and if he had been honest, he would have told her that it was the least of his thoughts. How did his father get into that situation, what could he have been thinking about, going to the Hussey club, how did he get to know of the involvement of the owner?

"Let's get you home, get that plaster off your face, get a decent dressing on it and stop the swelling on your black eye," Damston said walking towards the car.

Barton was glad she had decided to drive, didn't need the distraction. She must have guessed something was on his mind, for she never said a word all the way to the flat. Which they had arrived at too fast, he hadn't come up with an answer, why his father went to that club, or how he was going to get away from the situation he was in, to get there.

CHAPTER 26

Cecil couldn't retreat to his secret compartment behind the false sliding wall, had too many hostages in the cellar, didn't want them to hear the hissing sound of it moving. He could only hazard a guess when it would be safe to go upstairs to the lounge bar.

He cursed the loud creaking of the door as he carefully pushed it open, decided to get someone to oil the bloody hinges. The goons turned at the sound, guns still poised in their hands, smoke coming from the barrels. "What's happened?" he asked.

King Kong, standing head and shoulders above the rest, pushed forward, "they broke in, your man Purdy in the lead with five of them all hooded up with guns in their hands, we let them have it before they knew what hit them."

Cecil grinned, "did you recognise any of the others who were with him?"

The goons shook their heads, "I think we hit a couple of them," one of them replied, "but they didn't go down."

It didn't matter if nobody recognised them, Cecil knew Purdy would be back to get his girlfriend and his child. When he does returns, all he will get will be their corpses.

His feelings over the results of the raid were confusing, was relieved that the goons had beaten them off, but wished he had put more thought into it, and maybe, have captured Purdy. The next time Purdy tries his luck, will be a different story, it won't be a last-minute decision, a plan will be worked out to trap him. The club front door opened, Cecil and the goons swung around, guns still held in their hands and pointed at the day shift cleaners. "Put the irons away," Cecil commanded and pushed through to the front of them, he held up his hands at the two women, "I'll not be needing you, the guys will clean up," he said and pointed his thumb back at the goons. He steered the women out and studied the damaged door.

"One of you get that front door fixed," he said and wedged his way through them, sat himself on his seat at the bar, "the rest of you can start cleaning."

The bald-headed barman popped up from behind the bar, "would you like a drink?"

Startled, Cecil's natural reactions took over, like a firecracker going off inside his head, loosing all his rational senses, he picked up the empty glass in front of him and hurtled it, striking the man on the face.

The barman fell back against the wall holding his face, blood oozed between his fingers. He screamed and curled into a ball on the floor and sobbed like a child.

"Get that piece of shit out of here," he shouted at two of the nearest goons, "and clean his infested blood up.

"What will we do with him?" One of the goons asked.

"Bag him up and dump him in the back of that van, do the same with the two guys that put it there, make sure they can't make a noise or move about, don't want to attract unwanted attention.

After a shower and getting his wound cleaned and dressed, they decided, sleep was out of the question. They sat close together on the sofa, drinking coffee and trying to concentrate on television. "I think we should get a hold of Limping Lenny," Barton said, "see if he remembers any of Lumpy's associates."

"I doubt he'll be easy to find, after what we've done to him," Damston said, drinking the last from her cup.

"That's three hours we've been driving around, been in nearly every pub and, café and still no sign of him," Damston complained, "it wouldn't surprise me if he's buggered off."

Barton nodded and swerved the car into the shopping mall carpark, "let's go and get something to eat."

He followed close behind her along the footpath that led to the shops on the High Street. A solitary streetlamp shone from behind them in the carpark, casting their shadows in front of them, making it difficult to see where they were stepping. Up ahead the path passed between two buildings, the light from behind never reached this far. Without warning Damston stopped, Barton almost collided into her rear. The figure appeared from the darkness, but there was no mistaking that limping gait.

Lenny came hobbling towards them, head bent forward, hands dug deep into his pockets, hood pulled down over his face. The sudden shock of a strong arm around his neck, made him scream as he was pulled to the ground. Thinking he was being mugged, "I've no money!" he shouted, the grip on his neck held firm, could feel himself being dragged along the path and into the carpark.

Barton hauled Lenny over the bonnet of their car, held him down with a hand on his throat, his face now exposed in the light from the single lamp stand, the hood pushed back over his head. In the struggle the dressing came away from his injured ear, blood started to seep from it.

Damston pushed her gun against his nose, "we need more information from you."

Lenny had no idea who his attackers were, until he heard that female voice, had been having nightmares over it. He attempted to respond, but all that came out was a choking gabble of inaudible words.

Barton released his grip slightly, with his other hand gripped his arm and turned him face down on the bonnet.

"What was that you just said?" Damston asked, pushing her gun into his good ear.

"I've told you all I know."

"We want to jog your memory and give us the names of Limpy's associates." Barton said.

"I don't know the names of his associates."

"Well you better start remembering the names or describing who they are, or you're going to spend some time tied and gagged at that old farmhouse again until you do," Damston said.

Lenny remained silent, after a while Damston stepped back cocked her pistol, "tie him up and throw him in the boot."

Barton was relieved when she hadn't shot him and quickly got Lenny secured and in the boot of the car.

"Let's go and get something to eat now," she said when Barton closed the lid of the boot.

The waiters were standing at their stations, some glancing at their watches, looking anxious to get the place cleared up and get off home. Damston ignored the signals and drank slowly at her coffee, Barton on the other hand was beginning to feel uncomfortable, "I think we better get back and see if Lenny is still alive." He avoided the gazes of the staff, heard some of them clearing the tables behind him, the last of the other diners had long gone. He could see she was enjoying the attention, still sipping at the small cup in her hand, Barton had the feeling that the cup was empty, and she was revelling in the inconvenience she was causing, him and the staff.

She grinned at him, put her cup down, signalled for the waiter, "that coffee was delicious can we have more?"

Barton was relieved when the waiter informed her, that the coffee machine had been turned off.

"No problem," she replied, still grinning, got up and walked out leaving him to settle the bill.

"What was all that about?" he asked when he caught up with her at the car.

"A few years ago, just after I got out of the can, my clothes were a bit ragged and dirty, I looked down and out, I suppose. I went in there with a mate for a meal, they wouldn't let us in the door, so now anytime I go there, I give them a hard time."

She stood beside him as he opened the boot lid, they quickly recoiled as the smell hit them, Lenny had shit and urinated himself. "Shut it back down," she shouted.

When they opened the car doors, the smell was just as bad, she phoned the big man and got a car transported organised. The next call she made was for a taxi. This arrived before the transporter, "you have to be here to make sure the driver doesn't open the boot," she said climbing into the taxi, "direct him the office carpark, drop it as far away from the office as possible."

He watched the taxi drive off and out of sight, before he fished out his own mobile and called his father's number. It rang quite a few times before a strange voice answered, "who's that?" Barton demanded.

"Are you Richard Barton?" the stranger asked, in an effeminate voice.

"Who's asking?"

"Never mind that, are you Richard Barton?"

This could go on all night, Barton decided, "yes I am, why are you on my father's phone?"

"I have your father here, you also want to know about you brother, if you want to see your father alive again and want information on you brother you will have to come here."

"Where?"

"The Hussey Club."

"When?"

"Don't take too long or you might be too late."

The contact went dead, Barton cursed, glanced at his watch and wondered if he would have time to go there before that recovery truck arrived, knew it could only be a short walk there, but the typical had to happen, when expecting a recovery truck to take hours, it turns up in a few minutes. He cursed as he watched the vehicle pull up in front of the car. The driver got out slamming the door.

"You Mr. Barton?" The driver asked as he walked around the car, "will it start?"

Barton nodded, "yes but I wouldn't advise you to go inside, our dog had the runs and was sick in it."

"That bad," the driver grinned, "well I'll just have to hold my nose to let the hand brake off, then I'll get it loaded."

Barton pulled a few twenty-pound notes from his wallet, held them under the driver's nose, "could you come back in an hour?"

The driver grinned, "no problems mate, I've another job on anyway, and the smell might not be so bad then," he quickly plucked the notes from Barton's hand and got in his truck.

He watched the truck drive out the car park, turned and headed back along the foot path, heading for the Hussey Club.

CHAPTER 27

$\mathcal{P}$urdy turned to the two yobs, one sitting in the rear seat of the car the other beside him, "somebody must have tipped that little shit off, that we were coming, not the police."

"Well it wasn't one of us," the yob behind said, "that wouldn't make much sense for us to do that and risk getting blown away."

"When you got his number up on the phone, did you remember to restrict your own number?" the yob at his side asked.

Purdy went silent for a long moment, trying to remember fumbling with his mobile, "I'm not sure, if I did."

"If you didn't, that would explain how the little shit knew we were coming," the yob behind said.

Purdy started the car up, "the little shit won't be expecting us to rush back in so soon, and in the morning rush-hour."

Jerry, the youth sitting in the front next to him said, "I'm not so sure that would be a good idea, too many witnesses and somebody's bound to call the police.

"A risk I'm willing to take to get my family back," Purdy replied steering the car onto the main road causing other road users to brake, "pull your hoods up and keep your heads down, nobody'll be able to identify us."

Jerry still suffering from the shock of a near collision with other vehicles, turned to his mate in the back, "you okay Pat?"

"Pat nodded nervously, "I think so, when you consider we've been shot at, and nearly killed in a car crash, now we're going back to face those gunned up thugs again."

"Think of all that booze fags and drugs, you're going to get," Purdy said.

"I'm trying to," Pat replied, "but all I can see are all those guns pointing at us."

Jerry reached back and put an assuring hand on Pat's knee, "we'll be fine, they'll not be expecting us this time."

Heavy traffic held them back on the way to the centre carpark and had to drive around trying to find a vacant place. "Phone your mates, find out where they are," Purdy said driving the car onto the grass verge. He waited as Jerry got his mobile out and started fingering the numbers. On his third attempt Jerry got a reply. A few mumbled words were exchanged and he returned his phone to his pocket.

"Well?" Purdy asked, "where are they?"

"One got shot on the hand, another on the shoulder, their being attended to by a friend, the other two are with them, they say they've had enough, it's not worth the risk."

"Looks like we'll have to do it without them," Purdy said and got out of the car.

"How are we going to do that with three of us against at least half a dozen of them?" Jerry asked, when he and Pat joined Purdy as he made his way along the foot path.

"The goons will have been up all night they'll be upstairs in the bedroom sleeping with the whores."

"We hope," Pat said, striding behind them.

Purdy ignored him and stopped them when they reached the main street. The club door had been patched up with sheets of plywood, He cursed his luck, was hoping that the door hadn't been attended to and someone had been standing there for security. Being able to enter in silence was object of his plans, now they will have to force their way in, and the sound of smashing plywood will alert them. "We need a crowbar, to prize that wood off silently."

Jerry and Pat shrugged their shoulders, "don't know where we could get hold of one in a hurry," Jerry said.

Purdy noticed that the new sheets of wood were attracting quite a lot of attention from passing pedestrians. "This is not looking good," he said to the yobs, "somebody's bound to call the law when we try to get in, I'd like to get my hands on the fucker who invented mobile phones."

"Well every new invention has it's downfalls," Pat said, "can't drop a fag-end without somebody phoning up to tell their friends about it."

A tall heavy built man walked past them, Purdy wasn't sure what drew his attention to this man, wondered had he saw him before? Or was it the shoulder length black hair swept back over his ears, looking out of place on a mature guy? His eyes followed the stranger as he crossed the street in front of them. The shock came when the stranger walked up to the club door and banged on it with his fist. "Get over there now," Purdy said to the yobs, "dive in when somebody opens that door to let that gorilla in."

Jerry grabbed Purdy's arm, pulled him back onto the pavement as a large van drove past missing him by inches, the van driver blasting at his horn. "That was close," Jerry said.

Purdy jerked his arm free, "get over there, before that door closes," he shouted and dashed back onto the street. The two yobs followed, but they were wary of the traffic and waited for a safe gap. Purdy cursed to see that the goon was gone, and the door locked.

"What now?" Jerry asked.

"We've got two options," Pat interrupted, "we wait to see if someone comes out, which could take all day, or we find a shop that sells crowbars."

"We've got a third option," Purdy said, and walked to the end of the building. When the two yobs joined him at the end of the narrow lane. He pointed to the van parked at the bottom, "we move that and brake in through fire exit."

"They could have cameras down there," Pat said.

"That's how they managed to nab Bloch I bet," Jerry added.

"We assume there is cameras," Purdy said, "so the moment we hear that door open, we blast them through it and charge in."

"How do we move that van without being spotted?" Pat asked.

"We move fast, get down into that van, get it started and move it out the way, there's a chance whoever is watching the monitors could miss it."

"With all the action that's been going on," Jerry said, "with Bloch and the two guys that left the van there, they'll be keeping a close eye on this lane."

"We're going to have to take that chance," Purdy said, and ran towards the van.

The club door opened the moment Barton banged on the fresh plywood panels, as though the goon who stood behind it, had been expecting him at that moment. Must be a peep hole some where, he decided as he was escorted in with a goon on either side of him. The lighting inside was subdued, it took a few seconds for him to take in his surroundings. The odours of stale beer, cigarette smoke and marijuana hit his nostrils like a punch. The goons steered him to the far end of the bar to a little black man sitting in a stool, there was no question in his mind who this was, the description Wilma had given fitted.

Cecil turned in his chair, flashed his pure white teeth in a broad grin, held out a small hand, "so you are Richard Barton?"

Barton ignored the hand, "where's my father?" He asked, stepped towards the little man and felt the goons grip his arms.

"Your father is safe and well, you can have him back that way, but first you have to earn it."

"What do you mean earn it?"

Cecil's grin widened, "I want you to do a little job for me, when you complete it, you will get your father back."

Barton decided to bluff it out, "I'm not bothered about my father, you can stuff your little job where the sun doesn't shine."

"Then why are you here?"

"I've heard that you were involved in my brother's death?"

The grin vanished, Cecil turned away, lifted his glass, stared into it, "I had nothing to do with Corrie's death," he tipped the glass and drank the dregs from it, "I asked him to do a job for me, had he done the job properly, he and his pal Danny would still be alive."

"You expect me to believe that?"

Cecil banged his glass on the bar, the bald-headed barman pranced over and refilled it, "you can believe what you like," he went on when the barman returned to his work at the other side of the bar. "I heard there was a shooter involved, nobody seems to know who it was, you find that shooter and you find who killed your brother."

"Where did they dump his body?"

"Do this job for me and I'll tell you what I've learned, and you will get your father back."

"What's the job?" Barton asked, glanced at his watch," I have to get back somebody's expecting me."

Cecil held up his hand, "get back here soon and I'll tell you, if you don't turn up, you'll not see your father again."

The driver of the car carrier was pacing around the vehicles when Barton approached, he stepped over held his hand out, "give me the keys mate, I've another job on."

Barton's mobile sounded as the driver opened the car. Even at a few paces the odour hit him, he stepped back pulled his phone out and saw Damston's number.

"Where the fuck, are you?" Her voice rang in his ear.

"The trucks just pulled up we're getting the car loaded now." The contact went dead, and he watched the driver wind the windows down before he got in the vehicle. Barton jumped out the carrier, told the driver to drop the car off at the far side of the carpark. He headed towards the office door and met Damston striding towards him.

"What the fucks the hold up, where have you been?" She glanced at her watch and stopped a few feet away from him, her blue eyes glaring at him, shoulders hunched up arms swinging.

"It seems the driver had a more urgent job on."

She strutted past him towards the car, "we have to take that shit somewhere and get more information out of him."

"Will you be able to stand the smell?" Barton asked, as he trotted around to the driver's door.

"We're not going far, we'll just have to suffer it," the tissues were at her mouth and nose as she opened the door and got in.

Barton got settled in beside her, "it's not as bad as it was," he said, fanning his face with his hand. They pulled up at the warehouse in Allotment street, "get him out of the boot," she said, got out at the same time as the security guard opened the doors. They had a few words, while Barton lifted the boot, wondering if he could get time away from her to get back to the Hussey Club. He slammed the lid back down, was his eye deceiving him? Slowly he opened it up and was assured that he had seen right. Lenny was gone but the stench was still there. He turned to see her standing at his side holding the tissues at her mouth.

She dropped the tissues punched him on the arm, "you were supposed to be keeping an eye on this, you couldn't have missed seeing him get out."

"He must have got out when the carrier stopped at traffic lights or something, sitting in the cab I couldn't see the back end of the car."

"You fuckin tied him up, you must not have made a very good job of it."

"You saw me put the cable ties on him, hands behind his back and his feet, masking tape on his mouth. Somebody must have released him."

"There's no way somebody could have jumped on that car carrier at traffic lights and had time to cut him loose."

Barton slammed the boot lid down, "are you insinuating that I cut him loose?"

She stared into his eyes for a long moment as if trying to detect if he was lying, then her shoulders relaxed, she shook her head, "that wouldn't make much sense considering the trouble we had finding him. We're going to have to find him again."

"The quickest way is if we split up, I'll take this smelly car you can have mine," He dug into his pocket and handed her the keys.

She pushed his hand away, "no way, we both go in this thing," she opened the passenger door.

"Well if you can stand the stink," Barton jumped in the driver's seat, fanning the foul odour away with his hand.

With the tissue held to her mouth she edged her way in beside him. "We need to go back and tell the boss man and get some of the team to help, he won't be too pleased but what else can we do?"

CHAPTER 28

Randell was sat in his chair blowing cigar smoke at the three men in front of his desk, Barton noticed his usual pale complexion had turned scarlet. He glared at Damston then at the man sat between the Carter brothers, "is this who you are looking for?" He roared pointing a fat finger at Lenny.

The brothers turned and gazed at Damston, grins all over their faces, "noticed your car parked in the town centre parking area," Tommy said, "heard banging coming from the boot, when we got it opened guess what we found?"

Damston gave Barton her evil eyes, he turned and closed the door as a distraction from her gaze. When this was done, he noticed all eyes were on him except Lenny's whose head was bent over in in his hands.

The big man slapped his hand on the desk and pointed his cigar held fingers at him, "you were left in charge of that vehicle, where were you when these boys opened the boot and took this piece of shit out of it?"

The few moments he took to close the door gave him a chance to come up with an excuse. "I had to go to the toilet, sorry Mr. Randell but I was in agony, I ran down the street and into the nearest pub, I couldn't have been more than ten minutes."

Randell sat back on his chair, "well these things happen, but if it happens again get someone to relieve you. You're lucky on this occasion no harm was done, but remember the next time you desert what you've been left to mind, you're a dead man."

CHAPTER 29

Purdy got in the backdoors of the van and had to climbed over the three men that had been gagged and bagged, told Pat to cut them free and chase them. he got behind the steering wheel. Pat and Jerry remained in the rear. After numerous attempts, the engine fired, without any hesitation Purdy rammed it into reverse, the engine screamed as the vehicle careered up the narrow lane, a few times scraping off the wall smashing both its side mirrors. This had attracted a lot of attention from pedestrians who had to stop to avoid being hit and gasped in horror as the van drove straight into the path of an oncoming taxi, the driver just managed to avoid the collision by a few inches. Purdy slammed the van into forward gear and charged off up the street, the two in the back landed on top of each other against the rear door. "That's fucked up that idea," Purdy shouted back at them.

"What now?" Pat asked when Purdy had pulled into the carpark behind the shops.

Purdy shrugged his shoulders, "we hang on here till the club opens and the streets quieten." In silence they sat and smoked. A few yards away he watched the driver of a car carrier loading a vehicle onto the back, Purdy watched this with little interest, it helped to pass the time, until he noticed the gorilla with his hair tied back climb into the passenger side of the truck. That's when the warning light flashed. "That's the guy that went into the Hussey club earlier."

Jerry leaned over the seat, "I saw him to, maybe went in for a quick drink while waiting for his car to be uplifted."

"You don't go into the Hussey club for a quick drink," Purdy said, "you go into a place like that at night, buy drugs illegal booze and finish the up sleeping with a whore."

"Maybe he got chucked out," Pat said crawling forward.

Purdy put the van into gear, "I'm going to follow that carrier, got a bad feeling about that guy."

"What about your family?" Jerry asked.

"They should be safe for a while longer, "Purdy said and swung the van onto the main road. They caught the carrier at the second set of traffic lights pulled up close behind. When the lights changed, they followed close behind, never said a word until it pulled into the carpark of an industrial estate. Purdy pulled the van up on the roadway leading to a selection of offices. From here they could observe the activity of the car being off loaded. When the job was done the truck drove off leaving the tall character with the tied back hair standing, "something bugs me about that guy," said Purdy, pointed a finger at the tall figure who turned and headed for the offices. After a few seconds of silent thought, he started up the van, "let's get back, have another go at Hussey."

"You better heed that warning you bastard," Damston snarled at him through clenched teeth, "you won't get a second chance and I could go down with you." They headed across the carpark, saw Lenny being dragged into the boot of the Carter's car. Barton stopped grasped her arm, she swung round out of his grip.

"Where are they taking him?" He asked.

"To get some information out of him, that we were supposed to have done," she strutted away her head held high towards the car. She halted at the passenger door, "you better have a good explanation," she said as he opened his driver's door.

"I've already explained,"

"Don't give me that crap about you going to the toilet

"Well that's what happened, I needed a shit, I was desperate was in pain." He started the car, slipped it into gear and moved off, "where are we going?"

"Just drive where I tell you."

Barton soon realised where they were heading and drove in silence until they arrived at the quarry. She got out slowly and vigilantly made her way to the door of the red brick building, he stayed close behind her, constantly glancing around and scouring the top of the rock face. The cabin door of the old digger was lying open and swaying in the breeze, making an eerie squeaking sound. Before entering the building, he surveyed the machine and decided that there was no way a person could have been concealed inside it without one of them noticing.

She slammed the door and reached for the light-switch, Barton received an ice-cold glance from her, before she swung around and stamped her way to the office. He puckered his lips in a gesture of a mock kiss behind her back, grinned and followed her, "Why are we here?" He asked when she got seated behind the desk.

"To take over the Carters job, thanks to you."

"What is the job" he asked pulling up a chair in front of the desk.

She fished her phone from her pocket and began playing with it, "Mr. Randell has people coming here to move all that debris and boulders from the yard," she said without looking at him, "we've to oversee the work."

Barton immediately thought of the little black man's threat, "how long is it going to take?"

She tore her attention from her phone, for a long moment stared into his brown eyes. "why do you ask?"

Barton shrugged his shoulders, "just asking."

She returned her to her phone, "why have you somewhere else you want to be?"

"Unless they have a big team with them it could take days".

"You'll find out when these people come."

Barton got his own phone out and like Damston, began to play games. He stole a glance at his watch it was coming close to nine p.m. If those people were builders, they don't usually start work till about eight in the morning. He thought he detected a slight grin and a nod of her head as she stared at the screen on her mobile. Had she guessed he was up to something, or was it something she noticed on her phone either way, he was feeling uncomfortable. They both jumped when a sudden bang came from the outer door.

Damston shot up from her seat, "that must be the builders." Never-the-less, she pulled her gun out and cocked it and held it ready. Barton did likewise and followed her out the office. When they got close to the outer door he caught her arm restraining her from opening it.

"Builders at this time?" Barton said, "I don't think so, who's there?" he cried.

They got no response, Barton shouted again, much louder, a moment later the door was thumped again. He jerked the handle with one hand, weapon ready to fire on the other, the heavy door flew open. They charged out found themselves staring out into the empty darkness, he grabbed Damston arm and pulled her behind the door. It felt like they had stood there in silence, listening to each other's breath for an hour but it was only a few minutes. Damston could stand it no longer and dashed out. She was well clear of the door when he caught up with her.

In the rush Barton had no time to close the door, they stood exposed in the dim light from inside the building, he pulled her by the upper arm into the darkness and made her crouch down on her knees. He got down beside her and they monkey crawled their way to the old digger.

Damston reached up and opened the cabin door, the old hinges resisted with a loud squeak, they ducked down behind the bucket expecting shots, but nothing happened. Barton raised his head and chanced a look now that their eyes had become accustomed to the darkness.

"They could have ducked around the back of the building," Damstom whispered at the same time pulling him down by his leather jacket, "we need to find them before the builders arrive."

Barton remembered his last encounter behind that building, was still getting waves of pain from the wound on his face, he let out a deep sigh, "oh. kay. You stay close behind." On their hands and knees they made it to the nearest corner and painfully stood up pressing their backs against the building. They made their way along, side stepping all the way keeping tight to the wall. At the corner Barton stopped, held his breath and glanced around, could see nothing in the total darkness. He exhaled and let the tension slip from his body when he heard the crunching of gravel under a footstep. Although he couldn't see Damston's expression he sensed she heard it. "You go back the way we came," he whispered, "be as quiet as you can,

I'll carry on this way, if there is somebody here, we should be able to trap them at the front."

She was stood at the open door when Barton rounded the corner, pointed a finger at the inside. He cursed himself for not having took the time to lock it.

They charged in ready to shoot at anything that moved. Nothing did, after a thorough search of the building they found nothing out of place and no sign of the intruders.

"What the fucks going on?" She said when they got seated back in the office. Her face was chalk white, her hands shacking when she placed her gun on the desk.

Barton wasn't feeling any better, this had always been one of his greatest fears, fighting an unseen enemy, "there's one thing I'm certain of, that was someone banging on that door>"

She stood up, picked up her weapon, "well I think we better find whoever it was, before the builders arrive." She walked around the desk carrying her gun at arms-length into the warehouse.

Barton got up to follow her when the door banged again. This time she didn't wait for him to open it and emptied her magazine into it.

Barton barged past her, jerked the door open expecting to find a body lying on the steps

CHAPTER 30

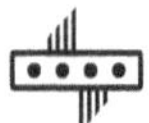

ecil looked at the clock behind the bar, it had been almost five hours since that guy Barton had left, had been down to the cellar got the package and placed it behind the bar under the sink He knew the only way he could get him to place the bomb in the warehouse in Allotment street was to use his father as a lever, but with Barton taking so long to return, the lever was looking as if it was having no effect. He waved to one of his goons to refill his glass, while he watched the goon pour his drink, a sudden idea flashed. Another half hour, was all the time he was going to wait for Barton, if he hadn't showed face, the idea would be put into practice.

Two drinks later, Cecil decided he had waited long enough, he waved two of his goons over, "go down the cellar and bring the old man up." A few minutes later the goons were at his side holding Tom Barton by the arms, Cecil turned in his seat stared into the oldster watery blue eyes, ripped the duck-tape from his mouth, Tom winced at the sudden pain and tried to fight free from the grip of the goons, this resulted on the grip tightening. When Cecil saw that the fight had gone out of the old man, he said, "if you want to know what happened to your sons remains, you'll have to do a little job for me first."

"You can fuck off," the old man spat at him,

Cecil nodded to the men holding him up, they in turn dragged Tom to the floor behind the bar and each landed a few kicks into his ribs. When Cecil called a halt to the beating, the old man lay in the foetal position moaning, "well, what's it to be, are you going to do this little job? When you were talking to that girl I took a photo of you both together, I could show it to your wife, tell her you spent time with her in one of the rooms." A few minutes passed as Cecil waited for a response, all the oldster could do was moan and try to curl up into a tighter ball. "If you don't agree to do this job you'll never know about your son, and on top of that I'll use your phone to text your oldest son to come here and collect you, but he won't get that chance, I'm going to get my boys to jump him the moment he steps in that door, so you'll lose both of them what's it to be?

Tom went silent and nodded his head slightly.

Cecil grinned widely down at the old man, "a wise decision, Mr. Barton," he turned to the goon nearest, "take him up to one of the beds, he'll need a rest before doing the job." The sound of a heated argument from the direction of the fire door drew his attention as well as quite a few of the patrons. Cecil jumped off his seat and rushed over to the two goons involved, "what the fucks going on?"

The goons turned together, "that van's gone," they shouted.

It took a moment for it to dawn on Cecil what they were talking about, when it did, he felt a little more at ease. One thing less to worry about. "How could that have happened?"

Seeing little concern on the little black man's demeanour the two big men grinned, "one of those men we dumped in it must have gotten loose," they looked at each other in agreement.

"You were supposed to have been tied up?"

The two men dropped their grin, shrugged their shoulders and shook their heads.

"What can we see on c.c.tv?" Cecil asked without showing much interest.

"All we could see was the van reversing out of the lane," one of the goons said.

Shaking his head Cecil turned and swaggered back to his seat at the bar. As he sipped his drink, he began to wonder why he had so readily ignored the incident of the van being pushed down the lane, remembered thinking at the time that it could have been nicked and the thief tried to get rid of it. He picked up the old man's mobile from the bar, found the eldest son's number and sent him a text. A moment after he pressed send a message came on the screen saying it was unsent. In a burst of rage Cecil threw his glass, smashed it against the wall at the back of the bar. He waved to the goon who taken the old man up to the rooms. "show me where you took that old guy." The big man nodded and led the way.

Tom Barton was sitting on the side of the bed, his head in his hands, when Cecil and the goon barged in. He jumped up, felt his head spin and fell back onto the hard mattress.

"Get him onto his feet," Cecil said to the goon.

Tom's legs gave way under him and the big man had to hold him up. Cecil pushed his face right up to the oldster's, "I've got a bag behind the bar. I'll give you ten minutes to pull yourself together, come down and I'll give you the instructions where to deliver it."

The goon let Tom go and they watched him crumple to the floor. He watched them leave and close the door behind them before he made attempt to get up, using the bed for support. Ten minutes would never be enough, the burning pain in his ribs was so severe he was having difficulty breathing, never mind trying to walk.

Purdy pulled the van into the same spot in the town centre car park, he got out and waited for the two men to climb out of the back. "Hussey should be relaxed now it's been a few hours since we charged into his place, we'll hang about across the street from it make sure things have settled.

As he was about to head across the car park, Jerry gripped his arm and stopped him. "I'm not too confident the goons will be relaxed, they'll be keeping an eye on the place, Hussey will be too scared to let them."

In the dim light of the car park Purdy could tell by the look on Pats face, he agreed with his mate.

"Well if you both don't want to come, I'll do it myself," he jerked his arm free and started walking. By the time Purdy got to the end of the lane, the mates were standing beside him Purdy looked at them and grinned, "changed your minds. Okay, the street is almost deserted, so let's get on with it." Side by side they sprinted across the street and stopped a few feet from the makeshift door. Had to dart to the side out of sight when the door flew open and an elderly man stumbled out carrying a holdall, as suddenly as the door had opened, it shut again.

"What the fucks going on?" Pat said as the old man staggered past them.

They retreated to the shadows of a shop doorway. "Could be a punter getting tossed out," Jerry said.

"Why the hold all?" Purdy said, "you don't carry a bag like that into a nightclub, I think he picked it up in there."

"What could be in it? "Jerry asked.

"If you want to know, let's go find out," Purdy said and began striding after the old man. Tom hadn't gone far before the three men surrounded him, the tallest of them grabbed the bag out of his hand, "What's in the bag old man?" he asked. Tom shook his head and walked away.

Purdy reached out and pulled him back, "let's see what's in your bag," the three of them gazed at it, while Tom slipped away

"What's in it?" Pat asked.

"One way of finding out," Purdy said placing the bag on the ground and was about to pull open the zip when Jerry kicked it out of his reach. "What did you do that for?" Purdy shouted.

"I did a tour in Belfast," Jerry replied, "I learned never to open a suspicious bag."

"What do we do with it?" Purdy asked.

"Take it somewhere safe, "Jerry said, "slit the side carefully to see what's inside."

"Fine," Purdy agreed, "we'll take it back to the carpark."

Under the dim glow of the only streetlamp in the carpark, Jerry gently slit the side of the holdall. while Pat and Purdy held it up," fucking hell." he gasped, "it's a fucking bomb."

Purdy and Jerry placed the bag on the ground, jumped back a few paces. "Has it got a timing device? Purdy asked.

Jerry shook his head, "there's an old mobile phone in there, it's set to go off remotely and there's another problem, It's wired to the zip, had you opened it we would have been raw meat scattered all over this carpark."

Purdy approached, looked over Jerry's shoulder, "what are we going to do with it?"

Jerry looked up at him and shrugged his shoulder.

Pat came closer, "we could find that old man and give it back to him?"

"Or we could just leave it here, Jerry said and stood up.

The three of them stood staring down at the bag, "I know what I would like to do with it," Purdy said, "take it back to that club and place it at the fire exit, but my family's in there. We'll just have to find that old man and ask him what he was intending to do with it."

They didn't have to go far the oldster was standing on the kerb side trying to wave a taxi. Purdy pulled him by the arm into a narrow passageway, pointed to the bag in Jerry's hands "where were you taking this?" He asked.

Tom drew deeply on his cigarette turned his head to the side and exhaled the smoke, "I was told to take it to a warehouse in Allotment street."

"Who told you?" Purdy asked.

"The little black man in the club."

"Do you know what's in it?"

Tom shook his head, took a long pull at his cigarette.

Jerry stepped towards him, opened the slit at the side of the bag, "that's a fucking bomb."

The old man gasped and stepped back, "I had no idea what it was, I was told to leave at the door,"

He pointed at the bag, "that looks like my mobile in there."

Well you better hope nobody calls you on it, or we're all dead meat and if the zip gets opened , the same results," Jerry shouted at him.

Purdy grabbed the old man by the collar, "get hold of that bag, we'll take you to that warehouse, you can deliver it, just hope that little shit doesn't decide to call your mobile before we get there.

CHAPTER 31

The Carter brothers had decided to take Lenny to the warehouse in Allotment street. After three hours of interrogation and constant beatings they had learned nothing. Lenny drifted into unconsciousness and the brothers dragged him by the ankles all the way out the warehouse into the street and dumped him into the boot of their car. The security guard had been locked in the toilet, when Tommy let him out, he grabbed the guard, "you open your mouth about this and you're next."

They dumped Lenny on the town centre carpark, dragged him behind litter bins and headed for the Hussey Club. When they reached the end of the narrow lane they stopped suddenly, "what the fucks been going on here?" Ben said nodding towards the sheets of plywood on the door.

"It looks like somebody's beat us to it," Tommy replied grinning.

"I don't think so, if that was the case the door wouldn't have been patched up yet and the place would be crawling with police."

Tommy decided his brother was right on his assumption, "that should make it easier for us to barge in and shoot that piece of shit before he tries to kill us again."

"I don't think that's going to be that easy, whoever it was that smashed the door has put them on the alert. The goons will be ready for another attack," Ben said.

From out of a lane four men appeared on the opposite side of the street. On noticing them the brothers darted into the shadow at the back of a shop. They watched the men as they walked briskly towards them. A grey-haired older man was between two younger guys and one behind, they seemed to be forcibly rushing the oldster who was carrying a holdall. The brothers shrank farther into the shadows when the four men crossed the street and turned into the lane, headed for the carpark. "What do you make of that?" Ben asked when the four men were out of hearing distance.

"I'm not sure," Tommy replied, "but that bag looked very much like the one that little shit gave us."

"That tall thin guy at the back looked familiar,"

Tommy placed a hand on his brother's shoulder, come on let's see what they're up to."

They got to the end of the lane in time to see a van racing out the carpark, instinctively they scrambled to their car, "don't be too hasty, "Ben said as he got into the passenger's seat, "don't want them to see us following them."

At that time in the morning the traffic was sparse, Tommy had to hold back quite a distance and almost lost them when the van made a last-minute left turn into Allotment street. "What are they up to?" He shouted, swinging the car over to the side of the road. They both jumped out, rushed to the end of the street and saw the van pull up at the warehouse door.

"We better phone Randell about this," Ben said standing in front of his brother with his mobile in his hand. Without waiting for a reply, he started scrolling for the contact. The instructions were sharp and brief. He rammed his phone into his pocket, "we've to get a hold of that bag and dump into the canal."

"How the fuck are we supposed to do that? It's obvious it's a bomb it could go off any time."

"You don't know for sure it's a bomb, we didn't see them leave Hussey's club."

"Hussey could have conned that old guy and those other three into delivering the bag same way as he conned us into doing it."

The rear door of the van opened and in the dim light they could just about make out the old man climbing out with the bag in his hand. Using the darkest side of the street the brother made their way towards the vehicle when with a sudden screech of the tyres it swung around and charged up the street past them, leaving the old man standing holding the bag.

Without hesitation they rushed over to the oldster, Ben grabbed the bag from his hand, "what have you got in this?" he asked.

Tom, still shacking by the suddenness of the attack, staggered back against Tommy who caught him under his arm, "I think it's a bomb."

"What are you doing walking about with a bomb? "Tommy asked steadying the oldster onto his feet.

"I got it from the owner of the Hussey Club, he told me to deliver it here."

Ben swung around and walked away.

"Where are you going," Tommy shouted after him.

"Taking this back its rightful owner."

Ben gripped the old man by the upper arm and rushed him toward their car.

CHAPTER 32

The man lay face up on the step, his high vis. Jacket had a large patch of blood in the area of his heart. His three work mates had retreated behind the pickup truck. Barton leaped out and put a finger to the man's jugular, could feel no pulse, turned to Damson who was now standing behind his shoulder looking down at the man, "you've killed one of the builders."

"How was I to know he was one of the builders, "she said, "they were not supposed to arrive here until eight o clock."

Barton glanced at his watch, pulled out his A.S.P. 9mm auto pistol, holding it ready and made his way towards the three men at the pickup truck. Behind his back he could hear Damson loading another magazine into her weapon.

Three figures stepped around the truck, when they saw the guns pointing at them, they put up their hands. Barton stopped about six feet away from them, out the corner of his eyes he saw Damson at his side. "Who are you? "Barton asked.

One of the men spoke up, took half a step forward, he wore bottle bottom glasses making his eyes look the size of golf balls, "we're here to do a job, not sure exactly what it is, you just shot the boss."

"You're not supposed to be here until eight' o'clock," Damson said.

"The boss wanted to get an early start."

"He should have phoned and let us know," she went on, "now he's got himself killed."

"We weren't expecting anybody to be here," one of the men from behind said.

She stepped aside and waved them past, "get started, I'll tell you what's to be done"

"What about our boss?" Bottle bottom glasses asked.

"That's your first job, get rid of him somewhere."

Barton moved over beside her when the men were a safe distance away, "what's to be done with them when the jobs finished?"

"I'm going to phone Mr. Randell, tell him what's happened, he'll arrange something.," she turned and walked away a few paces at the same time fishing her mobile from her pocket.

Barton's attention was split between watching Damson and the three men in the process of lifting their boss's body. The two tallest men took hold of the corpse's shoulders while the smaller bottle bottom glasses took the feet. They carried the body behind the old digger. He decided this could an ideal time to call his father's mobile, aware that the little owner of the club had possession of it, explain that he had been held up. Before Barton could get his mobile out of his hip pocket, she had finished her call and was standing next to him.

"Mr. Randell says that as soon as he can contact the Carter's he'll send them here," she said.

"Did you tell him that you shot and killed one of the builders?"

She nodded," the Carters will deal with the body, thar's their job."

The three builders appeared from behind the old digger, Barton followed Damson as she stepped over to meet them. "I want all this rubble cleared from the quarry floor," she indicated with her hand around the base," we've got shipping containers arriving here in a few days, this has to be cleared by then."

One of the men jumped onto the back of the pickup truck and handed the necessary tools to the other two, "where do you want us to start?" He asked getting down from the truck.

She didn't answer, instead started walking towards the building. The builders looked at Barton and he pointed to the far side of the base at huge rocks, "I think you'll have to start over there."

She was a very worried looking woman when Barton entered the office, slumped on the chair behind the desk, her head in her hands. He sat on the seat in front of her, "what's worrying you?"

He asked.

"The man we shot was a close friend of Crow's, the last thing Mr. Randell wants, is to lose the business relationship they have."

Barton wanted strongly to object to her using the word we, but held his temper, "It was an accident, did you tell him that?"

She shook her head, "he should know we wouldn't kill one of the builders deliberately."

Barton got up off his seat, walked to the door, "I've got a call to make," expecting some kind of reaction from her, he delayed a few moments studying her, when he didn't get it, he left closing the door gently.

Purdy drove the van out of Allotment street, the way he normally drives, foot flat to the floor with little or no consideration for other road users. Turned right on to the main road without easing off. Pat was in the passenger's seat, his eyes closed, Jerry in the back getting tossed about cursing and swearing. "Where are we going now?" Pat asked.

"Back to deal with Hussey?"

"Hope that old guy has got himself safe."

"Tough if he hasn't, his own fault for walking around the street carrying a bomb," Purdy said, pulling the van to a halt in the town canter carpark.

"How do you propose to deal with the little shit?" Jerry asked, still recovering from the rough ride.

"Patrons will be leaving at this time, the moment they open that door, we burst in guns blazing as they say in the movies,"

Pat glanced at his watch, "I think we best get moving now before people start heading into work."

"No not just yet," Purdy said, "wait till most of the patrons are away, that way nobody's going to get in the way when we rush in."

Jerry jumped out the back door making the vehicle rock slightly, Purdy and Pat turned as the rear door slammed shut, "where are you going?" Purdy shouted.

Jerry appeared at the driver's side window. Purdy wound it down, "what're you doing?"

"Trying to get some life back into my legs."

Purdy and Pat stepped out and joined him, "walk slowly," Purdy said, "by the time we get there it should be time to catch the last of the patrons leave."

By the time they reached the start of the narrow lane, a few cars had pulled into the car park and the one Tommy Carter drove in, didn't draw their attention. Purdy led the way along the lane onto the main street. This time they didn't hesitate and rushed across the street and barged in through the temporary door to find the place in total darkness with no signs of life.

"What the fucks going on?" Jerry shouted.

They stood in the darkness a few feet from the door, weapons ready fingers on the trigger twitching to fire at the slightest movement.

Like a flash the place was a blaze with blinding lights which for the intruders only lasted a few moments before sheer darkness and unconsciousness overcame them.

The desperate need to urinate woke Purdy, the darkness remained, his movement restricted, his wrists hurt could feel his hands begin to swell from lack of circulation. It didn't take him long to realise where he was. The pungent smell of cigarette smoke and stale beer, human excretion. The nightmare of his time in Hussey's cellar, he knew where he was, and this time Hussey would make sure, there would be no escape. The sound of muffled voices, told him Pat and Jerry were in the same predicament, He listened for the sound of his girlfriend and baby but could hear nothing above the noise the two mates were making. The sudden flow on hot liquid in the area of his crotch came as a relief from the pains in his bladder.

"Pissed yourself?" the familiar voice said as the tape was pulled from his mouth with such force Purdy thought his skin went with it.

"You bastard," he shouted and struggled against his re-strainers, which made the pains on his wrists worse.

Cecil grinned, was enjoying watching Purdy suffer, "shall we continued where we left off?"

The stinging from his mouth was bad enough, now the tape from his eyes was yanked away and felt as though his eye lids went with it. Purdy screamed, again he struggled, the bonds didn't give. He opened his eyes, this sent more stinging pain in them, his vision was blurred, could only make out shadowy outlines in front of him.

The sight of this big man brought back memories of Jaco, if it hadn't been for Purdy his lover would still be here with him. Cecil's pleasure was turning into resentment, the hate was boiling in his head, wanted to rip this man apart, piss all over his entrails, only then would he enjoy looking at him. That would have to wait, wanted Purdy to witness the further torture that was to be inflicted to his girlfriend and baby.

Purdy's eyes were beginning to come into to focus, the black face with the halo of frizzy hair was the first thing he could see, "if you've harmed my woman and baby, you bastard, I'll kill you."

Cecil pushed his face close to Purdy's, "I don't think you're in a position to threaten anybody," he stepped back. "If you want to see your family, They're over their behind those barrels," he nodded his head in the direction.

Purdy looked over but could only see a stack of metal beer barrels. The two mates were tied to chairs opposite him. Behind Cecil stood three goons, all armed and pointing their pistols at him.

"I want to see my family," he said. Cecil nodded to the goons and they headed in behind the barrels. They returned, two of them dragging his girlfriend by the arms her bare feet brushing along the stone floor, the other carrying the baby. She looked in a comatose state, they let her go and she slithered to the floor, the baby still in the other goon's arms, looked the same way. Purdy struggled with all his strength, when he had nothing left his head and body slumped over.

Cecil was about to slap Purdy's face when the cellar door burst open, he and the goons turned to see a duffle bag toppling down the stairs. At that same moment Barton's mobile connected to his father's phone, the signal set the detonator.

The club door had been left ajar, the brothers didn't hesitation, Tommy grabbed the bag from the old man and they both rushed across the street. Tom Barton made a hasty retreat, back to the carpark.

They were surprised to find the place deserted and wasted no time rushing to the cellar door, Ben opened it and Tommy lobbed the bag in with all the force he could muster, when he heard the bag hit the steps Ben slammed the door shut. They grinned at each other and darted back to the exit. At about three paces from the make sift door, the floor under their feet blasted upwards. The brothers never knew what happened as the blast blew from the basement all the way to the second story ripping its way up through the roof.

Tom Barton decided he had enough of being messed about with these thugs, had come very close to getting himself killed and at the end of it all still hadn't had closure on his youngest son. This time he wasn't going to wait for a taxi and started to take the short cut home through the carpark and cross into the playing field. He only got halfway across the parking area when the explosion came. At first, he thought it was a close clap of thunder, but that thought soon dissipated when he felt the ground beneath his feet shudder, the birds that had been nesting in the surrounding trees for the night set off in a burst of flight and shrills. Tom picked up speed to get clear of the area, he began to panic when he heard people scream and burst into a run. Two police constables were standing at his front door talking to his wife, they all turned when he opened the garden gate and walked up to them.

"Where the Hell have you been?" His wife Jean cried, "I reported you missing last night, these two policemen got me out of bed."

Tom approached her, his hands held out, "sorry love I'll explain it to you later."

After jotting down a few notes on their pads the two constables left. Tom followed his wife into their living room. After a few cups of tea, he explained all the events he had gone through missing out mentioning the bomb and the girl.

"Did you hear anything about the explosion in the town centre?" Jean asked.

Tom nodded, "I heard a loud bang on my way home, didn't know what it was," he could tell by her expression she wasn't convinced at what he had told her. Maybe she didn't want to know the truth, he decided when she got up and went into the kitchen with the empty cups.

"The reason the policemen had to leave so quickly, they were called to that explosion," she shouted from the kitchen, "or they would have wanted a few more detail from you."

CHAPTER 33

After failing to get a reply from his father's mobile, Barton went outside to be greeted with a grey dawn. The first thing he noticed was that the pick-up truck had gone, he jumped off the step and looked around to see if it had been moved and parked nearer where the men worked. There was no truck and no sign of the men.

"Have they fucked off?" Damson said, as she stepped out the door and walked towards him.

"Looks like it."

"Check and see if they've taken their dead friend with them."

"They've not taken him," Barton shouted from the back of the old digger and noticed she was on her phone again.

She put her phone back into her pocket "There's been an explosion at the Hussey Club," she cried.

Barton rushed over beside her, "say that again," not sure if he had heard right, when she repeated it, the reality of it came with a thud when the thought of his father being in there, "how bad is it?"

"Not sure, Mr Randell just got word of it, hasn't had the details yet."

"What do we do now?"

"We have to get back to the office as soon as," she locked the door and headed for their car.

Nevil pushed the big man in his wheelchair down the passageway from his office, Barton and Damson stepped into the reception area. He signalled for his driver to stop with a big hand. "I can't get the Carters on their mobiles, get into the centre see if they're hanging about where that explosion was."

They watched Nevil load the big man into the limousine before they set off, "I don't think we'll get anywhere near the centre car park," Barton said. Contrary to Barton's assumption they had a choice of places to park, "pull in over there," Damson said and pointed to a vacant space. When the vehicle stopped, she jumped out and walked around the car parked next to them. Barton got out, wondering what the hell's she was doing? "This is one of our cars, it must the one the Carter's were using, they must be around somewhere, probably watching the action at the explosion site."

They were stopped at the start of the lane by a young constable standing behind blue and white cordon tape, "we're looking for a couple of our work mates, their car is in the car park," Barton explained to the policeman.

"Nobody has been allowed through this way since six o clock," the constable said.

"What's happened?" Damson asked.

The constable shrugged his shoulders, "some kind of explosion, I've been informed."

"Has anybody been injured or what?" Barton asked.

Again, the young policeman shrugged his shoulders, "All I can tell you is that the ambulances have been in and out all morning."

Damson turned and walked away out of hearing distance and pulled out he mobile, Barton followed and passed her on his way to the car. He sat in the driver's seat watching as she paced back and forth in front of the vehicle.

She jumped in beside him, still talking on her phone. When she cut the signal she said, "head for the hospital we've got to find those two, if they've been injured or whatever that's the best place to find out."

"Don't you need to be a relative or something to get information from the hospital?"

"You could say you are one of their partners, don't need any proof of that."

Barton almost choked, "Do I look that way inclined?"

Damson chuckled, "Oh kay, I'll say I'm their sister or something."

"You can't say that," Barton interrupter her, "if they've been killed the police will want you to identify them, I don't think Mr. Randell would want that.

They approached the receptionist, Damson put on her concerned expression, "I think two of our colleagues, may have been injured and bought in here."

The woman grinned and lifted a pen, "can I have the names of your colleagues please?"

"Carter, Ben and Tommy."

After answering many questions, the woman picked up the phone and said a few words into it, put it down and said, "sorry no one by that name has been admitted, but some unidentified bodies were brought in D.O.A. To identify them you'll have to contact the police."

Damson did a quick about turn and strode out the building, Barton rushed after her, "what're you going to do now? You can't get the police involved."

She said nothing until they were seated in the car, "we're not a hundred per cent sure the Carters were among those D.O.A."

"How are you going to find out?"

"I'll try their mobiles," she rummaged in her pockets.

He gripped her arm and stopped her using her phone, "If they are among the dead or injured and their phones have managed to still be in use, a copper or a fireman even an ambulance member of staff could hear it and pick it up. Better just take it, that they were among the bodies."

"I'll call Mr. Randell, see what he says."

Barton listened to her explain the situation to the big man, for a while she went silent listening to to his advice. She replaced her phone, "we have to go back to the office and wait for him to return."

CHAPTER 34

They had spent an hour in Damson's broom cupboard sized office before the big man returned, Damson had passed the time on her desk top computer, Barton played games on his mobile, every now and then getting up to stretch his cramped legs, this and his tuneless whistling was getting to her but she never said anything. When Nevil opened the door and nodded, they both jumped up relieved to come to the end of the monotony.

Randell looked flushed behind the cloud of cigar smoke as though he had rushed to get back, but Barton knew that it would have been Nevil who did all the rushing. He pulled up a seat for Damson and one for himself but didn't sit until the big man gestured for them to.

He gazed at them both, "what's the story?" he placed the thick cigar between his hair line lips.

"We think they were both caught up in that explosion." Damson said. He removed the cigar, held it between two fat fingers and pointed it at them, "I've had it in good authority that it was a bomb, That's the second time in so many months that those two have been involved with bombs. The next problem is we've got some action on our C.C.TV. He nodded to Nevil who quickly darted out and returned with a screen and a recorder. Within a few minutes he had it operating. "As you can tell this is the front of the warehouse in Allotment street." The recording showed a white van pull up at the door, a grey-haired elderly man got out of the back carrying a holdall, the van sped away out of view leaving the old man standing holding the bag.

It took Barton a few moments to believe his eyes, had his father been threatened into delivering that bag because he couldn't get back to the Hussey Club in time, He could feel his heart beating off his ribs and could only hope that he wasn't showing any outward signs of it.

For about three minutes the camera showed the oldster standing looking at the door as if deciding what to do when two other men approached him, exchanged a few words then walked away out of sight. "that was the Carters," Randell roared and pointed at the screen, "what happened after that is any bodies guess. I'm thinking that the contents of that bag's the bomb."

It was at that moment it struck Barton that his father could be among the injured or the D.O.A. Now his heart jumped up another gear and was sure the big man would be able to see it on his face. Damson spoke and drew the big man's attention, "what could they have been doing in the Hussey Club?"

"Well," Randell grinned," if they were the ones who planted that bomb and got caught up in it, I don't think we'll ever know."

Barton urgently needed to get out of this office and try his father's mobile again, wanted to make sure, he was still alive, but how to do that without arousing suspicion? Randell took a long draw at his cigar and stumped it out in the glass ashtray in front of him, it smouldered for a while, all eyes were on it. The big man made no attempt to put it out, he looked around the room as if the place was strange to him. His gaze rested on Damson, "you will have to return to the quarry, get rid of that body, now the Carters are out the picture."

"What will we do with it?" Damson asked.

"The same way that had to be done in Allotment Street last year, I bought another storage place, I've arranged for a machine to dig a trench, dump any bodies in and fill it in with concrete."

The shock at what he had just heard sent an icy cold shiver through Barton's body, could hardly believe what he had just heard. This man sat behind his desk and the woman next to him, knew where Corrie's body lay all this time, he was sure that Hussey was responsible for both the death and the disposable of his brother's body. It took him all his willpower to supress his anger and to shoot them both there on the spot, knew it would be too dangerous with Nevil standing at the rear of the big man's chair. The picture was forming in his mind, Hussey was responsible for the bomb, Randell's organisation for the disposal of the body, the problem was, who was the shooter? The newspaper report said that Dany had been shot, Corrie must have come to the same end. Was this the shooter who killed the girl in the forest and killed Lumpy? Damson sprung up out her seat and disturbed his thoughts, "we better get going and move that body before the rest of those workmen start mouthing off about it and the police get wind of it."

Randell held up a big arm, "that's all been taken care of, just get there and get that body, I'll let you know where to take it.

"Have you got other builders to clear up the rubble on the quarry floor? "she asked.

The big man nodded and drew anther cigar from his top pocket, "when you pick up that body stay there."

Out in the corridor, Barton told her he was going to the toilet, she nodded and carried on to the reception area. Two or three times he tried his father's mobile and got no signal. With only a minute or so to spare he called his parent's house number it rang a few times but had to give up when he heard Damston banging on the door.

"What were you doing in there," She said, "giving birth or what?"

Barton grimaced and followed her to the car. This time she got in the driver's seat, "do you not trust my driving?"

"After that carry on with Lenny, I don't trust anything you do."

Barton was glad she had decided to drive, gave him time to think, to work out a plan of action for no way was this lot getting away with murdering his brother and possibly his father.

At the end of the estate road she stopped the car.

"What's wrong?" he asked. She didn't answer didn't need to when two of the course members got in the back. "Why the reinforcements?" He jabbed his thumb at the two men.

The silence remained all the way to the quarry. The men in the back were quick to jump out, had their guns out and pointing at him, "what's going on?" He asked, staring at Damson, noticed she too had her weapon out aligned at his face.

"Get out," she said, "and gently drop the metal work on the ground."

Barton had no other choice but to comply and watched her climb out, noticed that cold grin on her face, knew what it meant, had seen it before and knew the consequences, "I don't understand, what are you doing, what have I done to deserve this treatment?"

She stepped up to his face, "you think I'm stupid I saw the look on your face when you noticed that old man on the C.C. TV. And your body language at the mention of bodies being buried in concrete in the warehouse in Allotment Street."

"What did you expect that was the same place where someone took a shot at us, as for the old boy, he didn't look like the normal bums that live there, and the bodies in the concrete, I just wondered how the Carters managed to get rid of the corpses."

Pain sored through his shoulder as the butt of a gun from one of the men behind sent Barton stumbling forward almost landing on his knees. Two sets of hand grabbed his arms and dragged him towards the building. Damson skipped past them and opened the door, she stepped back and he felt himself being pushed inside. He managed to stay on his feet after staggering towards a stack of wooden boxes and was glad of the support.

Damson approached with the men on either side of her, all their weapons pointed at him, again she stepped up close, her blue eyes staring into his, pushed the barrel of her gun hard under his chin. "Have you any last requests?" She laughed took a step back and aimed her piston at his head. The shot rang in his ears, he ducked to the floor, landed on a body and rolled off it, His hands felt wet sticky and warm, could see fresh blood on them but could feel no pain. He realised Damston hadn't had a chance to get her shot off, where was the blood coming from? He struggled onto his knees and saw her lying next to him, he looked around for the two men and couldn't see them, got up onto his feet, felt a bit unsteady, looked down at her she was barely alive her eyes were open and tried to put her hand out to him, her arm never reached the full stretch and it slumped down by her side. Barton didn't need to check her for pulse, knew she was gone. He rushed outside looking for the two men, needed answers, was it one of them who shot her, if so why? The quarry forecourt was deserted and the car was gone.

The limousine crunched its way along the narrow gravel track and pulled up next to Barton as he stood in the deserted courtyard, Nevil got out and got the wheelchair from the boot. Barton held the chair steady while the tall black driver helped Randell into it.

"What the hell's been going on here?" The big man asked looking up at Barton.

"You tell me?" Barton said.

The big man's snowman shaped head coloured, the sunken blue eyes widening in anger, "how the fuck am I supposed to know, I wasn't here."

"Damson's lying in there," Barton said, pointing his thumb at the building, "she's been shot, I don't know who fired the shot, but whoever it was, saved me from being shot by her.

Randell waved a hand at Nevil, "Take me inside, don't feel safe here, too much lead's been flying around."

Barton followed behind the tall driver as he pushed the wheelchair towards the building, noticed his pistol lying on the ground where he was made drop it. He delayed a while until he saw them enter through the door, he dashed over, picked it up and tucked it into the back of his jeans.

Randell was behind the desk, when Barton entered the office, his driver was standing behind him. The big man gestured for him to be seated with a nod of his head, He pulled one of his thick cigars from his top pocket stuck in his mouth, turned his head towards Nevil and the driver instantly produced a plastic lighter. "If you can remember," the big man said, "I asked you and Damson to find out who Lumpy's assistant was," he delayed a moment to let his driver light his cigar, "that was a bit of a sham, because she knew all along who this assistant was, and I suspected as much, just needed proof. It's all over with now, all went with that explosion, the little black man who owned the club had a secret workshop and according to investigators this place was full of bomb making materiel, explosives and enough weapons to start a war."

The big man went silent to let Barton take this in, the silence didn't last long when a knock came from the door and in stepped the two men who had previously abducted him. They took up position standing on either side of him, Barton glanced up at them and back at the big man whose head was shrouded in smoke. "The problem I have now is working out if you were in collusion with her and we have a few questions to ask you about it."

Barton made to get up, but two hands clasped his shoulders and forced him back down. "I can assure you I didn't know she knew who Lumpy's assistant was."

Randel grinned but his eyes remained cold, "then why would she want to kill you?"

Barton could only shrug his shoulders and shake his head, he remembered her accusations, had spoken them out loud in front of the two men standing next to him, had they informed the big man of it? "She got the wrong impression of my reactions to that C.C.TV. footage."

"What was your reaction?"

"No reaction, I was desperate to go to the toilet,"

"I seem to remember you using that excuse before, do you have a problem with your bowels?"

Barton shook his head, "don't think so,"

Randell stumped his cigar out on the desktop, "was it you who shot the builder?"

"That was Damson, she fired blindly through the door, you must have seen the bullet holes in the door when you came in."

The big man glanced at his driver, who nodded in confirmation. "That builder was a close friend of a business associate who wanted retribution, I'm glad I made the right decision."

Some of the tension drained from Barton's body and he realised the big man had noticed, cursed himself for that moment of weakness, "her body's lying at the side of that crate near the door."

"I've been doing a bit of research on you," Randell said manoeuvring his wheelchair closer to the desk and leaning on his elbows, "you're not like the rest of these convicts, are you?"

"I'm not sure what you mean, I did time for assaulting someone, I'm sure you must have others in the same situation."

"But you did your time in a military clink, that is the difference, you assaulted an officer because you must have been provoked, the villains I recruit would have assaulted him for his money. If you want to stay with this organisation you have to prove I can trust you. That old man, we saw on C.C.TV. I want you to hunt him down and kill him," he pointed a finger at the two men standing on either side of Barton. "These two will accompany you to make sure you do it."

CHAPTER 35

Barton was escorted to the car at the point of two pistols, pushed into the backseat, one of the men got in beside him while the other jumped in the driver's seat, "where are we going? Barton asked.

"You heard Mr. Randell, to find that old man," the driver said.

"Where are you going to start looking?"

"That's your decision," the one sat beside him said.

"Well," Barton said, "I've decided we stop in at a service for something to eat."

"Oh kay," said the driver, "but you try anything, and we won't hesitate to shoot you."

"Why should I try anything, I've to kill an old man, not such a big deal, I could have done it without you two supervising, all the big man had to say was go get it done I don't know why he sent you two."

"We're doing what we are told," the driver said.

The driver had decided to take the M65 as it had the nearest service station, Barton cursed silently when he noticed very few vehicles in the carpark, had pinned his hopes on it being full, thus making it easier to dodge amongst the cars and escape. Now a new tactic would have to be thought out. The old hostage trick he had been taught in the army came to mind, "I remember during the course we weren't to use our names, now that's over, my name is Richard Barton, what do I call you two?"

The driver parked the car close to the restaurant, a clever trick thought Barton, less chance of him making a run for it. They sat in silence, making no attempt to get out the car. He started to think they were waiting for something or someone. "What's your names?" Barton asked again.

As if by some telepathic signal they both got out the car together. The driver opened Barton's door and with a jerk of his head signalled for him to get out. The other man was soon at his back, Jabbing his pistol into Barton's back. "You are not going to tell me your names then?"

The driver led the way into restaurant the man at Barton's back pushed him forward and put his pistol in the pocket of his leather jacket, making sure Barton saw it. There were plenty of vacant seats. The driver went to the counter while his armed escort steered him to a table farthest away from the exit. The gun man sat opposite Barton signalled he had his weapon pointed at him under the table.

Barton leaned forward on the table looked, into the man's eyes, "was it you who shot Damson?"

Before he got a reaction, the driver appeared at the table carrying a tray with food and drinks.

"We didn't shoot her," the driver said as he sat down," the shot came through the open door, we ran outside all we saw was a car racing up the drive." He handed out the food and drinks, "who ever it was must have took the shot from inside his car, the only way he could have got away so quick."

"You seem so sure it was a man?" Barton asked, taking a drink from his cup.

Nothing else was said till after they finished their meal and got back into the car. "So where do we start looking for this old man?" Barton said.

"According to Randell by the reaction you showed when that old man appeared on the C.C.TV. He thought you knew him"

"You heard me telling Randell, the reaction he saw was me bursting to go to the toilet."

The driver turned and glanced at his mate in the back, they nodded to each other, he started up the car and pulled out the carpark and joined the motorway.

Barton noticed the man sitting beside him no longer pointed his pistol at him, "the only place I could suggest we start looking would be the centre carpark," he got a slight nod from the driver.

There were still a lot of emergency and clean up vehicles in the car park, the driver pulled into a vacant space far away from them. A group of uniformed police were standing at the beginning of the lane in conversation with what they thought were plane clothed officers.

"No way am I going anywhere near that lot," the man sitting next to Barton said.

"I don't fancy it either," the driver added.

"If you both are frightened to go near the police, I'll go myself,"

The driver turned, pistol in his hand aimed at Barton's face, "don't even think about it."

"We need to know if that old man had been caught up in the explosion, we could be looking to kill somebody who is already dead."

The driver looked at his mate, who nodded in agreement, he turned to Barton," how are we supposed to find out?"

"If you two don't want to go to the police, I'll have to do it," Barton said, "I'll tell them I think one of my relatives may have been killed, could I go and identify him, they will ask me for a description, because I doubt if they have identified any of the bodies yet."

"They'll want a name," the man beside Barton said.

"I'll make up a name, they'll tell me where the bodies and the injured are and we go looking there."

"What if he's not there?" the driver asked.

"Then we have to start looking somewhere else," Barton could see that he had created a dilemma, could see the indecision in their eyes, "or if one of you could come up with a better idea?"

"I'll phone Mr. Randell," the driver said after a few minutes of thought, "see if he can come up with something."

Barton shook his head, "not a good idea, my experience with him is he leaves a lot to your discretion, if you get it wrong, he'll roar and shout at you rip you apart, that way he can manipulate you and keep control. On the other hand, if you get it right, he will wonder if you are a bit too smart and devious, not trustworthy."

"What are you trying to say?" the man next to him asked.

Barton turned to the man, "what I'm trying to say is, you've been sent on a fool's errand, you saw that old man with the bag, the Carter brothers take him away with it, the next thing a bomb explodes in the Hussy Club, the Carters are nowhere to be seen and neither is that old man, so what conclusion do you think Randell has come up with?"

The driver turned glanced at his mate and back at Barton, "why send you to kill a man he thinks is dead?"

"Because I think he's testing us for something big." Barton could see his reasoning was getting through, but decided to be careful not to over play it.

The Driver pulled a cigarette packet from his pocket, pulled one out and lit it, wound down his window and blew the smoke out, "so if we discover that this old man has blew himself up with the rest of them, do you recon that should be the end of the story?"

"I don't know," Barton replied and shrugged his shoulders.

After another pull at his cigarette he said, "oh kay, you go over there and enquire, but bare-in-mind, two guns are aimed at you, we can shoot you and be out of here before those coppers could get a description of this vehicle." He tossed his smoke out the window, pulled a silencer out and screwed it onto his pistol and nodded to his mate to do the same. Barton had no intentions of asking the policemen about his father, instead made some idle enquiries on what had happened and managed to slip in behind them, luckily the lane bad been opened and made his way to the High street. The Hussey Club was just a blackened shell cordoned off with blue and white police tape. Workmen were sweeping up debris and shovelling it into a skip. Pedestrians were crowding along the pavements on both sides of the street. He edged his way over close to the tape and asked an elderly woman if there were many casualties?

"Oh yes," the woman replied, "ambulances have been in and out all morning, have to have been at least ten, I think most of them were killed."

He edged his way along the tape and waved a constable over, "there's a vehicle in the carpark, I just walked past it and I'm sure I saw one of the men in it with a firearm." Barton walked away after describing the vehicle.

Another call to his parent's house resulted in him getting the engaged tone. A glance at his own mobile showed he was almost out of power. It took quite some time to get to the end of the street, although workmen were busy clearing up debris there was still a lot scattered about, pedestrian pushing their way down towards the cordon to see what was going on, cost him a lot of time trying to push his way through them, most of them were taking videos on their phones.

It cost him another half hour to get a taxi. He had parked his car in the area near Randell's offices, and hoped that nobody noticed him walking towards it and, also he wasn't' too confident it would start if it did would the brakes be seized. He got sat in it and was about to start the engine when the limousine drove past him and pulled up at the office door. Barton slid forward in his seat as low as he could, not easy for a man his size and build. Nevil got out on his own and leaped up the step into the offices. This was unprecedented, the first time he had seen the driver without the big man in the car, was Randell in his office or had he sent the driver back and remained at the quarry. There was one way of finding out, he got out the car and using the overgrown shrubs made his way around the back of the building, if the big man were in his office, he would surely be seen through the large window.

Barton was angry at himself for not having thought about it, had to be obvious knowing the big man, all he could see was brown tinted glass the afternoon sun reflecting off it. He retreated being careful not to draw attention to himself, this was an open lawn and any sudden move and it would be game over. They were standing at his car, Nevil and two other men that Barton had never seen before, he ducked back behind the building, hoped that he had not been seen, there he stood back pressed against the wall. A few minutes passed before risking a quick glance at them. They were gone, this could only mean they were searching for him and in this place, they would soon find him. He made a quick sprint across the lawn, down a slight embankment and found himself at the rear of another unit.

Contrary to his military training he relaxed thinking he was safe and walked to the far end of the building and right into them as he turned the corner. Nevil had a sawn-off shotgun over his shoulder and dawned a smile, not one of surprise, more in anticipation. The two strangers were behind him armed with pistols pointed his way.

"Mr. Randell would like a word with you," Nevil said, and waved the men past him, they frisk searched Barton taking the pistol from the back of his jeans.

With a gun pressed into his back, he was forced along the narrow road and turned onto a footpath leading to the Randell offices. Nevil took the lead and opened the main door, Barton felt himself being pushed through them into the reception area.

The receptionist jumped out of her seat and took a step backwards, but said nothing, she stared at Barton shook her head and walked outside, not wanting to be a witness of what might happen next.

"Keep him hear," the tall black driver said, "keep an eye on him," he turned and headed for Randell's office.

The two men half carried half dragged Barton up the corridor into the big man's office, Nevil placed a chair in front of the desk and he was forced into it facing Randell, who was at his usual belching smoke from a fat cigar and looking as though he had just sat on hot coals.

He drew the cigar from his mouth and leaned over the desk on his elbows, "what the fucks your game Barton?"

"I don't know what you mean, I don't have any game, just doing what I'm told."

The big man leaned back and pointed the hand holding his cigar at Barton's face, "why is it that the two men I sent with you are in police custody and you're not?"

"I didn't know, I left them in the car and went to make enquiries about that old man, when I got back the car was gone, I thought they had come back here."

"Did you find the old man?"

Barton shook his head, "looks like he was among casualties, might have been killed." Randell didn't look convinced, but not wanting to over stretch the lie, Barton kept quiet.

"What were you doing snooping about at the back of this building?"

"When I got back, I decided to use my own car to find out for sure about that old man, I got into it and was about to get it started when I saw a man running in the direction of this building. I decided to go after him, find out what he was up to."

"Do I look fucking stupid," the big man roared.

I would like to tell you what you look like, thought Barton, but decided the best thing to do was to act dumb. "of course not."

He pushed back his wheelchair, took a few long drags from his cigar and smiled, his small mouth hardly moved, "one good thing came out of it," he mumbled, "we know now who Lumpy's apprentice was and the informant."

It was on the tip of Barton's tongue to ask who but decided against it.

"Take this piece of shit to that new warehouse and bury him in the concrete," he pointed a fat finger at Barton and looked at the two men standing behind, "he'll be able to keep Damson company," he chortled, Nevil and the two men joined in . One of the men prodded Barton on the shoulder with his gun, "on your feet," he said, at the same time the other man gripped his arm and pulled him up from the chair.

"Secure his hands and feet and dump him in the boot of your car," Randell ordered as Nevil pushed him in the wheelchair around the desk, "no need to rush the mixer trucks will not arrive there for another three hours. We'll meet you there, I want to see this, that way I'll know the job has been done properly."

In the reception area the two men fought Barton to the floor on his knees and secured his hands behind his back with cable ties. During the struggle he saw Nevil push the big man out the door in his chair. That was last thing he saw before they blind folded him, he was gripped by the arm pits and lifted to his feet and pushed out the building.

Barton guessed he was being led across the carpark, the walk was quite far, and he asserted that they were going to use his own car. He pinned his hopes on it not starting or the wheels being seized. He got pulled to a stop and tripped over onto his back. One man sat on his chest the other secured his ankles. Now he felt himself being lifted and tossed into the boot, heard the lid close. Soon after the car started and pulled away with no trouble.

CHAPTER 36

They cut the cable ties from his ankles and dragged him out of the boot onto his feet, but after three hours of being cramped up in that small space his legs gave way under him. Two sets of hands took hold of his shoulders and held him up. It struck him like the flash from a camera when the blind fold was ripped from his head, had no time for his vision to adjust when he was pushed forward, his legs buckled again, he was caught and dragged along a rough gravel road.

The building he was pushed into was a redundant Royal Air Force hanger, the interior was massive and void of remnants of the previous owners, the only thing Barton could see in the place was the huge black limousine parked at the far end. He was steered into an office on the left-hand side. Randell was sat behind a small desk, but not in his wheelchair. Barton managed a quick glance around looking for it before being pushed onto a wooden chair.

The small desk was bare except for a mug that sat in front of the big man, he lifted it up in a fat hand and took a sip from it before replacing it and grimaced, "well Barton have you any last wishes?"

With his hands still fast behind his back, Barton was struggling to keep from sliding off the small chair, "I would like to know who shot Damston?"

Randell plucked one of his cigars from his top pocket, "so would I," he replied, rolling the cigar between his fingers, "in reality, whoever it was did me a favour." He saw the puzzled look on Barton's face, "I suspected that she was the informant, thanks to your blundering I got the proof and as a bonus I now know who Lumpy's apprentice was."

"What's that got to do with me?" Barton asked.

The big man glared at him, "you've been sleeping with the bloody woman, don't tell me you didn't know what she was up to?"

Barton shook his head, "I've learned that it's wise not to ask questions."

"As I have said to you before, you're not one of the usual cons I recruit, that makes me wonder what you are, why you joined my organisation and what Crow was thinking about when he sent you here?

"I attacked an officer, that in the forces is a serious offence, I served time and got thrown out and since then, I've been involved in flogging dodgy cars, I don't have a civilian record because I've never been nabbed."

Randell stuck the cigar in his mouth, Nevil reached over and lit it with his plastic lighter, "Oh I know all that. It's what I don't know that bothers me, even Damston couldn't enlighten me, and I don't like not knowing everything about the people in my company, the only way I know if I can trust them."

Barton lent forward, pushed his body back to get more room on the chair, "I basically told Crow my life story, if there's somethings you don't know, he has decided not to tell you."

"You tell me your story and I'll know what he's left out."

Barton told his story, left out the part about Corrie and his father, he never had a good memory and hoped he hadn't left anything out from his meeting with Crow.

"Most of what you say fits in with what Crow had informed me, I know he has good contacts in the prison service, but I never knew he had any in the armed forces."

"I got the impression he was a commissioned officer," Barton said, "he never said what regiment."

He took a long drag at his cigar, blew the smoke into Barton's face, waved a big arm and said, "take him down to that locker room at the bottom of the hanger, make sure he's secured and lock him in until the concrete trucks arrive. I'm going to make a few calls to find out if they are on there way and have a word with our friend Mr. Crow about him."

Barton was on his feet before the two men had a chance to grab his arms, causing more pain in his shoulders. He was punched kicked and pushed to the far corner of the hanger to a steel door that creaked, the sound echoing through the empty building. He realised there would be no way he could get out of this locker room without that sound alerting them.

The men kicked his feet from under him and he ended up on the floor on his stomach, they secured his ankles and tied him to a radiator. Satisfied with their work they felt and locked the door. He could hear them laughing and swearing, their voices fading as they walked away.

With his back tight against the radiator, hands behind his back and legs stretched out in front of him, there was a chance if he could get his feet up and under his buttocks, he could get up and wrench the old pipes from the wall. It would make a bit of noise but with the door locked it would be muffled. Getting his feet into the right position proved to be a problem and a painful one. After numerous attempts he got there but couldn't get them far enough but decided to give it a go. The first attempt failed, almost pulled his shoulders out, pain shot through his body. When the ache subsided he gave it another shot. This time he got onto his feet but was bent over so much he had difficulty keeping his balance, had to lean his lower back against the radiator and discovered that there was slight movement from it. With every muscle available and all his strength, he straitened up. The pipe came free from the bracket on the wall and with a few more painful tugs, he was able to get the rope off. The cable ties on his ankles hadn't been tight enough due to the struggle he put up when the two men put them on and he managed to shuffle his feet, eventually getting one foot out. By rubbing his wrists ties against the corner of a locker they fell off.

The only light that came in was from a small skylight window with bars. One wall was lined with steel lockers he counted ten, none of them had a padlock. One after another he opened them but couldn't find anything he could use for a weapon.

He returned his attention to the radiator, noticed the pipes leading to it, was the old lead type. The bracket that attached it to the wall had been dislodged from his earlier struggle, a good pull and a few twists, and it broke off giving him about four feet, just the right size for a lethal truncheon. There was no way he could break down that door and settled down in front of the radiator to wait for the men to return.

Tommy Carter with a bandage around his head, a plaster on his left leg hobbled on crutches to his brother's bed, a nurse was removing a bed pan when he approached, she covered it with tissues and departed. Ben was on a ventilator, with drips and tubes in both his arms a heartbeat monitor kept bleeping at regular intervals, he didn't need to ask to know his brother was in a coma, had seen it many times before when he and Ben had to question people, they had dealt with but never got the information they wanted, "If you can hear me bro. That little shit Hussey had to be scraped off the floor of his cellar, him and a few others. He wondered if Ben could hear, had read stories of people who had been in a coma had recalled conversations when they recovered.

He managed to get himself seated at the bed side seat and sat there listening to the constant bleep until he could stand it no longer, was about to attempt to get up when two men entered the room.

"I understand you were one of the people injured in that explosion?" The tallest of the two said.

Tommy ignored him and continued to get up off the chair.

The other man approached and tried to help him up, "we need to establish the names of all the Injured and dead so we can contact the relatives," he said with a hint of sympathy in his voice.

Tommy shrugged him off and struggled to his feet using the crutch to pull himself up, "well your asking the wrong person, I didn't know anybody in there."

"You seem to know this person," the tallest man said pointing at Ben.

Tommy shook his head, "had a few drinks with him, shared the same whore, that's it."

"So, you didn't get a name?" He asked.

Tommy shook his head.

"What's your name?" the shortest man said pulling a notebook and a pen from his pocket

Tommy pointed to the bandage on his head, "I can't remember."

They grinned at each other and walked towards the door, "we'll come back when your memory returns, the tall man said.

"Don't hold your breath." Tommy called as they closed the door. He hobbled out the room and made his way along the corridor. Looking through the windows of every cubicle at the same time making sure the nurses or other patients didn't appear and see him acting suspicious.

Two nurses stepped out of a room a short way along and stared at him, Tommy smiled and gave them a wave, they returned the smile and carried on their way. He waited until they were out the swing doors at the bottom of the ward and continued his search. He had almost ran out of rooms before he found what he was looking for. A cubicle where the patient looked comatose with a mobile phone lying on the bedside cabinet. He was sure somebody must have heard him clambering his way through the door, and delayed a moment listening for a reaction, let out a sigh when none came. The phone was old style with push button keypad, he scooped it up and got out as fast as his injuries would allow.

He sat on his bed in his own cubicle and phoned the big man, giving him an update. Randell's voice boomed in his ear, demanding to know what they were doing in the Hussey Club? "As Ben informed you, were driving past Allotment street when he noticed an old man standing at the warehouse door. We parked at the end of the street and sneaked up on him, asked him what his game was it seemed that he didn't know where he was, we bundled him in the car and dropped him off in town." The contact cut off, Tommy hadn't finished, wanted to explain a lot more, but knew not to call back, experience had thought when the big man hangs up that's end of conversation, you recall at your own peril.

Getting into bed was a hazardous task with one leg in plaster, he tried getting in on the left side and couldn't bend over to lift his broken leg and almost fell out. He got in successfully on the right side, although even that took a lot of time and effort. Sleep was impossible, could only lie on his back and his leg throbbed, regretted refusing the pain killers he had been offered.

The cubicle door opened, a female voice rang out wishing him a good morning, he sat up a bit too quick pain shot through him like a bolt of lightning, he yelled and lay back down.

"I'll help you out of bed," she glanced at the name on the card above his bed, "Mr. Brown."

Another nurse entered and they both got him out of bed and onto a chair, he watched while they changed the sheets. His thoughts drifted to the previous evening in Ben's cubicle and the two men who entered asking questions about the explosion and if he knew any of the dead or injured, it dawned on him and he almost sprang up out of the seat, but at the last moment remembered his plastered leg. Those men couldn't have been police, they would have informed him if they were, so, who were they? The phone he had left on the bed was now on the cabinet and out of reach, the crutches were leaning against the wall next to it, he had no other choice but wait until the nurses left.

No sooner had the nurses gone when a lady doctor came in. She looked closely into his eyes, asked him to follow her finger, which she waved from side to side, after a few questions told him he could get discharged later that day and to make appointments at outpatients.

Left on his own, Tommy struggled over and retained the crutches, hobbled out the door and down the corridor to Ben's cubicle. Through the window he saw a gathering of doctors and nurses standing around the bed. A wave of panic made him barge in, "is something wrong with my friend?" he cried.

All eyes turned to him, a moment later a man in a suit stepped over, "can I ask who you are?"

"A friend,"

"I'm sorry to tell you but your friend is no longer here," he indicated to the bed with his hand.

Tommy gazed at the empty bed, all the medical equipment lay strewn over the pillows and covers, "where have you taken him?"

"We haven't taken him anywhere, when the nurses came in to attend to him, he was no longer in the bed," one of the doctors from behind said.

"I don't think he was in a condition to get up and walk out," Tommy quickly replied.

"The police have been informed and should be here any moment," the man in the suit said.

Tommy decided he wasn't going to wait around for them and got the crutch moving out the door and back to his cubicle. The para medics had cut his jeans and he had little trouble getting them on. In a matter of minutes, he was hobbling along the corridor, through the swing doors and followed the exit sign until he was out.

CHAPTER 37

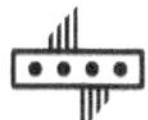

The locker room was in darkness before he heard footsteps approaching, he jumped to his feet and took up position in front of the door, remembered that it opened outwards. The key rattled in the old lock, the hinges creaked and the moment a face appeared, Barton drew the lead pipe down on it with all the strength he could muster. Nevil fell backwards, didn't have a chance to scream, the force of the blow knocked him out instantly. He stepped over the tall black man, ready to strike at anyone else. The chauffeur had been on his own, which made Barton worry about where the two men were. He knew where Nevil kept his revolver, had seen him draw it out a few times, it was a weapon Barton always wanted, the Korth.357 Magnum a lovely weapon small and easy to conceal. He dropped the pipe next to the driver, checked the gun was ready to fire and headed for the office.

The lighting in the hanger was subdued, old metal lampshades hung from long cables with large clear glass bulbs casting faint shadows in the corners. He didn't want to take the shortest rout across the open floor and risk being spotted, instead he kept close to the walls, trying to conceal himself as best as he could.

As his hand touched the door handle, a truck entered through the large open doors, it's headlights in full beam blinding him, there was no time to hide or run. It stopped just inside the entrance and the driver got out. He rushed over and made a sudden stop when he saw the weapon in Barton's hand.

"I've got drum full of concrete," the driver said putting his hands up, "I got held up and need to get it emptied before it solidifies."

"Take it outside and dump it where you like," Barton said and waved the gun at him. He watched the driver jumped back into his cabin when the office door behind him opened with Randell standing with a gun in his hand.

The shock of seeing the big man standing knocked his concentration off for that moment, a moment too late, the big man knocked the revolver out of his hand with his gun. Barton made a dive at him, but once again Randell was too fast and stepped back, striking him on the shoulder, sending Barton stumbling to the floor. He scrambled to his knees and when he turned round the big man had the gun pointed at his face.

"Get on your feet," Randel shouted.

Barton climbed to his feet, felt the big man's hand heave him around to face the office, next he felt the gun being pushed into his spine. The door had been left agar an idea struck, to dash for it and slam it on the big man's face. As if Randell had read his thoughts, the pressure of the weapon relaxed and at a backward glance, saw that the big man had stopped to let him enter. Seeing Randell on his feet was shock enough, but what faced him when he entered the office added to it.

Damson and Ben Carter's bodies lay placed out on the floor next to each other, Ben was still wearing a hospital gown with blood stains down the front of it. Barton felt the gun in his back again.

"Get down on your knees," Randell's voice boomed, "what have you done with my driver?"

"The last I saw him he was having a nap."

"You'll soon be having one with those two," Randell nodded towards the bodies . Barton decided it was time to change the subject, "what happened to the wheelchair?"

A grinned dawned across his thin lips, "Did you think I was a helpless cripple, that's what I wanted everybody to think, gives me an advantage, you soon got a shock when you saw me standing next to you, if you must know it's folded up behind the desk. Keeping the weapon pointed at Barton he waddled over and picked it up, gave it a good shake it unfolded, he settled into it, pulled out one of his cigars from his top pocket and lit it.

"You said you discovered who Lumpy's assistant was, can I ask who?"

"It wouldn't do you any good now, as he's gone, blew himself up," he pointed to Ben's body, "one of the victims, him and his brother, who incidentally survived."

"Where's Tommy now?"

"You ask a lot of questions for a condemned man."

"Does he know you have his brother's body here?"

Randell shook his head, the loose flash on his neck wobbling over his tight collar, "not yet but he will soon get to know and he'll come looking for him."

A loud knock on the open door drew their attention and four men and a girl walked in, Barton recognised them as members of the course all had weapons of different descriptions in their hands, he noticed one of the men carried a Heckler and Koch MP5.

"Are you going to start a war?" Barton said to the big man.

Randell grimaced, "no finish a war that you started."

"I don't understand what you mean by a war that I started?"

"According to Tommy Carter, who is a good pick pocket, that old man we saw on C.C.TV. the name on his bank card was Thomas Barton, he also told the brothers that it was his mobile phone that was used in that bomb," he dug his hand into his pocket and pulled out a mobile, held it in front of Barton." This is the one we took from you, I got one of our boys to do some research on this and discovered you called that old man's number at the same moment as that Hussey Club blew up."

Barton attempted to get up off his knees, felt himself being pushed back down.

The four men and the girl crowded around, all weapons pointed down at him, Randell placed his on the desk, took a pull at his cigar, "It doesn't take a rocket scientist to work out the connection between you and that old man and when I got in touch with Crow to do some investigating into your family, another man by the name of Corrie Barton came to light and that this man met his end in another bombing related incident."

Barton tried to get up again and earned himself a painful thump on the back of his ribs by the but of a gun. He slumped down gasping for breath the blow had winded him badly. "It's a common name," he managed to gasp out.

Randell was about to reply when Nevil staggered in, his face covered in blood and holding his head, "what the fuck happened to you? The big man shouted.

Nevil leaned on the desk for support and pointed to Barton, "that's what happened."

The big man shook his head, "you're a nasty piece of work Barton, I intended to kill you then bury you in the concrete, now I'm going to you put in it alive and watch you squirm for your life."

"What the fuck are you waiting for?" Barton shouted.

"Thanks to you the concrete lorry emptied in the wrong place, now I need to wait for another load to arrive," he waved a big arm at the group standing around Barton, "take him back to the locker room, one of you stay with him, if he tries anything shoot him but don't kill him."

Once more he was dragged to the locker room and tied, but this time there was no place for them to secure him to. Barton lay face down on the floor he could hear shuffling of feet and whispering as they debated who should stay behind, this went on for a while and eventually heard them leaving, Barton wondered who had been left behind, hoped that it was the girl. The room was lit this time by a single bulb hanging from the ceiling. He turned his head in both directions but couldn't see the person who was to stay behind and wondered if they had all left. He swung himself round onto his back and froze at the sound of gun being cocked. His hopes were answered she stood a few feet away, legs apart weapon pointed at him. "I need the toilet," he said, "don't think I can hold on much longer."

She stood like a manikin, never even batted an eyelid, Not even when the door behind her opened and the four men entered carrying the two bodies, the two men with Damsons corpse came in first, unceremoniously dumped her remains on the floor next to Barton, Ben's corpse landed next to hers.

"He wants to go to the toilet," the girls said, as the men were about to go out the door.

"He can piss himself," the last man out the said, the door banged, and the old lock rattled into place.

Left alone with the girl he decided she wasn't so tensed up, looked more frightened, maybe she didn't like being locked up beside dead bodies. The gun hand trembled and her eyes weren't so expressionless and fixed, Barton decided to take advantage of this weakness, "if I piss myself and these bodies start do decay, the smell in here will make you puke." He watched her eyes lids flicker, but she said nothing, "how long are they going to keep us in here?" Still no reply.

"Is somebody going to relieve you?"

This time he got a reaction, she lowered her head and relaxed her gun hand and let it drop down By her knee. A little progress, "it could be three days before another concrete truck turns up."

The reaction he got this time was unexpected, she stepped over and kicked his feet, "you think I don't know what you're playing at," came another step closer, bent over, her eyes staring fire at him. "you forget I'm an ex-con. as well as you, I've got that tee shirt, so shut the fuck up."

Barton timed it dead right, judged the distance, lifted his bound feet and kicked striking her on the pelvis, she doubled over gasping for air, he wriggled closer, this time his feet landed squarely on the side of her head. A few minutes passed and she hadn't stirred, he repeated what he had previously done and got his hands free, a heartbeat later he was leaning over her, with her pistol pointed at her face. She still hadn't moved, he shook her arm, still nothing, slapped her face, this time she moaned and opened her eyes. A few flickers of her eyelashes and it struck her where she was and what had just happened, she tried to get up, but Barton pushed her down, was about to strike out at him but held back when he pushed the weapon into her face. "Lie still and shut up,"

He stepped away from her, "now slowly get onto your feet, keep your hands where I can see them." He backed up to the wall, watched her get onto her feet, felt some regret for hitting her, there was no way he could have talked her into releasing him." Go over and topple one of those lockers on its side, give us something to sit on, but make no sound doing it. Hell knows how long we're going to be here."

She never got the chance to get a hand to the locker when he heard the old lock clatter, he rushed over to it held his back against the wall and waited till the four men got inside and fired a shot wounding the last one on the leg. The rest turned quickly and tried to rush him. But Barton was out the door and turned the key. He made his way to the office, hopped that the sound of the shot and the banging on the door wouldn't be heard from there.

Randell and Nevil were not in the office, the limousine was still parked in the hanger. Barton about turned and dived out, stopped at the door and scanned the hanger in all directions, they were no where in sight, the only signs of life was the persistent banging on the locker room door and voices yelling. The grey light of dawn was shining through the wide entrance. He edged his way towards it keeping close to the wall.

He stood inside the huge sliding door, from somewhere close by the sound of a powerful engine was labouring. He followed the noise creeping along the outer wall, at the corner he stopped and peeked around it, the sound was coming from a digger, it's gib working away at a deep trench. Standing at the side watching the action was the big man in his wheelchair and beside him Nevil dawning a large bandage around his head.

Barton delayed there long enough to decide if they were going to stay there talking for a while longer. Satisfied they would be, he retreated into the hanger, once inside he ran towards the limousine, luck was on his side once more the keys had been left in the ignition. He got the vehicle started and at full throttle raced for the open door when the wheelchair appeared in front of him. The big man let out a scream, Nevil moved at lighten speed and drew the chair back,

Barton was sure, he hit something but didn't take the time to give them a backward glance.

His escape didn't get him far, when he came to the end of the camp road a large steel security gate confronted him. He could see it was operated by a keypad. He abandoned the limousine and trotted along the high chain link fence hoping to find a place to climb over. Barton knew it wouldn't be long before they found the abandoned vehicle and started searching for him. He ran for what he reckoned must have been a mile when he came across another gate. On the other side he could see open fields that stretched far into the distance. This one wasn't as high and decided to climb over. His main worry was how far and fast will he be able to nun in all this open ground before being spotted. One way of finding out, he decided and climbed over and began running.

He struggled to keep up the pace, cursing for not keeping to his fitness program, his heart was pounding in his chest, could hardly breath, was beginning to think he was having a heart attack. He glanced behind him and could see no pursuers, was tempted to stop and catch his breath, argued with himself just minute, but it was out of the question. Keep going he repeated to himself numerous times.

At first, he could hear the unmistakable sound of traffic, wondered if his hearing was playing tricks on him and there it was about half a mile in front of him. He slowed his pace getting his breath back and walked the last hundred yards. Barton had no idea what road he had reached, wasn't too bothered all he needed was to thumb a lift and get away.

CHAPTER 38

*H*obbling across the hospital carpark searching for a taxi rank, Tommy Carter just remembered he didn't have his wallet, cursed himself when it dawned on him, he had left it in the bedside cabinet. All his money was in it but thankfully no identification. An elderly woman walked past him, he followed her, luckily, she didn't walk too fast or she would have reached her car and drove off before he got halfway there. As she dug into her handbag for the keys Tommy hit her on the back of her head with one of his crutches, he put so much effort into it he fell on top of her. He struggled to his feet, found her handbag, found the car keys and some money. A problem he had never gave a thought to, how to get into the driver's seat of an old-style Volkswagen Beatle with a plastered leg. When he got the vehicle started, discovered he couldn't press the accelerator pedal without hitting the brakes.

The little car jumped and screeched out the car park and continued doing so along the road until he found a way to master it, had to lift his plastered leg by hand. Luck was on his side when he approached the first set of traffic lights and got them at green, but not so lucky at a roundabout where he knocked a motorcyclist off his bike and didn't stopped. He made a wild swing into the road that led to the parking area in front of Randell's offices and had to crawl out the car on his hands and dragged his body out, his broken leg fell, the full weight of it landing on his bare toes. Using the open door, he pulled himself up and hopped to the passenger's side to get his crutches.

The girl in reception gave him a concerned look, "I heard about your accident," she said and stood up, came around her desk to assess the extent of his injuries, "how is Ben?"

Tommy shook his head, "I don't know, the last I saw of him he looked in a bad way and according to the hospital staff he's been abducted, where is Randell? I didn't notice his car."

She shrugged her shoulders and sat herself down behind her desk again, "there was nobody in here when I arrived this morning, the last I heard they were visiting a new site in Oxfordshire."

"I've lost my mobile, can you give him a call and get the address for me."

She shook her head and exhaled deeply, "I've instructions not to call in less it's an emergency."

"Well this is an emergency my brothers been abducted, and I need his help to find him."

She picked up the phone from her desk and handed it to him, "you phone him."

Tommy reluctantly took it from her and dialled the number expecting a rebuff from the big man and was surprised when Randell sounded pleased, wanted him to gather a team of his goons and get down there a.s.a.p.

Tommy instructed the driver of the twelve-seater to stop outside the hanger door and leave, "find a layby and stay there, I'll call you when we need you."

Two of the squad of ten helped him out the bus and set him up on the crutched," hang about out here," he told them and hobbled his way to what looked like an office.

Randell sat in his wheelchair behind the desk Nevil sat on a padded seat next to him a bandage around his head, the whites of his eyes were red as if he had been crying or just woke up from a deep sleep. "How many bodies could you muster?" The big man asked.

"Eleven counting myself."

"You're not going to be any good, the condition your in."

"I need your help Mr. Randell."

"Why do you need my help?"

"To find Ben, he's been abducted from hospital, need your help to find him."

Randell pulled out one of his cigars, stared at it for a while, changed his mind and put it on the desk, gave a deep sigh, "the reason I asked you to bring some of our boys down, is to search this area to find Barton."

Tommy painfully eased himself onto the nearest chair, "I don't understand, what's that clown been up to?"

"It was him that set that bomb off, he must have known that it had been detonated by that phone. We nabbed him brought him down here and questioned him. He shot Damson and I'm sure that it was him that dragged your brother out of hospital and if Benn was as bad as you say, I doubt he will still be alive."

Tommy made to get up, Randell held up his hand, "you sit there, you're not fit to go anywhere, Nevil here will get the boys sorted they'll soon find Barton."

The team that had been locked in the locker room entered Randell glared at them, "Bloody five of you and you couldn't contain one man," he turned to Tommy, "that's the clowns that let him get away."

Tommy glanced at them, a girl and four men, it was one of the men that made him take a second more intensive look, something familiar about him, had seen him recently but couldn't place where. It was when one of the other men shuffled to the front it clicked. The two that came into Benn's cubicle asking question, giving the impression they were police. He turned to see Randell's deep set eyes studying him, reading what he had just discovered.

Randell picked up his cigar, waved a big hand at Tommy, looked at the team, "take this piece of shit to the locker room and this time don't let him get away. I don't suppose in his condition he'll get far, but with you lot, nothing would surprise me."

Tommy struggled and fought the four men off as much as he could, they dragged him out the chair, "you bastard," he shouted at the big man, but he was out the office, the girl slammed the door so Randell wouldn't hear the abuse that was getting shouted at him.

The four men decided there was no need to tie Tommy's feet, they knocked him over and cable tied his wrists and locked the door. The girl was put on guard, but this time outside.

Before he climbed over the fence, he had a good look around to see if he was being chased, could see no sign of anyone in the open fields. Barton had no idea what this road he was trudging along trying to thumb a lift, was starting to wonder if this was a good idea keeping to the road, all it took was for them to look at a map and work out the obvious.

He had decided to take his chances sticking to the road. About two miles later still hadn't been offered a lift. The traffic was too busy and too fast for anyone to stop, a disadvantage also an advantage, meaning that it would be dangerous for his pursuers to try pick him up. His fear now was, would they shoot him from their moving vehicle? Too much of a risk with all those cars and trucks going past, would they be desperate enough to chance it?

Up ahead he spotted a layby with a bus parked behind a truck, he quickened his pace and discovered it was empty of passengers only the driver sitting behind the wheel playing with his phone. Barton knocked on his window, the driver jumped and almost dropped his mobile, "Where are you heading?" Barton shouted.

The driver wound down his window, "I don't know yet," he said, "I dropped a load of passengers off at the old air force base, I'm waiting them calling back to go pick them up."

Barton was about to ask roughly how many people he had dropped off when a car pulled in behind the bus. He gave it no more than a casual glance and continued conversing with the driver. He stopped mid-sentence when he heard the car door closing, saw the dapper little man heading towards him, "Mr. Crow, this is a surprise," Barton said and walked towards him, "what brings you out here in the sticks?"

The little man jabbed his thumb towards his vehicle, "get in the car Barton."

"I see you haven't changed your aftershave, still smells like a whore's handbag," Barton commented when they got seated in the car. Crow ignored the comment, "you're lucky I was passing, according to my informant Randell has pulled in about a dozen goons to find you. What have you done to upset him?"

Barton waited till he had the car going, "I'm not sure, he seems to think I killed Damson and set off that bomb in the Hussey Club."

"Did you?"

"No, I didn't kill Damson and no I didn't set that bomb off, not intentionally." He sat in silence as they approached a roundabout. Crow drove all the way around it and headed back the way they had come, "where are you taking me?" Barton said.

"Back to the airfield."

"What?" They'll bury me in concrete and you as well when they see you've helped me."

He held up a hand, "don't start pissing yourself, we're not going in, I'll park a short way up the road from the gate."

"Then what?"

"We wait until a shipping container turns up."

"Any idea when that will be?"

Crow shook his head, "I don't know, I've been driving up and down this road all morning, hoping to see it."

"Randell has hundreds of containers scattered all over the country, what's so special about this one?"

Crow drove past the gate and pulled into a layby about a hundred yards up the road, "the contents."

"I can't see it being any worse than the rest."

"It is trust me, it is, we're all career crooks, but this I don't want to be connected to, something has to be done."

The articulated truck rumbled past, a few seconds later the brakes screeched, "that's it," Crow said and jumped out the car, went into the boot and armed himself with an expensive camera, "let's go," he shouted.

"Where to?" Barton said and jumped out the car.

"Have some photos to take." Crow slung the camera around his neck, handed Barton a bag, and started walking back towards the gate."

Barton followed and protested, "you can't just walk in there, if Randell's got all those goons looking for me."

"It's okay, I know this airfield, did some service here, I know where we can observe what's going on without being spotted."

Barton lay beside him on a mound of earth that had been shaped into the letter c, to conceal ant-aircraft guns. Crow spent the next five minutes setting up his camera trying different lenses from the bag Barton held.

Crow aimed his camera at the truck, it had dropped the trailer by the side of the hanger where the digger still worked and pulled away, disappeared up the road.

"What do you think's happening?" Barton asked, pulled binoculars out of the bag and looked through them at the container.

"Just keep watching," Crow said, "and you'll soon find out."

The digger stopped the engine noise died down to a constant throb. Two concrete trucks appeared, must have been hidden inside the hanger. A group of men came out, some had shovels in their hands. The remainder opened the shipping container doors, Barton had seen this on the news, never thought it would arrive in this country, it sickened him so much he lowered the binoculars and turned away. Crow's camera shutters kept clattering, now and then he would stop to change lenses, then it would continue. "That's the lowest of the low," Barton said, "how could anyone take payment for doing that to other human beings, there's got to be about fifty dead bodies in that container."

"An anonymous call has been sent to the Oxford Police just hope they get here before that lot bury those bodies and concrete them in,"

"Who were those people?"

"Illegal immigrants, the container went missing for a few weeks, the men who organised it realised they must be dead and paid Randell to dispose of them."

The shutters in his camera stopped, Barton turned as Crow replaced the lens cover and packed the spares into the bag. "Time to make our-selves scares," he said and pointed towards the gate where a squad of police cars had pulled in.

"I think my car could still be in that area," Barton said, "it won't take them long to trace it back to me."

Crow was on his feet and began creeping his way back, Barton wasn't sure if he had heard and started after him. "Did you hear what I said back there?"

The little man stopped, shook his head and grinned, his watery blue eyes stared into Barton's, "you think that's your only problem, you've landed yourself right in it, Randell won't hesitate to point the finger at you, you have only one way out of this." He turned and continued towards his car.

Barton caught up with him as he opened the door to his vehicle, "what's my only way out?"

"Get in the car Barton, I'll drop you off near your flat and I'll be in touch."

Barton had a stormy reunion with his parents, was both shocked and elated to see his father, wanted to give him a hug but knew Tom wasn't the hugging type, would had pushed him away with embarrassment. After three of his mother's cups of tea he left, but didn't to tell them where Corrie's body was, knew what his mother's reactions would have been. She was sat in the same seat as before, Wilma leaned on the bar with her pint glass half full. "can I fill your glass?" The man's voice whispered in her ear, feeling his hot breath on her neck she turned, ready to run for the ladies, felt his hand on her shoulder she glared at him for a moment, her eyes lit up and a wide smile dawned across her face, "Richard, this is a surprise."

"Not as big a surprise as seeing you back here, I thought you had done a runner, for your own safety."

"I did but when I heard the Hussey Club had been bombed and he and his goons were killed, I thought it safe to come back."

Barton waved at the barman and got her a fresh drink and one for himself, "so what do you plan to do with yourself now your back?"

"Get a job somewhere."

"In another club?"

She vigorously shook her head, "no way that's too dangerous."

After a few drinks, they sat down at one of the tables, "how long have you been back?" He asked.

"Just arrived this morning."

"Where are you staying?"

"I gave up my flat when I left, haven't found another yet."

"I can put you up if you want, until you find a place."

She smiled and hooked her arm around his, "thanks Richard, I promise I won't get in your way."

"I'm not going to carry you over the threshold," Barton grinned and opened his flat the door, "the neighbours might get the wrong impression."

They sat on his sofa drinking coffee and watching television, didn't say much, she seemed engrossed on a film Barton remembered from his childhood. A sudden news flash came up that sent a chill through him to the point where he jumped up grabbed the remote and turned up the volume.

Wilma sprung up beside him, "what's wrong? She gripped his arm.

He sat back down, shook his head and sighed, "it's something you don't want to get involved in the less you know the better."

"Don't tell me your mixed up in that?" She pointed at the screen and got down next to him.

"I told you don't get involved."

The newscaster had reported that the Oxford police had apprehended a gang involved in people smuggling and had uncovered a shipping container with forty-seven dead illegal immigrants. Some of whom were women and children. The reporter concluded by saying that the head of the organisation had escaped and was suspected to have fled the country.

Barton replaced the remote Wilma still stared at him, he took no notice of her, his mind on the last words from that reporter. If the head of the organisation was Randell, he knew that there was no way the big man would leave his storage racket for someone else to run.

"A penny for them," Wilma said.

Barton grimaced, "sorry, I was miles away, I'm going to leave you to look after this place, I need to go away for a while." He tossed her the keys, put on his leather jacket and left.

He remembered Crow's warning words, (only one way out of this) as he waited to hail a taxi he checked his gun making sure the magazine was full and slipped it into his jacket pocket for easy access.

CHAPTER 39

The dapper little man sat on one of the park benches reading a newspaper, the headlines were the same on all the nationals and most locals. All front page in inch size letters. Full size pictures of the shipping container and the bodies lying next to it.

The tall thin man approached and sat down next to him his premature white hair ruffled by the wind, Crow glanced at his pallor complexion couldn't see the eye behind the dark glasses, with a slight nod he got up, walked away leaving an A4 manila envelope on the bench.

Judd as he called himself, picked up the envelope, looked around checking no one was observing him, satisfied, he carefully opened it. The face on the photo he didn't recognise, the name seemed familiar, had heard it mentioned somewhere. He grinned folded the envelope and put it in his pocket, this man will be an easy target, a grey-haired old man, easy to spot in a crowd, no problem, follow him to his house, get to know his routine, pick the perfect location and it's good by Tom Barton.

THE END

www.ingramcontent.com/pod-product-compliance
Lightning Source LLC
Chambersburg PA
CBHW051314190726
48290CB00001B/146